FIRED UP

Fever Falls

By Riley Hart

Copyright © 2018 by Riley Hart
Print Edition

All rights reserved.

No part of this book may be used, reproduced or transmitted in any form or by any means, electronic or mechanical, including photocopying, recording, or by any information storage and retrieval systems, without prior written permission of the author, except where permitted by law.

Published by:
Riley Hart

This book is a work of fiction. Names, characters, places and incidents are products of the author's imagination or are used fictitiously. Any similarity to actual persons, living or dead is coincidental and not intended by the author.

All products/brand names/Trademarks mentioned are registered trademarks of their respective holders/companies.

Cover Design by Black Jazz Designs
Cover Photo by Wander Aguiar Photography
Edited by Keren Reed Editing
Proofread by Judy's Proofreading and Lyrical Lines

So, what is Fever Falls? It's a fictitious series with the city of Fever Falls serving as the backdrop to Riley Hart and Devon McCormack's newest collaboration. Unlike our previous collabs, where we wrote books together, we'll be sharing the Fever Falls sandbox and creating solo titles within it. The books are intended to be read as standalones; however, because there are overlapping characters between the books, it'll be a lot more fun to read them all!

Fever Falls has it all, including an inordinate amount of hot, curious, and eligible bachelors who learn the hard way that there's an unexpected consequence to living here: you just might fall in love.

Visit the Fever Falls website
www.feverfalls.com

Synopsis

ASHTON

If there's one thing I know, it's how to play the game...both on and off the field. If it hadn't been for that one teenage slipup where I kissed Beau Campbell, I'd be able to keep fooling myself. Football is the one thing I use to distract myself from the truth, and when I screw-up and lose the game I love, I find myself right back in Fever Falls. And right back face-to-face with *Cranky Campbell*, who hates me even more than he did when we were kids. Whatever magic he held over me then is still there. As much as I fight it, I still want him. And I *always* get what I want...well, except with Beau, who constantly calls me on my crap. Why do I like that so much?

BEAU

I might've spent years watching Ash live out my dream—without the off-field antics and orgies with women, at least—but I've made a good life for myself. I'm a firefighter, and I coach my brother's football team for those with developmental disabilities. But when Ash swings back into town armed with his monster ego and an arsenal of stupid nicknames, everyone is in awe of him. Nope, not me. I don't care if our kiss years ago was responsible for my sexual awakening. I won't fall for Ashton Carmichael. Though that resolution would be a whole lot easier if he wasn't so tempting. Once he finds his way into my bed, I'm screwed—in more ways than one. But there's more to Ash than meets the eye, buried beneath his ego, sarcasm and how we burn up the sheets together. Soon, it's more than a game. We don't just get each other *fired up*, we just might win each other's hearts.

Too bad things are never that simple…

Special Thanks

Outside of reading articles and watching videos, I was lucky enough to have FIRED UP read by people who have loved ones with Down syndrome, and those who have up to thirty years of experience working with individuals with Downs. I would like to thank Wendy Richardson, Jackie Thorogood, Melissa Witt, and Leslie Lemerise for reading and offering feedback. Also, a big thanks to Beth Sweryda for answering questions. I couldn't have done it without you guys! Any mistakes are my own.

Also, I'd like to ask you to keep in mind that there are different levels of disability and functioning. Just like with anything in life, everyone with Down syndrome isn't the same.

Thanks for reading!

PROLOGUE

Beau

MY GUT TIGHTENED as I watched Ashton Carmichael dance on the coffee table with Sarah Pinkton. He grabbed her ass, and she giggled. Everyone cheered and laughed as they grinded against each other. He took a long swallow of beer from his red plastic party cup and then let it slosh over the sides. I didn't get it, the whole red-plastic-cup thing, but if there was beer and a keg, red cups always went right along with it.

And Ashton Carmichael, of course. I was pretty sure that in our four years of high school there hadn't been a party he hadn't attended…and acted like he was doing now…which people ate up like it was an ice-cream sundae on a hot day.

I couldn't stand him. I really couldn't stand Ash.

But he was also my friend…and obviously that made things difficult.

Strange how someone could grate on your every

nerve but you also considered them a friend...kind of...sometimes...okay, fine, he was a friend, but he was also annoying as shit.

Still, my eyes stayed firmly entranced by him even while I berated myself for it the whole time. Even while I told myself to ignore him. Like everyone else, I couldn't look away from Ash, and that truth made me even more frustrated with myself than I was with him.

The beer sloshed over the cup again. He laughed, dropping his head back with a rich, throaty sound. When he looked up, his gaze focused right on me. When I rolled my eyes, the right side of his mouth kicked up in a half grin. He winked at me while he danced with Sarah, and that was my wake-up call to turn away...which I did...only to look back at him a moment later and see Ash still watching me. There was a wrinkle on his forehead, a crease between his eyes as if he was thinking about something.

But then his eyes snapped away, and he jumped down off the table like he was trying to be Patrick Swayze in that movie my mom always went crazy about. He switched from Sarah to Crystal, and no one cared because he wasn't dating either of them. He just liked attention, to make a big fucking show of everything, and everyone around him got their jollies watching.

Did I mention Ashton Carmichael annoyed the shit out of me? It bore repeating.

And it was time to walk away.

As I headed toward the kitchen, weaving my way through the crowd, a body slammed into me. Shannon, my ex-girlfriend, looked up at me, her eyes sparkling and sort of dopey-looking. Not that Shannon wasn't smart, because she was. She came in third in our class with me in second and Ash fucking Carmichael in first, but alcohol always made her silly. "I miss you, Beau. Did I tell you how hot you look today?" She reached up and fingered my hair. "Your hair's soft. It's the color of chocolate. I really like chocolate."

Actually, my hair was black, not brown, and I hoped she wasn't planning on eating it. Regardless, this wasn't good. She was great, one of my close friends, but I just didn't feel *that way* about her. I kind of hated that I didn't. Shannon was perfect, perfect for me—only I couldn't make myself see her as more than a friend, and I couldn't figure out why that was. "Thanks, Shan. You look good too. How much have you had to drink?"

She held up her thumb and forefinger, making an inch. "Just a little bit, *Dad*."

I rolled my eyes. Was it such a bad thing to be responsible? Or as other people sometimes called it, boring, but whatever. I didn't think boring was such a bad thing.

Shannon stumbled into me, then frowned. "I don't feel so well, Beau."

"Shit," I groaned. "Come on. Let's get you outside."

I got her to the door just as Holly and Paulina, Shannon's closest friends, approached. "Thank God you found her, Beau. She slipped away," Holly said.

"We're gonna take her home," Paulina added. She was the designated driver. Anytime anyone partied, Paulina offered to drive people home because she didn't drink, which was a lifesaver more times than I could count. I wasn't out there drinking as often as most people I knew, but I did indulge sometimes.

"I'll walk you guys to the car."

"Thanks, Beau. You're the best." Holly squeezed my shoulder.

We made our way out of Wyatt's parents' lake house. They were the wealthiest family in Fever Falls, and Wyatt was Ash's best friend…not that I wasn't friends with Wyatt, because I was.

Ash and I hung out in the same social circles—being captain and co-captain of the football team—Ash was captain, of course. Hell, we were even in prom nominations together, which Ash won, not that I'd wanted to. He'd been to my house, and I'd been to his.

Considering we were supposed to be friends, I shouldn't have hated him, not as much as I did. Sure, he was obnoxious, got everything he wanted, always one-upped me, and would do anything in his power to be the center of attention, but we were chill with each other…outside of the mutual sarcasm and my secret dislike of him.

I could still hear the music thumping as we got farther away from the house. The driveway would have been dark if not for the new lights Wyatt's family had put in. Too much artificial lighting in the middle of the woods was so fucking strange to me. It took away the nature in nature, if that made sense.

When we got to Paulina's car, she opened the passenger door, and I helped Shannon inside. As I bent over to click her seat belt into place, her mouth moved in close to my ear. "My parents are gone… You could come home with me. I know we're not together anymore, but…just one more time?"

My muscles tensed up. "You're drunk, Shan. I'm not going home with you when you're drunk." I wouldn't go home with her anyway. It would just confuse an already fucked-up situation. But I knew I probably should want to go home with her, even if it wasn't to have sex with her. Oh, and I probably should have enjoyed having sex with her more than I had. She was beautiful, smart, kind…and staying in Fever Falls like me.

Staying… I was staying. My gut clenched.

"Beau…"

"Good night, Shan." I kissed her forehead and pulled back. Once I had the door closed, I asked, "Are you guys staying with her? I don't think she should be alone tonight."

"Yeah, we're sleeping over," Holly replied. "Thanks for the help."

I watched the three of them drive away. As I walked back to the house, I realized the party was the last place I wanted to be. Still, I had friends with me and couldn't bail on them. They'd give me shit about being a spoilsport, not acknowledging they all had stuff to celebrate and I didn't. Not really. My high school diploma didn't mean as much when my future was right there in town, living in the same house with my mom and my little brother, Kenny.

Stopping by my car, I grabbed a flashlight. Instead of going into the house, I walked around back to the path leading to the lake. It was darker back there, the lake out of view of the house. The dock belonged to Wyatt's family. We'd taken the boat from it numerous times, so I knew the way.

The wood creaked beneath my feet until I reached the edge of the dock, where I sat down. I could still hear the light *thump* of music in the distance, but it was nice to be away, to breathe for a minute.

This fucking sucked. I'd graduated high school today, but I was pouting by the lake instead of partying with my friends…because I didn't feel like celebrating…because my dream wasn't coming true.

"Playing hide-and-seek by yourself?"

I startled at the sound of Ash's voice behind me. Because of course Ash would show up. Why wouldn't he? I'd obviously pissed off the karma gods.

"Well, I'll play with you, and look, I found you. Freeze." Ash touched my shoulder.

"You mixed up hide-and-seek and freeze tag."

"I'm too drunk to care about details." He sat down beside me. I could smell the slight tinge of sweat on his skin from the dancing, mixed with something else I couldn't name…and wasn't sure why I wanted to.

"You know, you're entirely too serious for your own good, Beau. Loosen up and live a little. We graduated high school today!" He put an arm around me and shook me. "Ugh. I stink. Sorry."

Damn him for almost making me grin. "Yeah, you do."

"You're always so cheery. Such a fun guy to be around. Bubbly Beau, that's what I should call you."

"Gee, thanks, Ash."

"Seriously, Cranky Campbell, what gives?"

Which was it? Bubbly Beau, or Cranky Campbell, which was the name he typically called me.

"I hate it when you call me that, and I'm only pissy when you're around." Kind of…most of the time. Ugh. Why did Ash get to me so much?

"I guess that makes sense. It must be hard being around someone as kick-ass as me."

I rolled my eyes. The thing was, I thought he was probably serious. Ash didn't lack confidence in the least, which I respected and despised at the same time. "You're not helping."

"Dude, seriously. Be happy. You're as close to perfection as you can get."

Because I was always number two? "And you're perfection, right?"

Ash winked at me. "Obviously."

I turned away from him and looked out at the lake—the reflection of the moon on the water and how the shadows from the trees danced against it. With every fiber of my being, I wanted to be as happy as Ash was, wanted something to celebrate like he had.

"I'm sorry," he said after a few minutes.

"For what?" I replied, not looking at him.

"I don't know…everything?" He nudged me with his arm. "How's Kenny?"

I tensed up slightly at the mention of my brother's name. It wasn't as if he'd said anything wrong, but I was highly protective where Kenny was concerned. "He's doing well."

"That's good. I'm glad to hear it."

There was another pause. I didn't know what to say. It was strange that Ash was there with me instead of in the house partying, dancing, and making everyone smile. It was even more strange that he would bring up Kenny. Most of my friends didn't. They were cool to him and everything, but they never just asked me about my brother.

"It's so cool. He's always so happy."

My muscles went rigid at Ash's words. "No, he's not," I snapped. It was a stereotype that many people had about those with Downs…that they were always happy as though they didn't know better. And yeah, Kenny *was* happy a lot but he got mad and sad too. He felt things just like the rest of us only sometimes his emotions were much bigger, he was more expressive than most people. Kenny didn't guard his emotions.

"Did I say something wrong?"

I shrugged, not wanting to talk to him about it.

"You're going to Fever Falls Community College, right? That's what Wyatt said."

My initial reflex was to ask him why he and Wyatt had been talking about me, but instead, I held it in, letting my bitterness eat away at my insides. "I don't want to talk about it."

I didn't want to hear about Ash leaving for USC, about all the things he would do that I wouldn't.

"Shit. I'm sorry. I… You're a good brother, Beau."

My eyes snapped to his. How did he know I was staying because of Kenny? I sure as shit hadn't told him that. I'd known Ashton Carmichael all my life, and he'd never said anything like that to me.

I stared, dumbfounded. My mouth even hung open, and the only reason I knew was because Ash chuckled, then reached over, hooked his finger under my chin, and closed it. My body started misfiring, going haywire at his touch, though I couldn't figure out why. I hated Ash, but now goose bumps were dancing up and down my arms and my pulse sped up.

I didn't turn away, couldn't, and he didn't either. Then his tongue sneaked out and traced his bottom lip, and holy fuck did Ashton Carmichael have nice lips.

Whoa, where did that come from?

It clicked with me that he was closer, then closer again. My breathing picked up, and my brain malfunctioned even more because I didn't pull away, sit back, or ask him what in the fuck he was doing. Instead, I waited as he leaned in, felt the heat from his touch, realized that vanilla was the scent that clung to him, felt the electric current zipping from Ash to me when his lips pressed against mine.

Ashton fucking Carmichael was kissing me.

Ash was a guy.

And I liked it.

Mayday! Mayday! Mayday!

His tongue sneaked out again, pushed into my mouth, and…fuck, was I moaning? Jesus, I *was*. What in the hell was wrong with me? My fingers tingled as I reached up and held on to the back of Ash's head. His hair was wet with sweat, but I didn't care. He tasted so damn good. It didn't even matter anymore that sweat mixed with his vanilla, just the dance of his tongue and the way kissing him made me dizzy.

"Ash," I whispered when his mouth teased its way down my neck.

My words shocked him into action, or at least I assume they did, because Ash jerked away as though I'd burned him. Which of course made me do the same, only I fucked up again and jerked too far, toppling off the end of the dock and into the water.

"Oh shit," Ash said as he reached for me, and I'm not going to lie, for a brief moment I considered ducking under the water and hiding—drowning be damned.

I didn't want to die, though, so I let him pull me up, and we stood staring at each other, me in sopping wet jeans and a tee and Ashton fucking Carmichael looking gorgeous as ever.

Holy fuck. I thought Ash, with his blue eyes and tousled brown hair, was gorgeous. Had I always thought he was gorgeous?

"Whew. I'm really fucking drunk. It just hit me how drunk I am." He swayed for emphasis.

A frown pulled at my lips.

"You're sober, though, aren't you?" he asked, making heat and anger shoot through me. Was he going to blame this on me? Tell people I sober-kissed him and excuse himself because he was drunk?

I opened my mouth to reply, but Ash cut me off. "Catch you later, Cranky Campbell." Then he turned around and jogged away.

It took me a moment to realize I'd raised my hand, that I was touching my lips, thinking of Ash's there. In that second, it hit me why I couldn't feel for Shan the way I wanted to, why I'd never been as interested in girls and sex as my friends. That kiss with Ash did things to my body I didn't think possible. Made me feel alive, like I was flying and floating and shit, and I was pretty sure my dick had been hard before I hit the water.

I was gay and had a crush on my nemesis.

Fucking karma gods struck again.

CHAPTER ONE

Ashton
Ten Years Later

Ashton "Ride 'em hard" Carmichael strikes again!
Exclusive photos of the hotel orgy that could ruin
his career!

I GROANED AS I read the latest article in a magazine that had basically built its career on trying to ruin mine. My eyes scanned the pictures...me passed out in bed...alcohol all over the room...three women in various states of undress, with blurred spots hiding the goods. Obviously, the fourth—my ex—was behind the camera. The reason I knew that was because: 1. I'd gone to the hotel room with her, and 2. She filled me in on the leak before it happened, giving me the chance to stop it for a hefty sum of money I'd delivered upon.

But as my eyes scanned the article, my pulse sped up and sweat dripped down my face, because holy fuck, this was really happening...not that it was the first time for this sort of thing. I had a bit of a reputation, but it was the first time it happened right before contract negotiations and not long after my agent told me my team—the Los Angeles Avalanche—were worried. *Loose cannon* they'd called me, which of course I'd argued, but *oops*, they were right.

"Fuck," I cursed, rubbing a hand over my face just as my cell rang. There was no doubt in my mind who the call was from. I was pretty sure my agent, Andrea, had radar notification of any time I fucked up, which unfortunately was quite a bit. But it was so damn hard to be good. Why didn't they understand that?

For a moment I thought about ignoring her, but I knew there was no point. Andrea was likely calling from the road while she drove to my place, and nothing would stop her once she got there anyway. "I—"

"I told you, Ash. I fucking told you something was up with Bridget, but you never fucking listen when a fake pair of tits is involved."

Well…that was a little unfair, wasn't it? "I'm more of an ass man, myself."

"What?" she spit out. "Now isn't the time to be funny."

I wasn't being funny; I was being honest.

"You're a free fucking agent, Ash. Your team didn't

offer you a contract...no one else has either. If you haven't noticed, you played like shit last season."

I winced, feeling her words like a kick to the groin. It hadn't been a great year for me. It would be impossible not to notice that, because every time I turned around, someone was reminding me—reporters, coaches, teammates, social media...myself. Everyone always had an opinion and thought they had the right to share it. "Way to bust my balls, Andrea. And what's with all the F-bombs?"

She ignored my attempt to lighten the mood. "You don't pay me to lie to you, Ash; you pay for brutal fucking honesty. You've had a shit year, a shit couple of years, but this was the worst. You make headlines for all the wrong reasons, and you're a loose cannon with a bad attitude, who doesn't take anything seriously and cares more about putting his dick in someone than winning games."

"Hey! I resent that. I have a good attitude, and it's always smart to be serious about where one sticks their cock."

When she sighed again, I added, "I'm taking this seriously. My life has been about football for ten years. I'm just not freaking out right now, unlike someone else I know." My stomach was in knots, but I didn't know the actual reason for it yet. I was still trying to work through it all, which should have been a huge flashing neon sign for me. The reason I should be stressed out right now was my career, getting signed…only I felt like I should care about that more than I actually *did* care about it. After living and breathing football for so long, it was scary as fuck that it wasn't what fueled my lungs anymore…that I didn't know what did.

All I knew was I was tired…so damn tired. But I was also Ashton Carmichael. Football was my life. It always had been, even back to my dad teaching me how to play. It's who I was.

Andrea sighed again. I had a knack for making her do that. "You need to listen to me, Ash, really listen. Avalanche aren't excited about you anymore. When you first started, you were their golden boy, their star quarterback, and now you're—"

"I get it, Andrea, I get it." How could I not? Leaning forward, I put my phone on speaker, set it on the table, and rubbed my temples. "If not Avalanche, who else do we have? The Storm?"

"No."

My stomach dropped. "Houston?"

"No, Ash. We have feelers out…but no one is taking the bait."

My head swam, and I got dizzy. How was that possible? I was Ashton Carmichael—first-round pick, Rookie of the Year, MVP, the leader of a championship team. I was born to play football.

"What the hell were you thinking?" she asked again.

Excuses tangled in my brain—lies as well as the truth. What was wrong with consenting adults having sex? Even in groups. I didn't have an orgy. I was being blackmailed. But as I opened my mouth, I knew none of it mattered. "There's nothing I can do here, is there?" I asked, because what else could I say? Andrea was a miracle worker, but I could feel it in my gut—my football days were numbered.

"I don't know," she replied. "I'm going to try and work some magic. Elliott is out of the country, but Dax is going to meet me at your place." Elliott and Dax worked for the PR firm that represented me. Elliott was usually my guy, but Dax had been known to jump in from time to time.

"Okay," I replied. "Dax is a good man and good at what he does." If anyone could get me out of this, it was Andrea and Dax.

"I'll see you in a few minutes. Don't leave your damn house. Don't call or talk to anyone until we can figure out how to spin this. And if there's anything you can think of that'll help us here, for God's sake, share it with me. I know how proud you are sometimes. Now doesn't need to be one of those times."

"I know, I know," I replied. "See you in a few minutes."

The second she ended the call, I fell back into the armchair. "Fuck, Bridget." If she'd needed money, why hadn't she just come to me? Asked me? Why go through the risk of blackmailing me with the photos when I would have helped her regardless? And why, even after I paid, did she leak them?

The more important questions were: Why hadn't I told Andrea about the blackmail? Why didn't I plan to? And how had Bridget known that no matter what, I wouldn't? Not even to save my career.

CHAPTER TWO

Beau

My brother, Beau, is the best man I know.
~ Love, Kenny

"IT SMELLS GOOD in here," I said as I stepped into the house, the scent of basil and oregano filling my nose.

"I'm making meatballs!" Kenny looked over his shoulder at me and smiled as I came into the kitchen. The leather journal he often wrote in was on the counter beside him.

Mom cleared her throat from where she stood looking through a cabinet.

"*We're* making meatballs." Kenny caught my eye again and rolled his.

"That's better." Mom closed the cabinet, walked over, and kissed my cheek. She wore jeans and her Campbell's Confections shirt. It had been the name of the bakery before Dad left, before he'd decided it was too hard having kids, especially one with special needs, and bailed on us when I was eleven. People had asked her why she hadn't changed it and taken her maiden name back, but she always said her boys were Campbells and so was she.

Her brown hair was in a bun, short curls having slipped out around her ears. Her eyes were tired, yet happy in a way I'd grown up with. It hadn't been easy for her to raise Kenny and me alone, but she'd done it and she'd loved it. There wasn't a part of me that didn't know my mother would do it all over again, that we were her heart—especially Kenny. He was impossible not to love, they both were, which was why I fought never to feel sorry for myself for staying. That's what family did.

I walked over to my brother and ruffled his hair. "Don't worry, Kenny. I know you did all the work," I teased, and Mom laughed.

"Don't ruffle my hair, Beau. I'm not a baby!" Kenny gave me a playful evil eye, and I held up my hands in defeat.

"Oh, sorry. I didn't know you were too cool for affection from your brother now. Being twenty will do that to a guy." Kenny had turned twenty a few days before and hadn't stopped reminding us about it. He suddenly felt grown up, not being a teenager anymore.

"You're being sarcastic," he replied, and both Mom and I chuckled. Kenny's eyes glowed like they so often did, a smile pulling at his lips. The simplest things made him happy—laughter, birds, sunshine. The world would be a whole lot happier place if everyone looked at it through Kenny's eyes.

"Yeah, I am," I finally replied.

"Wash your hands. Dinner is almost done," Kenny told me.

"Yes, sir." God, I loved him.

A few minutes later we sat down for dinner. I tried to come over and eat with Mom and Kenny at least once a week, though it wasn't always easy between work and coaching Kenny's football team. But the three of us were all we had as far as family went.

"How's work?" Mom asked.

"Not too bad. That Hudson fire was brutal. Lost the whole damn building, but luckily, no lives."

It was an accident that I'd fallen into firefighting. I spent some time waiting for a football career to come find me in Fever Falls and make all my dreams come true. I don't know why that shit didn't happen. I forgot that yes, while we were an up-and-coming town with both urban and rural areas, and high school football was life, it stopped there. Had to head to the bigger cities for college or professional teams.

Then there'd been a kitchen fire at home. Luckily, there hadn't been much damage, nothing a slight remodel couldn't fix. I'd already moved out, but the thought of what could have happened to my mom and Kenny had given me a sort of jump start. And now I couldn't imagine doing anything else. Well, I could sort of imagine playing football, but obviously that wasn't going to happen. Still, I loved what I did. Gave me purpose, if that made sense.

"You're a hero!" Kenny said, and my pulse went crazy. He always said that of me, but I didn't deserve it. Not really.

"Nah, that's you." I winked at him, and he gave me another of those hundred-watt smiles.

We were quiet for a few moments. I made sure to *oooh* and *ahhh* about how good dinner was, which again made my brother practically bounce in his seat. When we finished eating, Mom offered to do the dishes, and Kenny and I didn't argue with her.

We went into the backyard and tossed my football back and forth for a little while, and I had to admit, feeling the leather against my skin made my chest ache…brought forth images of Ashton Carmichael—the muscles he'd put on since high school, his short, brown hair and those blue, blue eyes. Oh, and a career I would have killed for, which he'd recently thrown down the drain for a piece of ass. Or, as the articles had said, four of them.

Fucking Ashton Carmichael. I hadn't seen him since he left home, exactly one week after *that* night. When we'd run into each other after the kiss, we'd both acted like nothing had happened, but I'd been thinking about it. I'd hated myself for it, but I had.

Was Ash gay too?

Bisexual?

Did it make him realize he'd had feelings for me the way it had done for me?

Apparently, the answers to those questions had all been *no* because Ash had thrown himself into more than football when he left—he'd thrown himself into women. A lot of them. Apparently, sometimes in groups of four.

Pain shot through my nose, and I stumbled back as the football fell to the ground. "Shit!"

"I'm sorry, I'm sorry, I'm sorry!" Kenny's voice was frantic as he ran over.

"Hey. I'm fine. My fault for not paying attention, not yours."

I took my hand away. It wasn't even bleeding, just a bit sore.

Kenny's eyes found the ground, not looking convinced.

"Dude...I'm fine. Have I ever lied to you?" I wrapped an arm around his shoulder.

"No."

"And I'm not about to start now."

His cheeks got slightly red for a second, and I wondered what I could have said to make him bashful.

"Were you thinking about a boy?" Kenny asked.

Yes...yes, I was. I didn't plan to open *that* can of worms with him, though. "What makes you ask that?"

His cheeks turned three shades redder, and my stomach clenched while my heart swelled for him. Kenny had only had one real crush that he'd talked to me about, but it had been one of those things that never could have happened.

"There's this...girl. She's new to my group." He shoved his hands in his pockets and dug the toes of his shoes into the dirt.

Kenny met with a Down syndrome group called Pathway once a week. He'd made a lot of good friends there, and I was so happy he had it. That, along with his football team and the college classes he was taking, and Kenny had a more exciting life than I did. He'd always been what they considered high-functioning. He also hadn't had a lot of major health problems. He had a mild digestive issue, which a lot of people with Down syndrome had, but no heart defects, which were also common in people with his disability. He'd spoken late, and his speech had been hard to understand in the beginning, but after a lot of speech therapy, he was now pretty easy to understand.

There would never be anyone in the world I was more proud of than Kenny.

"And do you like this girl?" I asked him. "It's okay if you do, Kenny."

"I think so," he replied. "She's real pretty. She has red hair and freckles. And the other day I was thinking about her and I wasn't paying attention, so I ran into a pole…so I thought maybe you were thinking about a boy you liked too."

Goose bumps pebbled down my skin. I remembered what it had felt like when Ash's lips pressed down against mine—as if the whole world had suddenly made sense. Like I'd been living in the dark and didn't know why, and Ash had turned on the light. Not because he was Ash. I'd probably crushed on him, and had definitely thought he was hot, but it was more because he was a man.

I couldn't bring myself to admit it, though…that it

had been more than sexual awakening, because he was Ash and I'd hated him. How could I like him if I'd hated him? And I certainly didn't want to admit to thinking about him, because it meant conceding to the allure of Ashton Carmichael.

Still, I'd been telling the truth when I said I didn't lie to Kenny, so I answered as carefully as possible. "It's normal to think about someone you're attracted to or have a crush on. I've done it plenty of times. I've even tripped and ran into a pole while thinking about them too."

"Really?" Kenny's light-brown eyes glowed.

"Yep, seriously." I squeezed his shoulder and kissed his forehead. "Now, are you going to tell me about this girl, or what?" I asked him.

We sat down right there in the middle of the grass, and Kenny did just that.

CHAPTER THREE

Ashton

Playboy quarterback Ashton "Love 'em and leave 'em" Carmichael forced into early retirement!

I CLOSED MY Internet browser, exiting out of the shitty *news source* that didn't know crap about anything. No one had *forced* me out of anything. And Ashton *Love 'em and leave 'em*? How did they come by these corny names, anyway?

Because everyone thought I'd left Bridget after the foursome…that I'd had my way with her and her friends before finding someone else. I'd gotten what I'd wanted. That's what they all said.

Groaning, I shoved out of the desk chair and walked over to the window. The back lawn was lush, and behind it, a mass of trees that looked like they went on for eternity. I'd forgotten how green it was at home. Even in less urban areas of LA, the green was never that vivid. But then here, all I had to do was drive fifteen minutes into the city, and there would be the hustle and bustle, shopping, bars, restaurants. Fever Falls was the best of both worlds that way, and it had grown a lot over the years. What had once been a place we all wanted to escape was now a city people flocked to.

I'd been back in Fever Falls for two weeks, after spending time hiding out in LA, licking my wounds, ignoring the feeling of failure when my teammates went back to training camp. Now I was in the home I'd grown up in, with memories of my parents, of my childhood around every corner. Christ, they had a lot of photos of me…of us—swimming, hiking, laughing…loving.

My chest ached. I rubbed my hand over it as though I could massage the pain out. It had been eight years since I lost them in a car accident, the people who had chosen me as their child, who had loved me for me when others had given me away, and I hadn't slowed down enough to let myself realize I'd missed them. Hell, I hadn't even been back in the house until now. Eight years I'd stayed away. What had I been thinking? I paid for a cleaning service to come over and keep it clean, utilities to stay on, but I hadn't come back.

There was another squeeze in my chest, which wasn't pleasant at all, so I pretended it wasn't there. Masochist that I was, I almost went back to the computer to Google myself, to see what else was being said about me—comments on social media posts and memes that I sort of hated for being funny. It would have been a riot had they been about someone else.

Don't do it, Ash, don't Google yourself.

So instead I took a shower, considered jacking off but didn't. I'd spent two weeks alone; no one even knew I was back in town, which I'd liked. But I also needed to get the fuck out of the house. It was lonely as shit pouting for two weeks.

Maybe I also needed the feeling that came with being the *hometown hero.* I'd made it from Fever Falls to professional football, and that mattered here more than all the drama that had followed me the last few years...at least I thought it did. Please, fucking let me be right about that.

The thing was, I had two choices: I could go out that door with self-respect and my head held high, or I could stay in the house, have my groceries delivered from now on, and never go out in public again. Would that really be so bad? I had everything I could want here... *No!* I shook my head. What was wrong with me? I'd never run from anything in my life, and I didn't plan to start now. *Nothing? Really?*

Nope, I was filing that *Nothing? Really?* away with

other shit I ignored.

So I shot off a text that was answered almost immediately, and now I had a plan.

It didn't take long to get dressed—jeans and a blue-gray tee with three buttons at the top. The shirt was similar in color to my eyes and tight against the muscles in my arms. A few minutes later, I was out the door, climbing into my BMW and making my way down Cherry Blossom Lane.

See? This wasn't so hard.

You failed, Ash... Everyone's going to look at you and think you failed.

Why were personal demons so damn hard to lose? I'd made something of myself. I'd spent eight years playing professional football, plus another two before that in college, but there would always be that annoying voice nagging me and making me feel like a failure.

Trying to distract myself, I took in the lush, green scenery as I drove.

Wyatt lived in a brick house in an affluent community in Fever Falls. I'd just stepped out of my BMW when the door opened and Holly's blonde hair stuck around the corner. "Oh my God! It's Ashton Carmichael!" she playfully shrieked, making me laugh.

She jogged down the porch stairs and launched herself at me. I caught her, and she held on to my neck. "It's so good to see you!" she told me.

Holly and Wyatt had started dating not long after high school. They'd gone to the University of North Carolina together, moved back to Fever Falls together, and started their family.

The three of us had stayed in contact over the years. Holly was in real estate and helped keep an eye on the house for me. They even flew out to some of my games a few times. It felt good to hold her, but slightly awkward too. I couldn't help but wonder what she was thinking of me...of the articles and headlines that were all a mixture of truth and lies.

"It's good to see you too," I replied when we parted. Maybe it didn't make sense, but I was nervous. I knew how to be the Ashton Carmichael who flew friends out for his football games. I didn't know how to be Ashton Carmichael with my childhood friends, back in my hometown. It was as if I forgot who that person was.

"You two planning on hanging out here all day, or what?" Wyatt asked from the doorway, and my stomach immediately clenched. Wyatt was...a good man, a close friend...but also honest, sometimes to a fault, and starstruck of the life I'd lived since leaving home. "You're lucky I'm not a jealous man. I might be worried you'd try and have an orgy with my wife."

Because obviously he had to lead with that. I mean, forget that I'd probably have done the same thing, but it took everything in me not to slink away with my tail between my legs.

"Wyatt!" Holly swatted his arm.

"What? It's Ash. He knows I'm giving him shit." He turned to me. "Hey, buddy. How's it going?" We gave each other a sort of half-bro-hug thing.

"Not too bad. I can't stay long, though. I have a threesome scheduled in an hour." The joke just sort of jumped out of my mouth because it was easier to go along with it than not to.

Wyatt laughed, and Holly rolled her eyes at us.

"I'm going to be in trouble having the two of you together again, aren't I?" she asked.

"Obviously," Wyatt replied.

When we headed into the house, Holly asked, "Seriously, though. Do you want to stay for dinner?"

"I can't," I lied. "I really do have something to take care of tonight."

Continuing to hide out…or hell, maybe a private island was starting to sound like the best course of action.

CHAPTER FOUR

Beau

Sometimes I think Beau's sadder than he seems.
~ Love, Kenny

"CHRIST ON A cracker. I've died and gone to gay heaven. Who is *that*?"

I rolled my eyes at my best friend, Lincoln, before popping a tater tot into my mouth. Linc had a radar for pretty boys, and while there were times it had come in handy, I wasn't in the mood at the moment. "Who cares? Can't we just eat and not worry about sex for once?" Not that I typically minded thinking about sex. Hell, I quite enjoyed sex and thought about it often, but right then, I just wanted to eat and chat with my friend and relax.

"Who said anything about sex, hmmm?" Linc cocked a blond brow at me. "I was only commenting on a pretty face…and body…good *God* that body. It's better than yours."

That's what made me turn around in my seat. Not that I thought I had the hottest body around or anything, but it was pretty good. The second I did, my heart dropped to my stomach...nope, not there...it kept going, landing somewhere close to my feet.

My head suddenly throbbed. Jerking, I tried to whip around, duck down in my seat so he couldn't see me, but apparently my bad karma had returned because I saw the recognition in his blue eyes as I turned away from him.

"Beau? Holy shit, Beau Campbell," Ash nearly shouted as he stalked forward.

Linc's eyes went wide, obviously not realizing who it was. Linc hadn't gone to high school in Fever Falls, and though he'd of course heard about the football player who'd gone pro—because who the fuck *hadn't* heard of Ashton Carmichael—he wasn't into the sport and likely didn't put two and two together.

The moment Ash stepped up to the table, his muscular thighs were right fucking in front of me, enclosed in tight blue jeans...and they were sexy thighs. Not something I'd ever paid much attention to, but then these were Ash's thighs, and I had no doubt he was as charismatic as he'd always been.

But it wasn't nice to stare, was it? Especially not with straight football players who kissed you once and then never spoke to you again. Nope, not fair at all.

I knew I had to do something, knew I had to look up, but I couldn't quite make myself do it.

"Beau?" Ash asked, probably wondering if I'd lost my mind since he saw me last.

"Yes, Beau?" Linc added, because he was Lincoln and of course he could read me like a book.

As my head slowly angled upward, my eyes scanned his body. Ashton Carmichael... Ash was fucking there, back in Fever Falls. The second I reached his face, the corners of his mouth tilted up into a sexy, cocky smile, and I was taken back to that night, to the kiss, the feel of Ash's lips against mine, the feel of a *man's* lips against my own. He'd been both my nemesis—the man who would be able to live my dream—and my sexual awakening. And fuck, he was even more gorgeous than he had been ten years before. Somehow his eyes were bluer, this piercing dagger that went right through me. His jaw was squarer, his dark scruff sexier...well, he hadn't even had scruff back then, but he had it now. His hair looked a little lighter, but still very brown. His lips were sort of pouty, which he played to his advantage, or at least he had back then.

Wait. Had someone asked me a question? I couldn't remember.

"Hi, I'm Lincoln, Beau's very available and flexible friend. He seems to have lost his voice at the moment. You are…" Linc's words snapped me out of whatever trance Ash had put me into.

"Knock it off, Linc," I said just as Ash replied, "You don't know who I am?"

I rolled my eyes. Jesus, he hadn't changed a bit. "Oh, of course, because everyone has to know who Ashton Carmichael is."

"Obviously," Ash answered with a cocky grin that was just an older, sexier version of the one he'd had when we were teens.

"Wait…you're the football guy?" Linc asked, and I swear Ash lit up like someone stuffed the sun up his ass.

He held out his hand, and Lincoln took it. "Ashton Carmichael, nice to meet you." Lincoln pretended to swoon, and Ash frowned but recovered quickly. "Christ, it's been a long time, Beau. I think the last time I saw you was the night of our graduation party. Shit, I was drunk as hell that night."

Because he just had to throw that in so I was reminded that my sexual awakening had been his drunken mistake. I opened my mouth to reply but didn't get the chance before Ash was sitting down in the booth, making me automatically have to scoot over.

"Yes, please. Make yourself at home," I told him.

"There's the Cranky Campbell I remember."

Ash winked.

Lincoln laughed.

I groaned. How was this my life? I couldn't believe Ash was back. But then the headlines I'd obsessively read came back to me...the partying, the women, the orgy...not getting signed...Ash taking an early retirement.

A tornado formed in my chest, a mixture of sympathy and anger—hurting for him having lost everything; pissed that he threw it all away. Fuck, I would have done anything for the opportunities Ash had.

"Do you mind if I steal that?" Lincoln asked. "The guys will love it. Cranky Campbell fits him so well."

"Fuck you very much." I threw a tater tot at my ex-friend.

"Feel free." Ash told him, picking a tot off my plate as though it hadn't been ten years since I saw or spoke to him. What the hell was that?

He chewed, and it brought my attention to his strong, square jawline. This wasn't how I expected the day to go. There was no universe I could have imagined for myself where Ash would be sitting beside me, eating food off my plate.

"Wow...I knew about you, of course. Everyone in town talks about you, but Beau never mentioned you'd been friends. He actually made it sound like..."

I cocked a brow at Linc for nearly selling me out, and he closed his mouth.

"Like he hated me?" Ash asked.

"Well...now that you mention it..."

"I didn't hate you," I cut them off, but the truth was, I had. Or at least I always told myself I had, and in ten years, that hadn't changed.

"I think that might be the nicest thing you've ever said to me." Ash winked before eating more of my food.

I was so dumbstruck, I didn't know what to say, so instead I watched him as he made himself completely comfortable with us. Was there ever a situation where Ash was uncomfortable? Well, except for post-kiss with me, apparently.

"We love our Cranky Campbell," Linc added. "I have a feeling we'll love you too. Straight football player eating at Fever Pitch, one of the gayest restaurants in the gayborhood."

Oh fuck. There wasn't a doubt in my mind what Lincoln was doing. He was trying to figure out if Ash was straight.

"The gayborhood?" Ash's brows pulled together.

"And wait, there's such a thing as gay restaurants?"

I shook my head and groaned. This was going to be a long dinner. "No, it's not really a gay restaurant. I mean, it's frequented by a lot of members of the LGBTQ community, but anyone can come here, and yes, Fever Street is now basically the gay mecca of Fever Falls."

"Oh," Ash replied, and then his brows rose to his hairline as if he'd realized what it meant for me. "*Oh.*" His cheeks suddenly flushed, making me wonder if Ash was thinking about that night ten years ago, which had obviously been a fluke for him. Unless he kept his trysts with men secret, which was entirely possible. "Congratulations?" he asked, making Lincoln laugh again.

"Oh, honey, you're cute as hell."

"Cut it out, Linc," I told him. The last thing we needed was for Lincoln to fall in lust with Ash. He didn't do love, but he sure as shit did lust. I looked at Ash. "You don't have to congratulate me."

"Yeah...that was weird. Sorry. It just threw me for a second."

Because I'd kissed him like I'd been straight? I was pretty sure I'd kissed him like I'd wanted to crawl inside him. But then, he'd kissed me back, he'd kissed me *first*, and clearly it didn't mean the same thing for him.

"I'm not...gay, I mean. I'm an ally, though!" He said

the last part a little too enthusiastically, then looked around the restaurant as though the gays were all going to come and get him.

"Congratulations," I replied.

"You don't have to congratulate me," he said with a smirk.

"Bi?" Lincoln asked, hope making his voice rise an octave.

"Sorry, buddy, straight as straight can be."

Was it me, or had Ash turned away from me when he'd spoken? Likely, I was looking for signs that weren't there. It wasn't an enjoyable thought that my male-first-kiss only did it because he was drunk...that he wasn't attracted to me...or men in general.

"Damn it!" Lincoln cursed, and thankfully Ash laughed before popping another tater tot into this mouth.

"Ugh. These are cold. How about I order us some more? And potato skins. Maybe we can do some appetizer platters. Do you guys want a drink? Dinner's on me," Ash rambled on.

Before I could get the word *no* out, Linc replied, "I'm in."

Did I mention it was going to be a long night?

CHAPTER FIVE

Ashton

Ashton Carmichael, licking his wounds, suffers consequences for his actions!

I WASN'T SURE what had gotten into me, why I'd ordered food and drinks and basically inserted myself into Beau and Lincoln's night, other than the fact that I didn't want to go home to an empty house. I'd been there for weeks, drowning in gossip articles and my failed career. The idea of wallowing in my thoughts, my past, while the pictures lining the walls reminded me that I was utterly alone, was depressing as hell.

Shit. I didn't want to be alone. That was a revelation. Before all this had gone down, I tried to think of the last time I'd been truly alone, other than for a day or so, and nothing came to me. I was at the gym or training, at practice, at business meetings or endorsements, with friends, fake friends, and women…lots and lots of women. Christ, the thought of being alone, of talking to myself and dwelling on how far I'd fallen, made me sick to my stomach.

And for some reason, being with Wyatt had felt all wrong. There wasn't anything he'd done, outside of a few misplaced jokes. But Wyatt was so tied to Football Ash, and I wasn't that Ash anymore…at least I didn't think I was. In all honesty, I wasn't really sure *who* I was.

So I'd ordered a table of food and a round of drinks, which turned into two rounds of drinks, then three for me. Every so often, my eyes found the large TV screens by the bar—hoping, praying, that nothing about me popped up on the screen. Oh, and that no one recognized me. I'd come there hoping someone would, and now I was thankful they didn't.

Beau was pretty quiet. I felt his eyes on me more than once, so I'd look at him, make a joke or tease him. He'd get annoyed and roll his eyes, and Lincoln would laugh. The laughter was familiar in a time when nothing else was, so I clung to that, did everything I could to keep making Lincoln chuckle.

At one point there was a lull in the conversation, and damn it, nothing witty or funny was coming to me, so I asked a question that had waited impatiently on the tip of my tongue. "So…are you guys…"

"Together?" Beau asked.

"God no," Lincoln replied.

"Gee, thanks," Beau scoffed. "Tell me how you really feel."

"Oh, don't pretend you have any interest in me either," Lincoln answered, then looked at me. "I love Beau. He's my best friend/babysitter/there better never be anyone in his life more important than me, but it's not sexual. He's the most stable, responsible—"

"So basically, boring," Beau cut him off.

"Your word, not mine." Lincoln reached over and squeezed his hand. "Anyway…he's a great guy. Obviously hot as hell, but no, we're not like that. Never have been. I basically annoy the shit out of him and enjoy it."

"Hey! Me too," I added. "Or at least, I used to. What gives, Cranky Campbell?" I asked.

"Maybe the fact that you call me that?" he answered.

"Nah, that's not it. I annoyed you before that."

"And this is why we love our Beau. He wouldn't know how to have any fun without us. But again, not *that* kind of fun. We wouldn't be compatible in bed, if you know what I mean."

I stared at him, his body blurring a little around the edges—probably a mixture of alcohol and…okay, so probably just because of the alcohol. Also…I had no idea what he meant. "Actually, I don't."

"We're both catchers."

"Jesus Christ, Linc," Beau practically growled at him. "Could you not spread my business to the whole restaurant?"

"I didn't." Lincoln shook his head. "Just to Ash. Oh, look, he's blushing."

My face flamed to the extent I thought I might pass out. I wasn't quite sure why. It wasn't as if I didn't ever talk sex with my friends, but this was…*different*. This evening had to break some record. I was pretty sure I hadn't blushed this much in my life.

Beau liked to be on the bottom… Beau liked to be…fucked?

"Let's change the subject." Beau rubbed his hand over his face, and I noticed it looked like he hadn't shaved that day. A dusting of stubble danced across his jawline and cheek. He'd been smooth-shaven when we'd been in high school. It was a strange thing to remember about him, but I did.

His black hair was a little longer than it had been, a little wavier on top. The sides were shorter, though. It looked really fucking soft.

"Can I have one more?" I asked the waitress, and she said she'd be right back with my drink. Beau's eyes were on me again. I could feel them even though I wasn't looking at him, and I was positive he was frowning.

"What's the frown for?" Lincoln asked.

"I wasn't frowning," Beau replied, but he had been. I'd called it before Lincoln had spoken.

"Okay, we'll go with that." Lincoln winked at Beau, and I realized how much I liked him. He was a fun guy, friendly, and apparently didn't give a shit about football. He hadn't asked me about my career, what went wrong, or chastised me for throwing it all away. Neither he nor Beau had. That thought made my eyes get drawn to Beau again. He had his arms crossed on the table as he and Lincoln went back and forth about his frown. His arms were bigger than I remembered them being...not that I'd paid all that much attention to Beau's arms back then, and I wasn't now really either, but they were definitely bigger, more defined.

There were three small moles on his bicep, above a scar. I remembered that, but only because it had always looked like a happy face—two eyes, a nose, and a mouth.

We'd been about sixteen, I thought, when I saw it. We'd been lifting weights in PE, and much to Beau's annoyance, we'd been partnered with each other. I'd stood above him, spotting him, watching his arms for any sign that he needed help, when suddenly it looked like his muscle was smiling at me, or at least the little face on it was. Strange that I would remember something so small, that many years later.

The waitress set my fourth drink in front of me, and I swallowed half of it in long gulps.

"Are you sure you guys aren't together?" I asked as they continued bickering. It had come as a shock to me that Beau was gay, as in homosexual—he liked men, dated men, and that was something that everyone knew about him. Maybe it shouldn't have been so surprising to me, but it was.

"We're not. Why?" Beau asked.

"Just the nitpicking back and forth. It reminds me of someone in a relationship." After picking up my glass, I took another drink just as Lincoln spoke.

"Do you want to have a threesome with us? I'd be willing to make a sacrifice by sleeping with Beau if it was for the greater good, if that's what you keep hinting at."

Alcohol somehow got lodged in my throat, or went down the wrong pipe, and I snorted it. My nose burned. Shit, my fucking nose stung. I'd somehow gotten alcohol *in my nose*. My life flashed before my eyes, my vision blurring as Lincoln laughed and Beau's hand came down over and over on my back.

When I finally worked through it, Beau's hand slipped away. Shaking my head, I began, "I'm not... I said I wasn't... Not that I have anything against..."

"Relax. I'm kidding. Kind of. I *would* take one for the team, but you're straight, I get it. And as much fun as this is, I need to get going. I'm meeting Cam and Sawyer."

"Who are Cam and Sawyer?" I asked.

It was Beau who answered. "Camden and Sawyer are friends of ours." Then he asked Lincoln, "You guys are going out tonight?"

"Yeah, to Fever. We would have asked you, but we knew you wouldn't go to a club if it wasn't Saturgay."

Had he said Saturgay? Shit. I shook my head. I must have been drunker than I thought. I was hearing things.

"Here, let me give you some money toward the food and drinks." Lincoln pulled out his wallet, and I waved him off.

"No, like I said. It's on me. You can get it next time. Do you really have to go?" If Lincoln left, Beau would leave, and I would have to go home, which was the last thing I wanted to do.

"Next time?" Lincoln cocked a brow.

I shrugged. "Yeah...if it happens. If not, that's cool too."

Lincoln smiled. "I'll get it next time." Then he stood, followed by Beau, which meant I should stand up as well.

My legs wobbled, feeling slightly weak, as did I.

"Are you walking to Sawyer's?" Beau asked.

"Yeah. My car's already there. I left it before I came over. Rush has practice or training or some shit like that, so he's not around. But I don't think I'm the one you need to worry about driving."

My mouth opened, an argument right there, but the truth was, he was right. I had zero business behind the wheel of a car.

"Have fun, boys." Lincoln leaned over the table and kissed Beau's cheek. I watched his lips touch Beau's skin as Beau gave him a hug. Then, before I knew it, Lincoln was hugging me and I was standing there with my arms glued to my sides as if I'd never been touched before. What the fuck was wrong with me?

Lincoln left, and I fell back onto the bench. "You're frowning at me," I told Beau, who still stood.

"How would you know? You're not even looking at me."

"Because I remember what it feels like. You spent your whole life frowning at me. If I hadn't seen you smile at other people, I wouldn't have thought you knew how. I was always doing something to disappoint you. At one point, I was determined to get on the good side of

Cranky Campbell. Don't think I ever did, though." Fucking alcohol giving me loose lips. I did a lot of dumb shit when I drank too much—like have random orgies with women and apparently spilling my guts to Beau.

"Shit," Beau cursed quietly. "We'll talk about this in the car. I'm taking you home."

CHAPTER SIX

Beau

I asked Beau once if he was ever going to have a family...or a serious boyfriend, at least. He said Mom and I were all the family he needed. Maybe it was something I didn't get...there are things I don't get, but to me, that sounded sad. I thought Beau deserved better. ~ Love, Kenny

WHAT IN THE fuck was happening?

Without letting myself think about it much, I tossed money on the table.

"I was supposed to get the bill."

"You can get it next time," I told Ash, who looked up at me with glassy eyes.

"Next time?"

"According to you and Linc." I nudged him with my arm. "Come on, let's go."

To my surprise, Ash didn't argue. He stood, and we walked out of Fever Pitch together. Nodding my head toward the parking lot, I said, "I'm over there—Red Tundra."

He shoved his hands into his pockets as we walked. There was something different about him... Well, I was sure there were a lot of things different about him, but the most noticeable one was that he seemed sadder. That made sense—it wasn't a secret that he hadn't gotten a contract for another team.

We got into the truck, and as Ash struggled to buckle himself in, he said, "Sorry. I'm not usually like this. It's just...been a few tough months. Not sure why it's hitting me all of a sudden."

With a sigh, I helped him buckle in, took care of my own, and started the truck. "Where are you staying?"

"Home," he replied.

The answer made my pulse run circles. "How?"

Someone had purchased the house right after Ash's parents had passed. We never knew who it was, and no one ever moved in, but cleaning and yard workers came. It had always struck me as odd, but Ash wouldn't have had to buy it; he would have inherited it. And what would he have needed with a house in town he never saw?

"It's mine. It's always been mine. We just made it appear otherwise so it didn't look like Ashton Carmichael's home was empty."

I looked over at him, felt the corners of my mouth tip downward.

"Stop frowning at me."

Shit. "Stop being psychic." Or maybe I was predictable. That's what Linc would say. "It's not you. I frown at everyone." Other than Kenny, I guessed.

"Yeah, but you do it to me more."

"How would you know when we haven't seen each other in ten years?" Did he remember the kiss? Had he ever thought about it? Wished he still knew what I tasted like?

"Call it a good guess."

"I don't hate you," I found myself saying. But I wanted to. Part of me wanted to hate him now, and I'd definitely wanted to back then. Maybe because even before I'd admitted it to myself, I'd known I was gay and that I was attracted to Ash. It wasn't something I struggled with anymore—the out-and-proud part. I loved being gay and wasn't ashamed of that, but back then I likely had been.

"Okay," Ash replied, and we were quiet the whole way back to his house.

When we got there, I realized he had his head against the window and had fallen asleep. What in the hell was going on? Who was the man with me? When he first arrived, he'd been just like the Ash I remembered. He still was in many ways, but there was something else twined in; the sadness, yeah, but I thought maybe even more than that.

"Ash," I whispered, reached for him, almost brushed the back of my hand against his cheek. "Ash?"

His thick lashes rested on his cheek, but after I said his name again, he startled and his eyes jerked open. "Shit," he groaned. "I don't feel so great."

This was where I wanted to give him hell about drinking, make some kind of sarcastic remark, but then the last time we'd been together when Ash drank, he'd kissed me.

And…there I was, back at that again.

"Come on, I'll help you inside."

"Okay," he replied. "But only because I don't want to go in there alone."

My chest got tight, and I forced myself to hold back a frown. Was it just because he wasn't used to being alone? Always had someone there? Probably a woman. The thought made my skin itch, and I hated that Ash had that effect on me, that I cared either way how he spent his life or who he was attracted to.

I got out of the truck and walked around just as Ash

opened his door. He stumbled slightly when he got down, and on reflex, my arm went around him. He was strong, solid, his muscles hard and defined. Ash was about two inches taller than I was, not quite as stocky but equally muscular, if not more. Questions ran through my head. I wanted to ask him why football hadn't been enough to keep him happy. Why all the partying? If it had all been a joke to him.

If he remembered that night...if it had been a first for him or if it ever happened again.

Nope. Nope, nope, nope. I had no fucking business thinking that way. Not about Ashton Carmichael.

"Dude, I'm going to be so embarrassed in the morning."

Not when he called me *dude*.

He fumbled his keys out of his pocket, and I took them. The moment we stepped into the house, it was as if we'd walked into the room ten years ago—the same furniture, the same photos on his walls, his past completely intact.

Ash had been adopted. That wasn't something he'd ever kept a secret. We'd all known that, and it had always been one of the things I respected him for. He'd obviously loved his parents, felt like they were his, and seeing the house now, I saw how he'd tried to honor them. Maybe that wasn't the right word, but Ash's love for them was apparent everywhere...as was their love for him.

Ash didn't speak, just pulled away from me and walked down the hallway. For a moment I considered leaving, but instead I tossed the keys on the table and followed him down the hallway of the one-story ranch-style home.

I turned into a bedroom just as Ash went face-first onto a bed, his legs hanging off the side.

A chuckle fell out of my mouth as I saw the room covered in posters of women in bikinis, cheerleaders, and football players. Ash's old room...his old double bed. With all the money he had, he hadn't even changed that.

Who the fuck was he?

Why did I care?

"Shit," I mumbled as I walked over and began untying his shoes. The asshole was going to owe me for this. The last thing I ever thought I'd be doing was taking off a twenty-eight-year-old Ashton Carmichael's shoes because he was too drunk to do it himself.

"Thank you," he groaned into his pillow. "Christ. Embarrassed."

"I'm not sure he's embarrassed," I teased, but didn't get a sound out of him.

"Fucking alcohol. Always makes me do dumb shit."

It was said offhandedly, with a slur on the end for good measure, but still it was like a punch to the gut. Did he have to keep reminding me he had been drunk that night? That he hadn't wanted to kiss me?

"Don't worry. You're not my type anyway."

A soft snore was my only reply. I made it to the door but stopped, thought about the call we'd gotten a few years ago about someone who had been drunk and aspirated in their sleep. Grumbling, I walked over to the beanbag chair, which was better than the desk chair, and fell into it. Looked like I was sleeping there.

"Thank you," he whispered, his voice laced with sleep. Apparently, he was coming in and out of it.

"Don't want you to die, is all," I replied. "Can you imagine the shit I'd get if I left football legend Ashton Carmichael to die in a drunken stupor?"

"Not what I meant." He rolled over, put the pillow over his head. "For treating me like you always did…for not asking."

About the kiss or football? Or hell, maybe he meant both.

Fucking Ashton Carmichael. Somehow, he was wreaking havoc on my life again.

CHAPTER SEVEN

Ashton

Ashton "How about another drink" Carmichael is really in trouble this time!

THE SECOND I heard the front door close, I scrambled out of bed, which made my head spin, and made my way into the bathroom. My hands shook as I fumbled with my pants, dancing around despite my hangover. Once I had my dick out, the pressure inside me released and I emptied my bladder, which had been incredibly close to exploding.

I'd woken up at dawn, needing to take a leak like I never had in my life, but Beau had been there. The last thing I'd needed was to embarrass myself in front of him, and *thank God*, he didn't stay long after. He woke up, sneaked out, and now, as I finished taking my piss, I was moaning in pleasure like I'd just had the best orgasm of my life.

He'd stayed with me all night… Beau had stayed…

I was slightly embarrassed he'd had to and surprised that he would. Most people didn't just do nice things for me because they were nice. They did them because they could get something from me, even if I didn't figure out what it was until later. Yet somehow, I knew that wasn't Beau. He'd done it because he was a good guy, but then, that had always been Beau. He'd always been better than most people I knew.

I shook, washed my hands, tugged off my clothes, and fell back into bed. It was almost noon when I woke up the second time, my stomach growling and my head feeling too groggy. Rubbing a hand over my face, I walked naked to the bathroom, swallowed two ibuprofens, took a second piss, and then stumbled into the shower attached to my childhood bedroom. There was a familiarity I wanted in being there again, while at the same time, a part of me wanted to rebel against it. It was like going backward, falling from grace.

I'd failed. I'd fucking *failed*, and I didn't know how to deal with that.

Once my shower was finished, I used my face cleaner in hopes that it would make me look less hungover. The bags and dark circles were still there, and I was pretty sure my eyes were more bloodshot than they had been before.

Apparently, they made strong drinks at Fever Pitch.

I found some clean jeans and a tee, brushed my teeth, ran some gel through my hair, and decided I needed to get some food into my stomach before it began eating itself. Bypassing the fully stocked kitchen, I went straight to the door...where my feet rooted to the floor.

Shit. I didn't have my car. It wasn't the first time I'd woken up without my wheels, so I grumbled on my way out, planning to take an Uber, but when I opened the door, there it was. Holy fuck, Beau had gotten my Beamer home.

A smile pulled at my lips, and again, I wasn't surprised. That was Beau. He'd always been the first in line to help someone, only usually that someone wasn't me. He reserved frowns and scowls for me, not that I could blame him.

And then, before I realized what I was doing, I'd driven straight to Campbell's Confections, the bakery Beau's mom owned. Or at least she had ten years ago. It had been a favorite spot for our friends to go. Mrs. Campbell had often given us free goodies after we won a football game.

Warmth spread through my chest at the thought. I'd loved playing ball at Fever Falls High—lived and breathed it along with Beau, Wyatt, and our other friends. Playing in college had been an adjustment for me at first, because it had been so different from playing with the guys I'd grown up with. I didn't know them the way I knew Beau and Wyatt, the way I'd known the whole team. There had been comfort in that, familiarity. But I'd smiled, played it off, because that was what I did. I smiled and partied and worked my ass off on the field, trained in ways I hadn't known were possible, and eventually the ache in my chest had subsided, buried itself deep where I could forget it had been there and no one had to know.

Frowning, I wondered where that had come from, what made me think of those early days I did well pretending never existed. Being home, losing my career, was fucking with me in ways I didn't want to comprehend, so I pulled on my sunglasses, got out of my car, and went toward the building.

The white paint on the front looked fresh. They had a new pink-and-gray awning, and a few tables and chairs on the patio. None of that had been there ten years ago.

The bell over the door jingled when I walked inside. It was empty except for Kenny behind the counter. I almost stumbled seeing him. He was a few inches shorter than I was now, but holy shit, Kenny had grown up. Well, obviously, Kenny had grown up, but it was different knowing those things happened than seeing them.

My pulse sped up in a strange way as I took Kenny in—Beau's brother, the person he'd always cared for more than anyone in the world.

"Good afternoon, welcome to…" Kenny looked up at me, and his eyes widened. "Ashton Carmichael…Ashton Carmichael…Mom! Ashton Carmichael is here!"

My pulse jumped again at the realization that Kenny remembered me. It was a strange thought. Kenny was ten when I left; of course he remembered. Plus, I didn't mean to brag, but I was Ashton Carmichael. Most people knew who I was, but definitely people in Fever Falls.

"Hey, Kenny. Long time no see." I stepped up to the counter.

"Hi, Ashton Carmichael."

I smiled. "You can just call me Ash." I reached over and held my hand out for him. Kenny shook it.

"Okay, Ash. I think I'm supposed to be really happy to see you…everyone else in town makes a big deal about you, but I think you're just a person like everyone else, even if you do play football. We should all be happy to see someone else, no matter who they are, because everyone deserves that. It shouldn't matter what you do for a living. Do you mind if I treat you like everyone else?"

If it wouldn't have been strange, I would have hugged him. A weight fell off my chest that I hadn't realized had been there. It likely always was until I knew I could let my guard down. "It would make me the happiest person in town if you treated me like everyone else."

"Good!" Kenny gave me a huge smile. "Welcome to Campbell's Confections. I'm happy to see you, and I say that because I'm always happy to see people and not because you're Ashton Carmichael."

Joy burst in my chest, a giddy feeling I hadn't experienced in a long time showering me. "I like that attitude. I'm happy to see you too." Likely more than he knew. I'd done a lot of research on Down syndrome in high school because of Beau's brother—not that anyone would know that. Down syndrome had always been my charity of choice over the years. No one knew that either. But I'd always known how important he was to Beau, and that made me curious, especially because Beau was so protective of him.

I knew Kenny was high functioning, but I hadn't known he had a job. And when he smiled, I felt it in my chest because it was genuine in a way I didn't often see in the world. It always had been, and I'd forgotten.

I pulled off my sunglasses and asked, "What do you recommend?" just as Beau's mom came from the back.

"What are you yelling about? Oh, hi, Ash. Look at you! All grown up!" She offered a genuine smile, and I realized it was the same as Kenny's...the same as Beau's, on those rare occasions he sent one my way.

"Yes, ma'am," I replied. "I still prefer acting like a kid, though. It's a lot more fun."

Mrs. Campbell laughed, and I could tell it was the real kind, not just something she thought she had to do because she was talking to Ashton Carmichael. "Some things never change, I see. Such a charmer like always." She came around the counter and gave me a hug. I closed my eyes, savored it because she reminded me of my mom—the one who'd raised me, not the one who'd given me away.

"I try hard," I told her.

"Oh, don't you go pretending it doesn't come natural to you," she replied, and I thought maybe I'd like to sit in the bakery all day with them. I wasn't a pro football player in that building. Hell, I wasn't even a disgraced ex-football-player there. I was just Ash...the guy who'd grown up friends with her son. "Now, did I hear you asking for a recommendation out here? Unless Los

Angeles did something to the boy I know, you love my chocolate éclairs."

My stomach rumbled just at the name. Her chocolate éclairs had always been my favorite, and somehow I'd forgotten that too. "I'll take two...and a coffee, please. To go."

Kenny rang up my order as Mrs. Campbell pulled two fluffy éclairs from the case and put them in a bag. She just finished with my coffee after I paid, and I asked, "I'm looking for Beau. I ran into him last night, and he helped me out with something. I'd like to thank him, but I don't have his phone number...or know where he works or anything."

"Beau is a hero!" Kenny said, and Mrs. Campbell smiled. I could see that...Beau being a hero.

"Beau's a firefighter. He's actually right down the street at the firehouse. He works an early shift today."

Holy shit. First of all, thinking of Beau as a firefighter made my stomach flip strangely. Second of all...he worked today, yet he'd slept on my uncomfortable beanbag chair all night? Then managed to get my car to my house, which was still a feat I wasn't sure how he'd pulled off.

"You saw Beau?" Kenny asked. "He used to watch all your games. He wouldn't even let us talk if your game was on."

Well…that was an interesting development. My stomach flipped again, but I figured it was just because I was so damn hungry. "Does he still watch all my games?"

"Yep, the same Ash I remember. Don't you go fishing for compliments," Mrs. Campbell teased, then turned to Kenny. "Your brother just wanted to support Ash. He was one of Beau's very best friends."

This time my stomach dropped, and I felt slightly woozy. Had I been? I wasn't so sure about that. Yeah, we'd always hung out and had mutual friends, but I'd always known Beau didn't like me much. *Which is also why you gave him so much shit…to make it worse.*

I'd always tried to get under Beau's skin, though I didn't know the exact reason, other than Beau had needed to lighten up. "He was one of my best friends too." I cleared my throat. "Thanks. I'll see if I can find him. I don't want to interrupt him at work." But I absolutely was going to walk by the fire station. Where was the harm in that? Free country and all.

"It was good to see you again, Ash," Beau's mom said.

"Thanks. You too, Mrs. Campbell."

I made it halfway to the door when Mrs. Campbell's voice stopped me. "Beth. You can call me Beth, and I hope I'm not overstepping, but…they would be proud of you, Ash…your mama and daddy…they would be proud of you and all you've accomplished, just like I am. You remember that, okay?"

I inhaled a sharp breath, closed my eyes, hoped she was right about my parents. That despite all the ways I'd fucked up, they would be proud. I was honored Beth was proud, even though I wasn't sure I deserved it. "Thank you, Beth. I appreciate that. And bye, Kenny. It was good to see you too."

I walked out of Campbell's Confections with my stomach feeling uneasy. Beth's words settled into my skin, comforted me, yet at the same time made me feel like I'd screwed up even more. She was proud of me and she thought my parents would be too, but again, the truth was, I'd fucked up. A lot.

Pushing on, I continued up Cypress Lane toward the fire station.

Beau Campbell was a firefighter. Back in school, he'd loved football as much as I had. Hell, probably more, and he'd been damn good…maybe even better than I was. I knew he hadn't gone anywhere with it, but I also knew Beau well enough to know it had been his dream, that he'd wanted football to be his life but had chosen his family instead.

He was a good man in ways I wasn't, and hell, now he was…well, he was exactly what Kenny said he was. A hero. Beau saved people's lives. It was more than I could say about myself.

When I rounded the corner at Cypress and Willow Brook, there was a gleaming fire engine in front of a red-brick building with green around the windows. Huh, the green was new. A blond man was there, kneeling and petting a dog a woman had on a leash. As I got closer, he nuzzled the dog, and when the woman walked away, he stood and began wiping down the truck. He turned my way when I approached, then did a double take that I was all too familiar with.

"Holy shit. You're Ashton Carmichael."

I plastered on my best smile. "Guilty as charged." Great, after what had gone on in my career lately, maybe that wasn't the best term to use.

He wiped his hands on his jeans, then reached out with his right. "I'm Jace."

Transferring my coffee and bag into one hand, I shook his. "Hey, Jace. Nice to meet you." My eyes skirted around him, trying to look into the bay, hoping for a glimpse of Beau. It wasn't my fault if I happened to be walking down the street he worked on and one of his coworkers stopped me.

"Shit...this is kind of embarrassing, but do you mind if I get your autograph? It's, um...for my brother."

I nodded, feeling both a spike of adrenaline and the hairs on my arms stand on edge. It was strange the dichotomy I felt about fame. On the one hand, I fucking loved it. I'd always thrived on attention, and what more could I ask for than what I got as a professional football player? But on the other hand, it made my gut twist, an edge of discomfort that always made me feel like a liar...a fraud. "Yeah, sure. No problem."

"Great, man. Thanks a lot. I'll be right back." Jace disappeared inside, and I took a few steps toward the building, trying to look for Beau. I was bordering on creepy stalker, but at the moment, I couldn't find it in myself to care. Beau made me feel like I was the Ash I'd been when I grew up there, not the ex-football-player. Plus, I'd always been a little fascinated with Beau Campbell. There was no denying that. There had always been something about him that caught my attention. He was different, kind.

My pulse throbbed against my skin, pounded in my ears. I shook my head, forcing away whatever that feeling was.

Jace came back a moment later. He offered me a pen and a piece of paper, which I signed for him. He rubbed at the blond scruff along his jaw. "Thanks. This is great. My…brother will love it."

I smiled at him, peeked into the building again. "Glad I could help."

It was then that a shadow moved around the back of the fire engine. Before he came into view, I knew it was Beau, and sure enough, there was my very own, personal Beau-scowl, his dark hair covered with a backward ball cap.

"Ah, hell," Beau said, and I grinned.

"Hey, man. What a surprise. It's great to see you too!"

CHAPTER EIGHT

Beau

Beau says you should try to be kind to everyone…unless they're an asshole. ~ Love, Kenny

THE MOST FUCKED-UP thing about seeing Ashton Carmichael standing in front of the station was that I wasn't surprised. It felt like something I shouldn't know about him—that he would show up today, not considering the fact that we hadn't seen one another in so long—but I knew. He'd come because he knew it would fluster me, even though I hated that it did. He'd come because he liked to get under my skin. And he'd also come because I'd done something nice for him and he would want to thank me. I thought maybe that wasn't the Ash people usually took the time to acknowledge. Hell, I knew I didn't. It was hard to do it even now.

"I stopped by Campbell's Confections. Decided to take a walk around. It's been so damn long since I've roamed these streets," Ash said, then held up the bag with Mom's logo on it. "Want a chocolate éclair? I mean, I have an extra one and all, but if you can't while you're working, I understand."

My brows pulled together at the vulnerability in Ash's voice. I wasn't sure anyone else would hear it, didn't quite know how I could, other than I'd grown up paying too much attention to Ash, watching him because he drove me batshit crazy. Ash was basically the definition of confidence, and while I could see it in him then, there was something softer in his eyes too, and something in the unsure tone of his seemingly easygoing voice.

"I'm gonna take a break, Jace," I replied.

"Okay, I'll just be sitting here working," he teased, and I rolled my eyes.

"Let's go to the park." It was just a block away up Willow Brook.

We were quiet as we went, our footsteps falling in line with one another. A smile tugged at my lips when I realized Ash wasn't filling the quiet space with random jokes and lines about how good he was, the way he would have done when we were kids.

"Well, that's new. What's that smile for?" he asked.

Damn it. I hadn't known he'd looked over.

"It's not new. I smile."

"Not with me."

"We went over this last night. And I smile with you, Ash. My whole world doesn't revolve around you." Though I tended to act like it did when he was around. I needed to work on that.

"You have to admit I'm a pretty good thing to have your world revolve around."

"And there's the Ashton Carmichael I know," I replied as we sat down at a picnic table under a willow tree. Ash pulled an éclair from the bag, wrapped it in a napkin, and handed it over.

"God, you used to love my mom's éclairs." I'd forgotten about that, the way Ash would get an éclair after school or a game.

"I still do. When I first left for college, Mom used to send them to me."

That seemed like a waste. "What, they don't have éclairs in LA?" I teased.

Ash shrugged. "It wasn't the same." His words slid down my spine in a strange way. There was nostalgia in his voice, and I wasn't quite sure what to do with that. It was a puzzle, trying to put together the Ash I grew up with, with the one I read about in all the headlines, the one who dominated on the field until recently, and finally, the man I saw last night and the one in front of me today.

"Sorry about last night," Ash added. "I really am a grown-up now who can take care of himself, contrary to what it might look like sometimes."

It was there, sitting on the edge of my tongue to ask him if he truly was grown up, but I bit it back. "It's no problem. Happens to the best of us."

"You slept on a fifteen-year-old beanbag chair before you got up, got my car, and then went to work, where apparently you're a hero." He grinned. Obviously, he'd been speaking with Kenny.

"I'm not a hero."

"I think you are." His words were a jolt of electricity to my chest. "At least, that's what I heard."

And…that tamed it down a bit.

"How did you get my car back, anyway?"

"I know someone who owns a tow company. Figured you'd need your car. That's all."

"Thanks, Cranky Campbell."

"No problem, Cocky Carmichael."

He grinned, and damn if my dick didn't take notice. It would be a whole lot easier to dislike Ash if he wasn't so damn sexy.

Looking away, I forced myself to change the subject. "So, I get an éclair and no coffee?" I teased.

"You can share with me." He pushed it over.

"I was kidding."

"I promise you won't get cooties from drinking after me. Geez, so uptight." He winked, and damn it, I smiled.

I took the cup and let the warm coffee distract me. I needed it after how shitty I'd slept last night. A fifteen-year-old beanbag chair isn't the most comfortable thing I'd ever slept on.

"So…Kenny tells me you watch all my games. That you're so into them, no one is even allowed to talk when I'm playing."

And I felt it. I was frowning again. "Don't let it go to your head, Ash. I'm mostly just critiquing your game."

"Oh, my heart." Ash clutched at his chest and fell off the back of the bench and onto the grass. I couldn't help but laugh, the rumble starting deep in my gut. He was charming as hell and he knew it. I wanted to hate him for it.

He got back onto the seat, and I said, "I should head back." It was earlier than I needed to go, but I said it anyway.

"What time do you get off? I figure I owe you a dinner. I was supposed to pay last night, and you drove me home, babysat me, and had my car towed."

I was already shaking my head before he finished

speaking. I hadn't quite put together why Ash wanted to spend time with me. Wyatt was around. They'd always been closer anyway, and I knew they kept in touch because Wyatt went to a couple of his games a year. Regardless, I wasn't sure spending time with Ash was the best thing for me. "You don't owe me. We're good."

"Come on, Campbell. You did a nice thing. Let me do a nice thing."

"You brought me éclairs and shared your cootie coffee with me."

Ash chuckled like I hoped he would.

"We're even, Ash. You don't have to pay me back for anything."

I'd just begun standing when his words stopped me. "What if I just want to hang out with you?" His eyes darted away toward the table as heat spread across my skin—well, that and a heavy dose of confusion.

I sat back down, opened my mouth, and let myself say what had been weighing on me for years. "You kissed me, Ash. You kissed me, then ignored me and left for college. It wasn't as if I expected anything. I know a kiss isn't a contract, and hell, I didn't want one anyway, but did you ever think of what that moment did to me? *For* me? I was confused as shit, scared as shit, and yeah, I'm over it now. I'm gay and proud, but I just... Maybe it shouldn't matter. I know it's been ten years, but...I don't know. I guess I've been waiting ten years to ask you that."

And I was wishing I hadn't. What the hell? I sounded like a scorned lover. Like I'd spent my days pining over him, when I hadn't. "Actually, scratch that. Can we forget I brought it up? I should get back to work, and again, you don't owe me dinner."

"Dinner has nothing to do with that," Ash said. "That was... I don't know what that was. I was confused, but I'm not now; obviously, I'm not now. I'm straight. I just...thought we could be friends."

His words from last night slammed into me, his thanking me for treating him normally and for not mentioning football and the kiss. Christ, I was an asshole. I should have known better than to ask him. It was his life, his business. "That came out wrong. I'm not sure what got into me. Friendship has nothing to do with your sexuality, and I knew that's what you meant. I just think—hell, I'm sure—that I spent a whole lot of years thinking about something that didn't matter, that was likely forgotten right after it happened." I hated to admit it, but I *had* spent ten years wondering about it, seeing him on television and driving myself crazy about one small moment in time. After all these years, I needed to get over it.

"So...dinner tonight, or what?" I asked.

"I mean, if you insist..." Ash grinned, and again, I chuckled.

"Asshole."

"That's what I've been told."

"I need to get back to work. Fever Pitch at seven?"

"Okay," Ash replied. "See you then."

When I walked away I felt it, the same way Ash always knew when I frowned—I felt his eyes on me.

I could do this. I could be an adult and let go of the past. I could be friends with Ashton Carmichael.

I think...

CHAPTER NINE

Ashton

Ashton "Fake it till you make it" Carmichael pulls out a surprising win!

"COME ON, DUDE. Go chill with us. You're always making excuses." I looked at Beau as he adjusted the backward ball cap on his head. His arm muscles looked like they were getting bigger, a vein running down his forearm. My pulse thumped strangely, sped up in a weird way that made me frown.

"I can't. I have shit to do," Beau replied.

"You gotta work at your mom's shop?" Wyatt asked, and Beau shook his head.

His eyes caught mine and then quickly shot away, which made me do the same. "Lemme guess…ditching us to get your dick wet?" I asked.

"No, asshole. There are more important things than sex, but even if I was, let's not pretend you wouldn't do the same."

He had a point there. Ever since I lost my virginity, I hadn't really been able to stop getting my dick wet. "I don't chase girls; girls chase me."

Wyatt laughed and gave me a high five. Beau looked away as though I'd disappointed him, and my stomach tightened in response. I was always doing something to annoy or disappoint Beau. I didn't know why I cared. I tried not to, but that shit was always fucking there. It was weird. I didn't much care what anyone else thought of me, but I cared what Beau thought. On the other hand, I didn't want to care, so I purposefully tried to piss him off. It was a vicious cycle I participated in even though I didn't understand it. "You're scared my team will kick your ass, huh?"

We were trying to arrange a football game with some friends, and somehow, Beau and I always ended up on opposite teams.

"Fuck off," *Beau replied.*

"I'll go easy on you." *I winked, and when he flipped me off, I saw something in his eyes that made guilt rumble around inside me and my chest tighten.*

"You two attached at the hip or something? You can't play without Beau?" *Wyatt complained.*

My face got hot. "What? No. Fuck that. Let's go."

We said our goodbyes to Beau at the corner, then jumped into Wyatt's car as Beau turned and walked away.

"Should we give him a ride?" I asked.

"He would have asked if he wanted one. What the fuck, Carmichael? You're always so goddamned worked up about what Campbell's doing."

"Fuck you!" I shoved his arm, and he swerved slightly. "I don't give a shit what Campbell does." I didn't. I really fucking didn't.

We drove around and picked up a few more of our friends. We met another group at this café we went to, where they had really big to-go cups for cheap. Once we filled up on soda, we all climbed into a few cars and made our way toward Fever Falls High.

When we passed Willow Brook Park, I saw a familiar backward cap—Beau standing there, talking to a kid. It was like a light bulb went off in my head, knowledge smacking into me as I thought about the shit I've given him.

"Fuck, pull over," I told Wyatt.

"Huh?"

"Pull over. I was supposed to, um...meet Mom at the store and I forgot. I can't play today."

"What the fuck, Carmichael. You're the one who put this game together."

"And now I remembered I have something to do...with my mom. Pull over, man."

Wyatt grumbled under his breath but stopped the car.

"Dude, you're worse than Campbell right now," he told me.

"Hey...you'll be the best player on the field without me and Campbell there." I closed the door, and he flipped me off. I waited until the cars had driven around the corner, then jogged to the park. When I got there, making my way across the sidewalk and over one of the small, grassy hills, I saw Beau across the way, playing catch with Kenny.

I stopped, my feet rooted to the ground like the huge willow tree in the middle of the park. Beau made his way over to his little brother, said something to him, showed him the ball...maybe how to hold it?...before he pulled his arm back, likely explaining to him how to throw.

My stomach sort of ached, and goose bumps traveled up my arms. I should have known it had something to do with Kenny. There was only one thing Beau loved more than football, and that was his family, especially his brother.

The ache traveled from my stomach to my chest. I didn't know anyone like Beau. He was good at everything, confident, and a nice guy. He was more responsible than anyone I knew, like this old soul fitting into a body that looked similar to mine.

Only he had that happy face on his biceps... His arms were smaller than mine but getting bigger. His hair stuck out from under his hat, and there was mud on his thigh. He had a dimple beneath the left side of his mouth, and the way his forehead wrinkled when he talked to Kenny... And what in the fuck was I doing standing there describing Beau Campbell?

As I watched him throw to Kenny again, I thought about how much he loved him. Beau never asked for anything in return. He just always did the right thing, was always kind...and I wished I was more like him.

"Hey!" I said as I jogged over.

"What are you doing here?" Beau asked when I reached them.

"Cap-tain, right, Beau?" Kenny asked. He spoke slowly, as though he was trying to concentrate on his words. His speech was slightly hard to understand.

I grinned. "Yeah, I am. And Beau is second." I was trying to make sure his brother knew Beau was just as important on the team as me, but the way Beau groaned, I wasn't sure I had. "Can I play with you guys?" I asked.

Kenny said, "Yes!" right as Beau asked, "Why?"

I shrugged and said the first thing I could think of. "Because it sounds like fun. I can help you teach Kenny how to play."

"P-ease, Beau! P-ease!" Kenny begged, and I knew I had him. Beau wouldn't deny Kenny anything, and again, it struck me how noble he was.

Beau nodded. "Okay."

"But-er-fly, but-er-fly!" Kenny said, then began chasing it.

Beau chuckled. "So much for football... You don't have to, ya know? I'm sure you'd rather be with the guys...or Sarah."

"I'm not seeing Sarah."

"Olivia?"

"Nah, we broke up."

"You can go, Ash. You can't want to play catch with me and my little brother."

But I did, more than I could explain. "Sorry, Cranky Campbell, but Kenny wants me here, so you're stuck with me. Come on, let's go teach your brother the fine art of football."

And that's what we did. Sometimes it was hard for me to understand what Kenny said. I always felt bad when that happened, but Beau always seemed to understand every word. We were out there with him for nearly two hours before Kenny told Beau he was tired and ready to go home. It had been one of the things I couldn't make out.

Kenny smiled more than anyone I'd ever met. He was a fun kid, who obviously loved his brother like crazy. I envied them their relationship. I didn't have siblings, and as much as I loved Mom and Dad, I'd always wished for a bigger family.

As we waited for Kenny to get a drink at the fountain, Beau looked down, toed at something in the grass I couldn't see. "Thanks, man...for playing. He liked that. The other kids tease him sometimes, so he doesn't really have anyone but me. They made fun of him because he couldn't throw."

"He can now. How could he not learn with the best teacher there is showing him?"

Beau rolled his eyes. "You're so full of yourself."

"I wasn't talking about myself. I was talking about you."

His eyes snapped up, his lips pulling into a smile. Dizziness swept over me, twisted me up. My feet itched to run away, and I suddenly couldn't stand there a second longer. "Catch you later, Cranky Campbell," I said, then turned and took off as fast as I could go.

I SHOOK MY head, trying to wake myself up from my nap and wondering why in the hell my dream had gone to that day in the park with Kenny and Beau. It had to be because I'd seen Kenny for the first time in what felt like a hundred years. It hit me how much his speech had improved, and I smiled, proud of him for what he'd accomplished.

It was impossible not to think of Beau and Kenny as a sort of package deal. There wasn't anything Beau wouldn't do for his brother. It didn't matter that I hadn't seen him in ten years; I knew that was still true.

And like it had when I was younger, that did something to me. I envied it...respected it...was enamored by it. My parents would have done anything for me. I'd grown up knowing that, but outside of them, I wasn't sure I'd ever met someone who gave a shit about me on a real level, a deep level, and not because I was good-looking or popular or good at football. And I always wondered if I could do it, if I could have given up all the things Beau did for his family. I was pretty sure I was too selfish for that.

Those thoughts took me back to what Beau had admitted...when he'd asked about the kiss. I'd spent years in turmoil over it, not able to believe I'd done it, scared it would come back and bite me in the ass...wondering what Beau thought about it.

Nope. I wasn't going there.

I dragged myself out of bed, and for the second time that day, I took a shower. I thought about jacking off, but wasn't sure I had the energy, so I just stayed in until the water went cold, and then got out. Wearing only a towel, I went back into my room and tried to figure out what I was going to wear.

Realizing it didn't matter what the fuck I wore to a thank-you dinner with my old high school friend, I grabbed a pair of khaki shorts and a black Henley. Before I knew it, I was walking into Fever Pitch a whole half hour early and wondering what I was doing.

I should call Wyatt. It could be a reunion dinner of sorts. The three of us could hang out, touch base again. Wyatt had said he still saw Beau sometimes, though they didn't hang out like we did in high school. Thinking about that made me think about Beau's friend Lincoln...and the other guys he mentioned. I didn't recognize any of their names from friends of ours in school, so they were either new to town or had gone to a different high school.

And I was pretty sure they were all gay or bi.

Oh shit. Were all Beau's friends gay? Did that mean it was weird for me to want to go out to dinner with him?

My pulse sped up and my eyes went a little blurry before I reminded myself I was a grown-ass man and could be friends with whoever I wanted. What the hell did anyone's sexuality have to do with friendship? I was losing my damn mind.

Which brought me back to the point that maybe it

would be cool to call Wyatt, and we could hang for old times' sake. Still, I didn't call him. It would be nice to get to know Beau again, just the two of us.

"Excuse me...sir?" a man asked, and I could tell by his frown and the way his brows were pulled together that he'd been talking to me for a while. "Just you?"

"Um...no...two. I'm, um...early, and I'm meeting my friend Beau here. We were high school buddies and haven't seen each other in a long time. He should arrive soon." Because obviously I had to give the host my whole life story.

"I'll be sure to tell your friend you already arrived, sugar." He winked.

"No, no. We really are just friends," I replied as I followed behind him.

"I didn't say you weren't."

"Yeah, but the way you said that..."

"I didn't say it like anything. Honestly? It's none of my business. I'm just here to seat you."

Well, now I felt dumb. I believed what I was doing was called projection.

The host walked me to a booth toward the back. My overactive brain started to go crazy, wondering if he was seating me back there because he thought I was hiding. Did he really think Beau was more than a friend? Was I losing my goddamned mind? Yes, yes, I was.

He sat me, and the waitress came up right behind him.

"He's waiting for a *friend*," the host said.

Was it me, or did he stress the word *friend*? "Can I have a beer, please?" I asked, then told her which kind.

I fiddled with the black menu, kept looking up to see if she approached with my beer. Having dinner with Beau was strange in a way I hadn't expected, and I hadn't even started the having-dinner-together part yet. And then there was the fact that it was my idea...one that I couldn't let go and had pushed until Beau said yes. *Because I'm a nice guy...because I want to get to know an old friend...because there's always been something about Beau that gets to me.*

The waitress brought over my beer, and I drank half of it in a few quick swallows. The moment I set it down, a shadow crossed the table and Beau was there, his black hair kind of messy and looking a little wavier. He wore a T-shirt that said *Fever Falls Fire Department* and a pair of jeans. "You're early," I told him.

"Not as early as you." Beau cocked his right brow.

He had a point there, so I figured it best I ignore it. "You want a beer? I'll signal the waitress over."

Beau sat across from me, a smile tugging at the right

corner of his lips. There was a small scar there that I remembered from when we were kids, but I wasn't sure what had happened to him. What the hell was with me and his scars, I didn't know. "You're smiling again."

He frowned.

"Damn it! I ruined it. What happened to your lip?"

Beau raised a hand and rubbed his mouth. "There's something wrong with my lip?"

Shit. That wasn't what I meant. "No. Your lips are good. I meant the scar." *Your lips are good?* What the fuck was that?

Beau winked. "I've never had any complaints."

Okay, this wouldn't do. "Somehow, I believe we just traded places. I don't like it. I'm the cocky one, remember?"

"I'll keep that in mind." He shook his head as though he didn't know what to do with me…but he also smiled again. I liked making Beau smile. I decided it was my goal to do that more often.

CHAPTER TEN

Beau

Beau says sometimes life surprises you. I wonder how often it surprises him. ~ Love, Kenny

THE WAITRESS ARRIVED, I ordered a beer, and then Ash and I took in the menu. *Your lips are good.* Why had he said that? No matter how many times I tried to focus on burgers, fries, and salads, all I heard was Ash telling me my lips were *good.*

Lips he'd kissed.

And then promptly forgot about…ten years later reminding me it was a mistake because he was straight, yet there I was obsessing about it, something I was determined to stop doing.

"Okay, stop. What are you thinking? Right now, tell me what you're thinking? You're tightening your jaw so much, I'm worried you might break it."

"I'm wondering why you're watching me," I lied. Obviously, I wasn't going to tell him I couldn't forget the way his mouth moved when he told me he liked my lips...well, kind of told me that.

"I'm not watching you."

"Then how do you always know when I'm smiling or frowning? Or in this case, working my jaw?"

"You forget that I don't have to see you to know these things about you. You're easy to read, Campbell. Plus, I know you."

"Used to know me."

"Seems like I still do."

Yeah, yeah, it did. The strange thing was, I didn't feel like I knew Ash anymore. There was something different about him. The confidence was still there, but there was a vulnerability I'd never seen in him. Because of losing his career? I wondered... But then the partying and orgies surprised me too, even though they probably shouldn't have. Ash's main goal, even in high school, had been hooking up. "What are you going to eat?" I asked, figuring a change of subject was in order.

"I'm thinking about a lettuce-wrapped burger and maybe some sweet potato fries. I ate like shit yesterday. This is a little better, I guess."

"Ew," I replied.

"Ew, what?"

"Sweet potato fries, for one. Eating healthy in general, for two." I was exaggerating...at least a little bit. I wasn't the biggest fan of healthy eating, but I did try to do it enough to help me stay in shape.

"I'm getting fries and a burger. I think we're going overboard by calling it *eating healthy*."

I chuckled because it was true. "Point taken. If you'd gotten a salad, I might have had to leave." It was surprising that I didn't already feel like leaving. My emotions didn't want me to enjoy spending time with Ashton.

"I'll remember that for future reference."

Future reference? As though we would be doing this again?

The waitress approached and took our orders, Ash getting what he'd said, plus another beer. I got an order of boneless buffalo wings, regular fries, and a sweet tea.

"So...tell me about your life, Campbell."

Ugh. Campbell. It felt like such a straight-guy thing to do, always calling me by my last name. Forget that I sometimes called him Carmichael; that was different. "There's not much to tell. I'm a firefighter, I've been doing it for years, and I love it. I have a house on Hickory Lane." Not very far from Mom and Kenny, which was important to me. Maybe most people wouldn't understand it, but that was how I felt.

"You live close to them," Ash replied.

"Huh?" I asked, not because I hadn't heard him, but because I was surprised he'd said it—surprised he remembered where my family lived and that he would think to mention it.

"Your mom and brother. They're only two streets away, right? Unless I'm not remembering correctly."

"You are." My pulse did this strange dance, for absolutely no reason.

"You're good to your family, Beau. You always have been. You treat them right…take care of them…sacrifice for them… Those are admirable qualities."

My eyes darted away. It was too hard to look at Ash right then. He was saying something we both knew was true, something many people knew was true but never said it out loud—that I could have gone away to college, played college ball, had been offered scholarships, but I hadn't done any of it. And the truth was, as much as I'd wanted that dream, I didn't regret it. How could I?

"I made you uncomfortable."

A laugh jumped out of my mouth, even though a moment before I hadn't felt like laughing. "You still say whatever's on your mind…no-holds-barred." Though that didn't feel a hundred percent true anymore. I thought maybe Ashton Carmichael had secrets.

"I've been known to stick my foot in my mouth a time or two," he replied. "I've been told it can be a bit much. Actually, that's a lie. No one ever tells me that, except you. They just pretend it doesn't bother them."

Well, shit. Now I felt like an asshole. "It's an admirable quality too, Ash. You're honest, confident. Those aren't bad things. But if you tell anyone I said that or speak of it again, I'll deny it. And I'm sorry I always call you on it." In some ways, maybe I wasn't so different from Ash. I didn't know what it was about him that made me act the way I did, but it had always been there.

"Oh, I'm going to remind you every fucking day. You can bet on that. And…thanks, Campbell. That means a lot coming from you. Don't apologize for it. I appreciate always knowing where I stand with you, even if it's not the best place." He chuckled. "At least I know it's real."

My brows pulled together as I looked at him, and Ash glanced away, taking a drink of his beer. There was something incredibly sad in what he'd said, in the lower tone of his smooth, confident voice, in the way he wouldn't look me in the face. It was also sad that I'd always given Ash a hard time, always been standoffish with him in some ways. Hell, we hadn't seen each other in ten years, yet he was thanking me for how I treated him because it was *real*. How many people hadn't been honest with him? Had used him for who he was and what he had? It wasn't something I'd ever thought about before. "I—"

"Who got the low-carb burger?" a Fever Pitch employee asked.

"That's me," Ash replied. She set his plate down, then mine, and gave us our drinks before disappearing again. "Perfect timing. *That* could have been awkward."

That easily, I knew the conversation was over, and while part of me wanted to keep it going, to ask him what he meant, the other part was glad. I wasn't sure I could handle getting too close to Ashton Carmichael. Subconsciously, I'd known it since I was a teenager, but it had taken his kiss to make me see it.

"I HEARD THROUGH the gayvine that you had dinner with a gorgeous football player you supposedly hate."

I groaned at Linc as we jogged through Willow Brook Park. "First of all, what the fuck is a gayvine?"

"Gay version of grapevine. Hello, Beau?"

"I get it. I just think it's silly." I had no problem with who I was. I quite liked being gay, but I didn't get it when some of my friends playfully put the word *gay* in front of everything. "And second, you knew and it took you this long to bring it up? How the hell did you even hear?"

"One never outs someone from the gayvine. Get it together!" I glanced at Lincoln as we jogged, and he grinned. He hardly had any sweat on his forehead. Linc was smaller than me, shorter and skinnier. He wore the twink badge very proudly.

"I hate you."

"No you don't. You love me. We're best friends."

I really did love him, and he was my best friend. It didn't matter how different Linc and I were, we just fit. He was sometimes needy, drove me crazy, and I likely did him too, but I couldn't imagine my life without him. He was who I talked to if I needed someone. He knew things about me that no one else did. *Not that kiss with Ash…he doesn't know about that.* Jesus, why was I thinking about that again? "You're right, I do love you. It's the only reason I put up with you."

"Aww. If that's not love, I don't know what is!"

In sync like always, Lincoln and I slowed down at the same time. I plucked the towel from the waist of my shorts and wiped the sweat off my face as Lincoln sat at the picnic table—yeah, the one I'd shared with Ash.

I knew that if I didn't give him something, he'd hound me for days, or hell, weeks. "Yeah, I went out to dinner with him. It was just a thank-you for getting him and his car home. That's all you get." He opened his mouth, and I added, "And there's no more to get either. He's straight, remember?"

"Oh, come on, boo. I've landed plenty of straight boys for a night or two."

"I don't know about you, but to me, that seems like they're pretty bisexual."

"Yeah, I agree, but not according to them. Maybe your football player is the same?"

I shook my head. "Even if he is, I'm not interested, and he's not *my* football player." Sometimes, I wanted to kill my friend.

"You guys going to hang out again?" Linc asked.

"Nope." And we weren't, not that I knew of, at least. We'd had dinner together, the conversation much lighter after what Ash had admitted to me. We laughed, talked football. He gave me stories about some of his years playing, and even though I wanted to ask him why he'd thrown it all away, why he'd so obviously fallen out of love with it, I hadn't. It wasn't fair of me to ask, and it wasn't my business. But I did know Ash had fallen out of love with the game. I could see it in the way he'd played the past couple of years.

I talked to him some about work and Kenny, just life in general. I'd enjoyed it more than I'd expected. There had been no awkward silences or anything like that. It was a few hours later that I'd told Ash I needed to go home. He'd paid, and we went our separate ways.

I had to admit I'd thought about it a lot since dinner two days before. It was strange how easily we fell into place. When I looked at him, I didn't see an ex-professional-player like I thought I would. I saw annoying, sexy, cocky Ash.

And of course I'd had to throw *sexy* in there. Fucking Ashton. I didn't know why it was his fault I was attracted to him, but it was.

"For a minute, I thought I was going to have to be jealous of you." Linc nudged me. "But God, he's gorgeous as hell. It's simply not fair he's straight."

"No," I replied honestly. "It's not."

CHAPTER ELEVEN

Ashton

Ashton Carmichael needs to up his game. Play more like the MVP Ashton who led his team to a championship. He's not worth anything to them if he can't play ball.

"I'M SORRY. I know I'm staring, but I can't believe I'm sitting here with Ashton Carmichael, right now."

On reflex, I lowered the cap I wore, as if that would make a difference. My eyes immediately darted around, but it didn't look like anyone in the loud, bustling restaurant heard him.

Wyatt elbowed his friend…Pete, I thought his name was. Wyatt had called to ask me if I wanted to go out to lunch with him. It had been a week since I'd seen Beau, and I was bored out of my fucking mind, so I'd said yes. I hadn't expected to show up and find him there with someone else. Why in the hell would he do that? Why invite someone else along without telling me?

"Nah, it's just Ash. He's just like everyone else." Wyatt grinned at me, yet I couldn't help but wonder why he'd invited someone else without telling me if I was just like anyone else.

"You have to admit, I'm kind of a big deal." I winked, hoped I didn't come off as an asshole, but both Pete and Wyatt laughed, so I relaxed. It was hard to skate the line sometimes—being *on*, being light and carefree, confident, but also not coming off as a total prick.

"There's the Ashton I know," Wyatt replied, and we all laughed harder, but I felt a slight sting in my chest, like a bee got me, and then the pain somehow radiated out.

"I can't imagine the life you've been able to live for the past ten years," Pete said.

"One of my closest friends and high school football buddy playing professional football. You know I used that to my advantage over the years too," Wyatt replied.

"Forget the football, what about all the women," Pete added.

When I laughed, it sounded hollow, empty, but I didn't think either of them noticed. And really, why should they? Or at least, why should I sit there feeling sorry for myself? They were right. I'd been a fucking

king. I'd played a game I'd loved, made a whole hell of a lot of money, and Christ, the women. There had been a lot of them—every size, shape, and ethnicity. I didn't discriminate. I just loved women.

Do you? Do you really? a quiet voice asked inside my head. That fucking voice. It was bothering me more than it had in years.

But I did. I'd always loved women, losing myself inside someone else's body... "I'd tell you about it, but a gentleman never kisses and tells." My gut twisted, and my throat burned.

"Like you've ever been a gentleman!" Wyatt replied. "Even in high school, this fucker got more pussy than any of us combined. He was always with someone."

The bile—oh, that explained the burn—rose in my throat. It was as if I was seventeen again, sitting around talking about who we'd hooked up with or who we wanted to hook up with. I got it. They were fascinated with the bachelor lifestyle of a professional football player, but it didn't sit well with me, made my gut roll over.

"Do you guys remember that Christmas Eve game when we played the—"

"Wolves!" Pete finished for me, and like I hoped, the subject was effectively changed. We talked games and players and championships, but the longer the conversation went on, the more I fidgeted in my seat. Talking football with Beau last week didn't feel the same as it did with Wyatt and Pete now. Tonight it felt...fake, manufactured, as though I was on display.

I was thankful when we finished eating and both Wyatt and Pete had to head out. I waited until they left, jumped in my car, and found myself parking at Campbell's Confections...because it was some kind of rule that I needed a chocolate éclair after lunch. Who didn't?

I walked in, and Beau's mom was speaking with a customer while Kenny sat in one of the chairs, writing in what looked like a journal. His eyebrows rose and a smile curled his lips when he saw me. "Hi, Ashton."

"Hey, Kenny." I walked over to the table. "Do you mind if I sit down?"

"Of course not."

I sat, twisted my cap around so it was backward, and sighed.

"You don't sound like you had the best day."

I looked at him. "Not the worst." I'd definitely had days I wished I could erase from existence, but I didn't think I should tell him about wild parties and orgies.

"But you've had better?" he asked.

"I've definitely had better. I'm getting an éclair and

talking to you, so it's not so bad now."

"I guess that's my cue?" Mrs. Campbell set the sugary deliciousness in front of me.

"My hero." I teased.

"Beau's a hero too," Kenny said again.

"He is," I answered, and I believed that. I truly did. There had always been something special about Beau Campbell.

I took a bite of my treat and moaned. Fuck, I was going to gain fifty pounds if I stayed around Beau. I wouldn't be able to turn down the food.

"That good, huh?" My eyes darted up to see Beau had walked through the door. Apparently, I'd been enjoying my food more loudly than I thought if he heard it all the way over there.

I smiled, thankful he'd come in not looking like he wanted to kill me for something…or wondering why I continued to find myself in his presence. It was something I was trying not to think about. "I'm considering having all my meals here from now on." Kenny and Beau's mom laughed. "I'm serious, Mrs. Campbell. You're probably going to get tired of seeing me soon."

"Not possible." She patted my hand. "And it's Beth, remember?"

I didn't know why, but that made me smile. When I

looked up, Beau was watching me, his brows pulled together as if he was confused; then he turned away. "You ready, Kenny?" he asked.

"Yep!" Kenny replied. A stab of disappointment landed in my chest that they were leaving. "Do you want to go to my game with us?" Kenny asked.

I liked where this was going. "Game?"

"I play football like you and Beau. Beau's our coach." Kenny beamed with pride, and damned if it didn't do something to my chest. I saw the love of life in him, the love of his brother, hell, even of football.

"It's a mostly indoor league sponsored through a group called We Can Play, for those with special needs to play sports. Kenny kicks ass." Beau grinned at his brother. "But I'm sure you have—"

"I don't," I interrupted. "Have, I mean...anything to do. I'd love to go. That's where I'm going with this." A local football league that I was assuming was similar to Special Olympics? I didn't even know there was such a thing. It didn't surprise me that Beau did.

Beth said, "Beau fought like crazy to get us a team, but as we know, when Beau sets his mind to something..."

"It's nothing, Ma."

"It's absolutely not nothing," she replied.

"It's the best," Kenny added, and that made Beau nod. He would do anything for his brother.

"Yeah, it is." I thought maybe it was one of the most incredible things I'd ever heard.

"We should go." Beau nodded toward the door, obviously not liking the attention on him. He'd always been like that, and I thought that had always been part of the discord between us. Beau shied away from praise, whereas I'd always sought it out, even if it was in a playful way.

Kenny and I stood. Beth hugged him, telling him goodbye and apologizing for not being able to make it. I couldn't help it—my eyes were drawn to Beau. To the way he watched them, the slight pink to his cheeks, the stubble across his jaw, the sculpted shape of the muscles in his arms.

His eyes caught mine, and I realized I was staring. Holy fuck, I was staring, and I shouldn't have been, so I did the first thing that came to mind. I stuck my tongue out at him.

To my surprise, he did the same. There was a lightness in my chest with it, and when Kenny asked, "Why are you guys sticking your tongues out at each other?" Beau and I both barked out a loud laugh.

"Ash did it first," Beau replied.

So that's how it was going to be. Throwing me under the bus, huh? Forget that I actually had done it first, because apparently I was now five. "Yeah, but we all know I'm a big kid. You're supposed to be more mature than I am."

"Am not." From the glimmer in his eyes, I could tell he was playing along on purpose, and I had to admit I liked it. I enjoyed this light, silly Beau. I had no doubt it was more for his brother's benefit than mine, though.

"Are too."

"Am not."

"Children," Beth said, and we both looked up at her and answered simultaneously.

"Yes?"

Then we were all laughing, and I found myself wondering when I'd last had that much fun. We weren't even doing anything other than standing there, but I enjoyed it.

"Let's go, Kenny." Beau wrapped an arm around Kenny's shoulders, and the three of us walked out. When I glanced back, I saw Beth watching us with a small grin on her lips.

I followed Kenny and Beau to Beau's truck. For most of the twenty-minute drive, the two of them spoke about plays and the team they were going up against. I listened, took it all in, did my damnedest to bite my tongue and not give suggestions. It was one of the hardest things I've ever done. This was *football*, and it was football with Beau, and I hadn't realized how much that meant to me until I didn't have it anymore. But this was Beau's team and it wasn't my place, so I fidgeted in my seat and pretended I wasn't bursting at the seams. Beau knew what he was doing anyway. He didn't need my help.

"What do you think, Ash?" Beau asked, and it took me a minute to notice he wanted my opinion about something, though I couldn't say exactly what. I'd been too busy thinking about this thing he was doing and what it had been like to play with him.

When I didn't answer, he added, "It's flag football. Remember blue bird?"

Memories swam through my brain. I damn near felt the air change, taking me back to when we played in high school, to a time when things were simpler. When I could just be me...well, sort of. More so than I'd been me most of my life, at least.

"You know that was my play, don't you?" I teased.

"Ours," he countered, and he was right. We'd come up with the play together.

"What's blue bird?" Kenny patted Beau over and over on the shoulder, like a young child wanting attention.

"Your brother and I worked hard on that. It was our specialty. Beau always got free to make the catch. It always worked." Nostalgia burned through me, fired me up in a strange way.

"Nah, that's just because you could always find me no matter what. No one had an eye like you."

It was *him*. It had always been easy for me to find Beau. We'd worked well together. It was another reminder of how much I missed playing with him. "Nah, just got lucky. Couldn't have done it with anyone else. No one was as good as you at getting free."

I was pretty sure Beau's cheeks pinked, and my pulse shot up. There was something different about him today. He was more open, friendly, like he wasn't keeping a wall between us…and yeah, like he didn't hate me with a passion, but I didn't think Beau ever really hated me…maybe… Okay, he might have sometimes, and I'd probably deserved it, but it wasn't real hate. I thought he *wanted* to hate me more than he did. Mostly I just annoyed him.

None of that was evident now, though.

He pulled into a parking spot, and I watched his arms move as he did, as he reached and turned off the key. I noticed the happy face on his biceps and smiled myself. Don't ask me what was so damn exciting about Beau turning off his truck that I had to watch him, but I sure as hell was doing it.

He glanced my way, turned, then looked again. His jaw tightened, but I didn't think it was in anger.

This time when his eyes found mine, Beau didn't glance away. He cocked a brow, stared, and asked, "What?"

"What what?" I replied when obviously, I knew he wanted to know why my eyes were glued to him. I still hadn't figured out exactly why, though. He wasn't doing anything interesting.

Beau chuckled this rich, earthy sound, and yes, I was aware that calling a voice *earthy* didn't make sense, but that was the only way I could think to explain it. "What?" I asked.

"What what?" he replied with a grin, the bastard.

"Beau, hurry, can we go? We're gonna be late," Kenny rushed out before his words tangled together toward the end, making it so I couldn't quite figure out exactly what else he'd said.

"Slow down, buddy. We're good. We're going in now." Beau smiled at his brother, and it did something to me, twisted me up and sort of made me dizzy in this strange way. He was so damn good with Kenny. The love he had for his brother shone in every word he said to him.

We all climbed out of the truck, and I helped them with some of the equipment bags. Kenny jogged ahead of us, toward the building, and Beau said, "He gets a little excited sometimes and his words jumble together more. He loves playing."

"Like someone else I know?" I cocked a brow at Beau.

"Yeah, you always did love ball."

"I wasn't talking about myself," I replied.

"I know." Beau shrugged. There was a story there, but then, I had my own too. He was right; I'd always lived and breathed football, but I hadn't in years. A wave of melancholy rode down my spine.

When we got to the building's double door, Beau unlocked it. "Fancy," I teased, and he rolled his eyes but smiled too.

"Wow…this is a great," I said when we stepped inside. The inside looked as though it was either new or had recently been remodeled with state-of-the-art flooring, which was painted as though it was a football field.

"Yeah, we raised a lot of money to make this happen. It belongs to We Can Play, and they host all sorts of sporting events. I'm hoping to get the land on the other side as well. Then we can have an outdoor field for football, plus track-and-field events. We just didn't have the money for it all."

There was so much want in Beau's voice, it twisted up my insides. He was doing something important there, something he was passionate about, that despite my time in the pros, I thought was more important than anything I'd ever done. I opened my mouth to tell him so when Kenny cut me off from where he stood in the doorway, "Some of the team is here, Beau!"

On reflex, I grabbed my cap and twisted it around frontward, low on my eyes.

"Go watch from over there." Beau pointed to a corner, back on the side of the bleachers, that afforded a little privacy. "I'll bring you a chair."

He started to walk away when I said, "Thanks."

"It's just a chair."

"Not for the chair, Cranky Campbell." He shook his head as though he didn't know what to do with me. "For letting me be here. It means a lot to me."

Beau's brows knitted together as he took me in. There was something different in the way he looked at me, in the intensity of his whiskey-colored eyes.

"*Beau!*" Kenny called again, snapping Beau out of

whatever trance he'd been in.

"It's fine, Cocky Carmichael. It's not a big deal."

But it was, and I thought we both knew it.

CHAPTER TWELVE

Beau

Beau watches Ashton, but I don't think he knows it.
Ashton watches Beau even more. It's weird.
~ Love, Kenny

EVERY TIME I glanced Ash's way during the game, his eyes were firmly glued on me or the players. He wasn't like other people in the stands, who looked at their phones or seemed distracted. Hell, he'd hardly sat down the whole time, energy radiating off him in a way that was nearly visible in his movement, his pacing, in the way he fidgeted.

I hadn't expected him to be as into it as he was. Hell, I also never would have thought he would want to go to the game or that I'd walk into Mom's shop and see him there again, sitting with my brother.

When we'd won, he'd whooped so loud, a few people looked at him, and he'd lowered the hat on his head again.

My eyes kept finding him as we thanked the other team and celebrated with friends and family. Ash stayed back, this enigma I couldn't figure out anymore, and I wondered if I'd ever really known who Ashton Carmichael was. I wondered if he had the answer to that question himself.

It wasn't until the building emptied of everyone other than Kenny and me that Ash came out. "Dude, that was such an incredible game! That catch at the end, Kenny? Felt like I was watching Beau out there."

Kenny's smile lit up the damn building, and I felt my defenses softening even more toward Ash.

Kenny began speaking so fast, some of the words got tangled together. That was one thing the speech therapy hadn't helped as much with. Sometimes he just got so excited, it was hard for his mouth to keep up. Still, he made me proud every day.

"Slow down, Kenny," I reminded him.

He took a few deep breaths, then asked, "Do I really remind you of Beau?"

My heart clenched at that. He always placed me on a pedestal I was damn sure I didn't deserve to be on.

"You do," Ash told him. "Maybe even better."

When he threw me a grin, I found myself saying, "We're having pizza at Mickey's. It's a bit of a tradition.

I'm sure you're busy, but if you're not, you're welcome to join us."

"Well, you *are* my ride and all," Ash replied. "I guess I kind of have to go."

"Guess you do," I added.

"But, Beau, Ashton doesn't have to go. I want him to, but if he can't, we can always drop him off at his car." He cocked his head as though he was working through why we would think Ash had no choice but to go with us.

"You trying to get rid of me?" Ash teased, putting an arm around Kenny's shoulders.

"No," Kenny answered simply, but I was caught by how easily they took to each other. Ash treated him the way he would anyone, didn't talk to him as though he were a child, and didn't ignore him as though he didn't matter. Many people did both, but not Ash.

My memory flitted back to that day when Ash had helped me teach Kenny how to play in the park…and then to that night, before the kiss, when he'd asked about my brother. Even back then he'd treated Kenny with more respect than most people, hadn't he? I'd never given him enough credit for that. I'd always just seen the things I didn't like about Ash when I looked at him…well, that and the fact that I was pretty sure that even before I realized I was gay, part of me knew I'd wanted Ashton Carmichael. "Come on, you two knuckleheads, let's get out of here."

"Knuckleheads? Knuckleheads? Did you hear what he called us, Kenny?" Ash feigned offense. "That's why I call him Cranky Campbell."

"Cranky Campbell?" Kenny replied, chuckling sweetly.

"Oh, no. Don't tell me the two of you are going to start ganging up on me with that name."

"Guess you better be extra nice to me, huh, CC?" Ash teased.

"I'm not talking to you."

"But you just did," Kenny replied, and the three of us laughed again.

"I'm leaving without you guys." I went for the door, Kenny and Ash behind me. We tossed the equipment into the back of my truck and then made our way to Mickey's.

Kenny and Ash talked about the game, and most of the time I simply listened. It was different for me, hearing Kenny talk to someone other than me about things like that. He had his friends, of course, some of the people he met at the center he went to, and people from his college classes, but it was different coming from someone I knew. It wasn't that my friends weren't great with Kenny, because they were, Linc especially, but…well, hell, they weren't Ashton Carmichael. If I were honest with myself, I'd admit that had always been a thing for me. Maybe I held Ash to higher standards in some ways, and didn't expect as much of him in others.

Once we were at Mickey's, the three of us got out together. Luckily, the place wasn't too busy as we went to the counter to order.

"I hope you like pepperoni and double sausage. That's all we order. I love sausage." The moment the words fell out of my mouth, Ash cocked a brow at me, and I realized how it sounded.

"Big sausage fan, are you?" he teased in a way I'd never been teased by any of my straight male friends before. What the fuck was up with him? I couldn't figure Ash out.

"Quite interested in my preferences, aren't you?" His eyes darted away, and guilt immediately drowned me. Shit. For as hard a time as I always gave Ash, I was the one who was fucking up lately. "I'm giving you shit. I didn't mean anything by that."

"What could you mean by it?" Kenny asked.

"I can take the next customer in line," the man at the counter said, saving my ass from my dickheaded statement to Ash and explaining it to Kenny.

"Do you want something else?" I asked, and Ash shook his head.

"Nah. I'm good with...*that*."

Great. Now I'd ruined it so we couldn't even say the word *sausage*. Go Beau. I was killing it.

We ordered our pizza and a pitcher of soda, then sat in a booth close to the arcade, Kenny and me on one side, Ash on the other. We talked more about the game, Mom's éclairs, things like that. I couldn't help but notice Ash wasn't making eye contact with me like he had been before. Not that I could blame him.

It didn't take long for our food to come. We basically annihilated the pizza, and then Kenny made his way to the arcade. They had an old Pac-Man machine, which was his favorite. He didn't do any other games, wasn't into shooting or racing cars, but he could play for hours that old-school game that was even before my time.

"Listen...I'm sorry about the joke earlier. It was inappropriate—"

"It was a joke," Ash cut me off. "It's fine."

But it didn't feel like a joke with him. It felt like *more*. Maybe it was the kiss all those years ago or a fantasy I had about Ashton and me that I'd never allowed myself to truly voice. Maybe I was trying to see something that wasn't there because Ashton had always been better than me at everything, more secure than me, but in this, in being a proud gay man, I was more comfortable in my skin than he was. Or maybe he wasn't gay or bisexual at all, and I was projecting my own shit onto him...but yeah, it just felt like *more*, it felt important, and I didn't know any better way to explain it than that. "But it's not okay if it makes you uncomfortable."

"It didn't make me uncomfortable," Ash replied.

"Okay."

"Seriously, Campbell. I'm good. I can take a joke. I'm funny as shit, in case you don't remember."

I couldn't help but chuckle. Ash was good at that. "Well, you don't lack for confidence, that's for sure." But when his eyes darted away, my stomach dropped, and I suddenly felt like I'd done something wrong again. Or hell, maybe I saw that Ash wasn't quite as confident as I'd always thought he was. "It's true, ya know?"

He turned my way again. "What's true?"

"I watched all your stupid games. If I worked or was in school, I recorded them. I was proud of you, Ash...I still am. That isn't easy for me to say. I wanted what you had so badly, that at first I watched trying to tell myself it was a mistake, that I was better than you."

"You could have had what I had. You put your family first, is all."

"No." I shook my head, being honest with myself for the first time in years. "I was good. I could have played college ball, but I wasn't good enough to be professional. Even if I'd gone on to play, I wouldn't have accomplished what you did."

"Christ, Campbell. You're about to make me cry." He swiped at tears that weren't there.

"If I were you, I would take advantage of this. Within a few minutes, I'm likely to start hating you again," I teased, even though I wouldn't, and never truly had.

"There's the Cranky Campbell I know and love. Stop making me think you like me. It's weird."

We both laughed, took a drink of our sodas, distracted ourselves. At least that was what I was doing.

"Since we're playing nice, maybe now's the time to tell you you're amazing with him—your brother."

I shrugged. "You don't have to say that. He's family. I love him. There's nothing that makes what I do amazing. I'm just a big brother to my favorite person. The last thing I deserve is praise for that."

Ash was quiet, watching me, staring at me with those shadowy eyes of his that I thought held more secrets than I'd ever given him credit for...that had more depth to them than I'd ever let myself see. Finally, after what felt like an eternity stretched between us, he said, "I think you deserve a whole lot of things you don't see, Beau Campbell."

My breath caught, a mass forming in my throat. It took me a moment to be able to speak around it. "That's my thing."

"What?" he asked.

"Calling you by your first and last name."

Ash chuckled. "My bad."

"Thank you."

Ash shrugged. "Nothin' to thank me for. And he's amazing too." He nodded toward the arcade.

"He is. I'm so damn proud of him. He takes classes at the college, works with Mom. He's smart, kind, happy, fun as hell, and passionate about the world around him. It's impossible not to be in awe of him."

Ash's eyes darkened, his brows pulling together as two small wrinkles formed above them. His stare held mine with an intensity I couldn't explain or deny, and if I hadn't felt it, I'd probably laugh if someone else said they experienced it.

"You're looking at each other weird." The sound of Kenny's confused voice snapped me out of my Ash-trance. I'd seen many people fall into it before and never return. Despite our truce, or the fact that I was going to be an adult where he was concerned, that wasn't a place I could allow myself to get lost.

"That's because Ash is weird," I told Kenny.

"No, he's not," he replied.

"Yeah, no, I'm not!" He raised his voice, feigning offense. He was so theatrical and always had been.

"And the Oscar goes to…"

"Do you really think I'm that good?" Ash asked, and I laughed again. Damn it. He'd gotten me. The same way every person who'd ever crossed his path became enamored with him, I was officially a member of the Ashton Carmichael fan club.

Which basically meant I was fucked.

CHAPTER THIRTEEN

Ashton

Los Angeles Avalanche's Ashton Carmichael needs to figure out who he is as a football player.

"HELLO?" BEAU'S VOICE was sleep-roughened, gritty, telling me he'd either just woken up, or that I'd awakened him with my phone call.

"You're still in bed? Get up, lazy-ass," I teased. The tone of his voice still sort of echoed in my head, which obviously was weird as shit. "You sound like you just finished smoking two packs of cigarettes."

"Gee, thanks. Nothing I enjoy waking up to more than a critique of my morning voice."

"Morning voice…I like that. I've never heard it before. You're husky. Is this always your morning voice, or is it some blend of sleepiness and Ashton-annoyance?"

Beau groaned. He hadn't been doing that to me as much in the two weeks since the night we had pizza after Kenny's game, and we'd hung out quite a bit. We'd had dinner at Fever Pitch again, jogged in the park, and had gone bowling with Kenny. Besides that, I'd fallen into the habit of sugar for breakfast at Campbell's Confections, which I often shared just with Kenny. Beau also let me tag along to a couple of Kenny's practices, and the first time I'd hung around and signed autographs for everyone afterward. Beau had apologized, but I hadn't minded. They'd been some of the most respectful fans I'd met, and hell, I'd explained to him that it wasn't as though I didn't enjoy meeting fans, because I did, but sometimes I just wanted to be Ash and not Ashton Carmichael, ex-quarterback for the Avalanche. Most of the time, I didn't want to be reminded of my off-field antics, but this happened more than one might think. Why did people believe it was okay to throw people's mistakes at them?

Luckily, that hadn't happened there, and it had been fun…almost as enjoyable as watching Beau coach. His passion for it shone through, and he was good, though I thought Beau was good at more things than he gave himself credit for.

Beau's voice shook me out of my reverie. "I haven't been annoyed with you lately." He sounded as if he'd moved, maybe sat up, and I wondered what he was doing.

"Oh, come on. Even when we're getting along, you can't pretend there isn't always a little bit of annoyance there."

"Are you really arguing with me when I said you weren't annoying?"

"Annoying, right?" I countered, and he laughed. A flicker of pride lit up in my chest. I liked making Beau laugh.

"Okay, so you're still annoying, but why are you so interested in my morning voice?"

Hmm. He had a point there. "Because it's ten, which feels too late for a morning voice. You wanna hang out this afternoon?"

"I can't." Beau yawned. "I have to pick up an extra shift. I'm going in for a swing."

"You're such a grown-up. I try to adult as little as possible…but then, I'm not a hero."

"I guess you were right; you *are* still annoying."

It was fun irritating Beau. It had always been one of my favorite things to do. "That's because I'm always right."

"You're fucking weird." There was a smile in Beau's voice. Before I could reply, he added, "I gotta go."

"Oh yeah. Adulting," I teased.

"No, I actually have to take a piss. Someone woke me

up, and I haven't gotten to go yet, so unless you'd like to accompany me into the bathroom, we should probably hang up."

My pulse accelerated before dropping quickly. My mouth felt dry, and as I tried to think of a joke, some kind of wisecrack, my brain went blank.

"What are you doing tomorrow?" Beau asked.

"Please don't tell me you're peeing right now, Campbell."

It didn't matter that we were on the phone, I knew Beau rolled his eyes.

"I'm not going to try and be nice to you anymore," he joked.

"I was thinking about doing some work around the house. The old shed out back needs to be torn down, and I'm thinking the patio cover too. A few things like that."

"You need some help?" Beau asked. I was both surprised and not surprised. It was in Beau's nature to help people, but it was also typically me who initiated things when we hung out. Apparently, I was suddenly a needy fuck. Oh shit. Not a fuck, fuck. A person, a needy person.

"Yeah, that'd be great, if you don't mind. I'll supply the beer and food."

"I'll supply the muscle," Beau countered.

"Oh, fuck you very much. I have some of that too."

"I hadn't noticed."

I grinned. "Go pee, asshole. I'll see you in the morning." I heard Beau laughing as I hung up the phone.

WELL, SHIT. NOW I didn't know what to do, which was sad, yeah, but true. Sure, it had only been a couple of weeks, but I'd gotten used to the time I spent with Beau and Kenny.

I decided, though, if Beau was going to be an adult, I was going to be one too. I could keep myself busy without Beau or without calling Wyatt to see what he was up to.

The first thing I did was get up, clean the house, and wash my sheets. If Beau was coming over the following day, the house should be presentable. Not that he'd be seeing my sheets, but I figured those should be washed too.

Once that was done, I tortured myself with a few articles on the Internet about myself. I scanned some of the ones about the orgy, because I was a glutton for punishment. Beau obviously knew about it, and I wondered what he thought...if the details of it would matter. Shoving those thoughts from my head, I called and caught up with Andrea, and got a small amount of joy from the fact that the Avalanche weren't having a great season. Maybe that made me an asshole, but I was okay with that.

It was such a dichotomy...the way I felt when I thought about football. There was the part of me that missed it, that felt like a piece of my soul was gone without it, while another part of me didn't miss it at all. That second part maybe even wondered if the first was there because it was true, or because it felt like what I should feel.

But how could that be when it was something I'd lived and breathed? When it had been the thing that brought me the greatest joy? When it had made me feel good.

And...that was enough of that. I definitely wasn't in the mood to go that deep, so I closed my laptop and decided to go do some grocery shopping.

On my way out the door, I grabbed my baseball cap, which felt like my invisibility cloak or something.

It was a short drive into downtown Fever Falls. There were a hundred grocery stores in town, but for some reason, I chose one at the corner of Fever Street and Onyx Drive.

There was a slight buzzing feeling at the base of my spine as I wondered if anyone would recognize me. Honestly, I wasn't sure if I wanted them to or not. I liked the anonymity of my life at the moment, but I sure as shit didn't want to be forgotten either.

I made it down a couple of aisles when I heard, "Well, if it isn't Mr. Sexy Football Player."

I turned around at the sound of Lincoln's voice. "You recognized me from the back?" It wasn't as if I knew him well...or as if we'd spent a lot of time together.

"Football players have nice asses."

My stomach did this odd somersault thing.

"Oh, you're blushing. Isn't that cute. But I promised Beau I wouldn't flirt with you."

Well, this was interesting. I sort of forgot I was supposed to feel uncomfortable for a moment and said, "Beau asked you not to flirt with me? Why?"

"Um...because you're straight...?"

Oh...that would make sense. Christ, what was wrong with me?

"Probably because he has a secret crush on you too, but I don't have hard evidence on that yet."

This time it was as if my damn gut was in the Olympics—swoops and flips and all sorts of annoying feelings. "Who could blame him? Most people do," I teased, and

Lincoln laughed.

"Yeah, I assume they do. Come on, let's have a little fun with him. Lower your hat and put your head down so I can't see your face."

I did that, and Lincoln got close to me, held his phone out, and snapped a selfie.

"Is this okay?" he asked. He showed me the photo on his Instagram account—my face covered with the hat and Lincoln with a big-ass smile on his face. The caption read: *Wonder what kind of trouble we can get into…*

Okay, so I had to admit, I was maybe curious about Beau's reaction. Not that he had a reason to react any certain way, but obviously, I liked to get under Beau's skin, and I thought this might do it. "Yeah, go for it." I glanced at Lincoln's username as he posted it.

We spoke for a little longer, and then a woman came down the aisle, stared at me, swooped around, and came right back. There was a spark of recognition in her eyes that made my discomfort ride the dips and curves of my spine. "I think I better go," I told him.

I was surprised when Lincoln hugged me, my arms plastered against my sides because I wasn't really used to hugging people goodbye and grocery-store stalker-lady still had me in her sights.

From there I went straight to the registers, paid, and left. That was enough adulting for the day.

CHAPTER FOURTEEN

Beau

I asked Beau if he wanted to hang out today, but he said he had plans. For the first time, he didn't offer to cancel them for me, and that made me happy. Whatever Beau was doing must be important, and I wanted him to have a good time. ~ Love, Kenny

I PARKED IN the half-circle driveway in front of Ash's house around eight in the morning. We'd wanted a fairly early start to get a lot of the teardown done before it got too hot. It was so strange, spending time with him again. Spending time with him where I wasn't telling myself I hated him when in reality I'd wanted him to fuck me. Not anymore, but the deeply closeted, self-denial Beau had likely been jonesing for Ashton Carmichael's dick just like everyone else had been back then.

Just like they were now. Not me, of course, but everyone else.

Fuck. How had I gotten on the subject of Ash's cock?

Grumbling at myself, I got out of the truck. The window shook when I slammed the door a little too hard. I adjusted my cap backward on my head.

"What'd that door ever do to you?"

My heart did an embarrassing lurch as Ash walked around the side of the house and toward me. "Shit. I didn't see you there. Being a stalker is creepy, ya know?"

Ash grinned, a deep dimple forming beneath the left side of his mouth. He hadn't shaved that morning, and dark stubble covered his jaw. If Ash were someone else, I'd wonder what it would feel like as it scraped my skin—my neck, my face, my groin, my ass—but this was Ashton Carmichael, so I didn't wonder.

"Okay, who's creepy now? Why are you smiling at me like that? I'm so confused. You used to be all frowns around me, and now I get unexplainable smiles? What are you up to, Campbell?"

Well, shit. I shouldn't have been smiling while thinking about stubble burn that didn't belong to Ash. "Don't you wish you knew?" I threw in a wink for good measure. Nodding toward my truck, I added, "I brought some tools. I wasn't sure what you had or might need."

"Ugh. You're so responsible and always prepared. I guess that means we really have to work today."

The comment made me wonder what Ash planned to do now that his football career was over, but I didn't want to ask. It felt rude, and I'd been that to Ash too often in our lives. "Yes, we're working. Now help me get this shit out of the truck so we can get started before it gets too hot."

"Yes, sir."

"I like that better than Cranky Campbell. I think that should be your nickname for me."

"You wish."

"A man can try."

We unloaded my truck and carried everything around the back side of the house. The pool I'd swam in with him as a teenager was still there, but it surprised me that it was running. It couldn't have been all this time, so he must have had it serviced when he moved back.

The patio cover was over a slab of concrete behind the house. It had definitely seen better days, and I could understand why he wanted it torn down. The shed too, years of damage and sitting there having caught up with both of them. I wouldn't have expected him to do it himself, though. Someone with his money…hell, it still surprised me that Ash even chose to live in his family home. I hadn't thought about it since that first day. Early retirement or not, Ashton Carmichael had to have more money than I'd ever see in my lifetime. He could have had anything, yet when he'd left his home in LA, he'd come back to Fever Falls, back to the small, ranch-style home he'd grown up in.

"Why are you here, Ash?" I hadn't meant for the question to slip out, but now that it had, I couldn't take it back.

"Huh?" He used his hand to push his hair off his forehead and shield his eyes from the sun.

"Back home...Fever Falls, same house. I don't mean to sound like a dick when I ask that. I'm just curious. You could go anywhere, have anything, yet you're here."

He rubbed that same hand over his face before dropping his arm to his side. "Because this is my home. This is the place the parents who chose me raised me, and if there's anywhere I can figure out who in the hell I am, I guess I figured it was here."

He went to turn around, but my arm shot out, my fingers wrapping around his large wrist. His skin was hot, sun-kissed, the heat from his body penetrating mine. How could Ashton Carmichael not know who he was? He was what people strived to be—smart, confident, funny. "I don't think you give yourself enough credit." Those weren't words I'd ever imagined myself saying to Ash. He'd always seemed too full of himself, too over-the-top, which should have told me something right there. Maybe it had, and I hadn't wanted to see it.

"I can't believe you just said that to me."

"I was just thinking the same thing." I grinned, hoping to lighten the mood.

"Maybe hell's frozen over?"

"I'm sure it'll thaw out in a little while and things will be back to normal."

"Thank fuck for that. I'd hate to have you being nice or giving me compliments all the time. That's not us, Cranky Campbell."

I shook my head. Fucking Ash. Of course he had to go there. "No, I guess not, Cocky Carmichael."

His eyes darted down to my hand, and I realized I still held on to his wrist. Dropping it immediately, I said, "Sorry."

"No, no. It's fine. If you wanted to hold my hand, you just had to ask." He winked, and I rolled my eyes.

"Let's get started before I change my mind and refuse to help you."

"Please, let's not pretend you're not the guy who's always there to help someone in need. You're a hero, Beau." He moved toward me, and I sort of froze, wondering what in the hell he was doing, but then Ash stole my dark-blue Fever Falls Fire Department cap, fitting it over his head. "Sun was getting to me," he said before walking to the shed, and damn Ashton Carmichael, because I didn't even ask for my hat back.

CHAPTER FIFTEEN

Ashton

Ashton "Take a chance" Carmichael did just that...
Will it pay off?

WE SPENT HOURS tearing down the shed. The conversation hardly stopped. Beau talked about his job and his mom and his group of friends.

Rush was apparently a professional motocross racer. I didn't know much about the sport, but had always been interested in dirt bikes, even though I'd never ridden.

I realized Camden and Sawyer were actually brothers we'd gone to high school with, only they hadn't been friends with our group. Sawyer had been...shy...quiet, really fucking smart. He'd gotten picked on a lot, and Camden had always come to his rescue. Camden had been known as a troublemaker.

It just struck me that there had been Camden, Sawyer, and Beau around me, who were all gay and no one had ever known it. I mean, obviously I had to have had some inclination about Beau since I'd kissed him, but hell, it could have been a fluke with him the way it was with me.

"This is awful nice of you…helping me out like this," I told Beau.

He shrugged. "You're not an asshole."

"Huh?"

"Nothing. Just something I've told Kenny before."

Okay… "After we finish the shed, wanna take a break for lunch and beer?" I asked. He wiped the sweat off his forehead with the back of his hand, his bicep tightening as he did so. My eyes trained in on the ball of muscle, how firm and cut it was. Yeah, I definitely needed a beer break.

"Sure. And thanks for getting my hat sweaty."

I grinned, took it off, and held it out to him. "Want it back?"

"Fuck no."

Laughing, I slipped it back on my head. I didn't know what had made me take it and wear it all morning, but Beau always made me do weird shit. It was annoying as hell.

So we kept talking about random stuff as we finished up the shed, and then went inside. I ordered pizza, and first thing I did afterward was crack open a beer. "Want one?" I held the bottle up for Beau.

"Sure."

I pulled a second out of the fridge and handed it to him. When I did so, our fingers brushed. The heat must have begun to get to me because it was making me woozy. I needed to hurry up and get some food in my stomach.

"So, patio cover next?" Beau asked as he leaned against the counter, tilted his head back, and took a few long swallows of beer. And now my eyes were oddly glued to the muscles in his throat, to his Adam's apple as it moved.

"Yep." Looking away, I concentrated on a fly buzzing around the yellow kitchen. *Relax, dude. You've been through this before. Just gotta get your head on straight. It always goes away.*

"What are your plans?" Beau asked.

"I was going to build another—patio cover, I mean. I did some construction work in college, helping a buddy out. And that's what Dad always did. He used to take me to work with him, remember?"

"Yeah." Beau nodded. "I remember when Wyatt and I went with you guys too. Remember Wyatt nailed his finger to a two-by-four?"

We both chuckled. "Wyatt hated that shit."

"I loved it," Beau replied. "I used to wish my old man wanted to take me to work the way yours did. He wanted to leave us instead."

His words landed in my chest, and I couldn't help but let my eyes snap to Beau again. He drank the rest of his beer, then turned and washed his hands in the sink. I stared at him from behind, which was strange, I knew. Still, I couldn't pull my gaze away. It traveled from his sweaty hair, down his back, to his ass before I went to drink the rest of my beer, only to realize it was gone, and I did my best to force my eyes away from him.

"He didn't deserve you guys. I know that's not true comfort. I tell that to myself about my birth parents." Not because they gave me away. No, I was glad they'd done what was best for me there. It was what had happened later, afterward. That dumbass thing I'd done in college that no one knew about.

"Kenny deserved better."

"So did you," I replied. "And damn, he's lucky to have you."

Okay, so I got that our eyes were always meeting, but it happened again, like they were drawn together. Something shifted in Beau's expression as he took me in. It was intense, strong as a touch running the length of my body. We didn't talk like this when we were kids.

Hell, I didn't talk like this with anyone.

He opened his mouth. I waited with bated breath to know what he was going to say and—*ding-dong!* We both jumped at the sound of the doorbell. I could tell he noticed it in me too because he looked down, shook his head, and snickered. "So luckily, that was just the doorbell and not a serial killer coming to get us."

"How do you know that's not who's at the door?" Beau asked.

"Good point. But would he ring the bell?"

"Maybe to throw suspicion off his true motives." He took a step toward me, and another. "You go first. I got your back."

"Oh, I see how it is. You're sacrificing me?" I teased, even though I liked the idea of Beau by my side, sacrifice or not.

"Your house."

"Pfft. I'm not taking the fall because of that. If I go down, you're going down with me." Damned if I didn't grab his arm and tugged a laughing Beau along with me.

WE ATE THE pizza that had been delivered and then went right back out to work. The conversation continued to flow, and Christ, he was funny. Beau could always make me laugh, but what made it even better was the fact that he didn't try. I didn't think it ever occurred to him to try and be funny the way it did with me.

The thing that was making things tricky was that I couldn't stop watching him. I hated myself for it in some ways, but I was drawn to him, always had been—to his kindness, his humor, his work ethic…just *Beau*. When he'd look at me, I always jerked my gaze away. I made sure to drink a few beers, which helped dull the part of me that worried about how much I looked at him or talked to him or enjoyed being around him.

When we finished, I realized I wasn't ready for Beau to leave yet. "Wanna swim and cool off?" I asked. "We can grill up some dinner. I went grocery shopping." That wasn't a strange question. Two friends swim and have dinner together.

"That when you saw *Linc*?" he asked.

"Why do you say it like that?"

"Like what? I didn't say it like anything."

"You—"

"You want me to go swimming with you?" His brows knitted together as if it *was* a strange question. "I don't have swim trunks."

Then my brain started going haywire because I

couldn't figure out why he was looking at me or why I was so nervous about asking him to swim with me. I almost backed out of it, but that meant he would leave, and I really wanted to hang out with him. "Oh no. Whatever will we do? I mean, I don't have clothes or anything," I said sarcastically.

"You want me to borrow swim trunks from you?"

"The only other option is skinny dipping, and I like you, Campbell, but I don't want to see your ass." I didn't. There was nothing wrong with wanting to if I did, but I didn't. *I don't, I don't, I don't.*

"Your loss, Carmichael, because it's a fine ass. I've never had anyone complain."

I trembled. Fuck, why in the hell was I trembling? I gripped the porch railing, trying to ignore the waves tracing down my spine. "Eh, I've seen better." I shrugged as my brain fired off questions: *Why did you say that? Have you, Carmichael? Have you really seen better?*

Stop it!

"Come on. I'll get you something to cover that hairy ass of yours, and get us another beer."

"I'm okay on the beer, and you say that as if there's something wrong with a hairy ass," Beau replied as we went back inside.

"You like hairy asses?" sort of tumbled out of my

mouth. Why had I asked that? What the fuck was with my mouth and the shit that came out of it?

"I'm sure you don't want to talk about that."

"What? Just because I'm straight, I can't want to talk to my friend about his preferences?" Well, now I *had* to talk about it, to prove a point and all. I grabbed a beer from the fridge, opened it, and took a swallow.

"Typically, yes," Beau replied.

Again, now I had to keep going to prove to him I wasn't like the guys he was talking about. "That's not me. You're free to talk about hairy or non-hairy asses as much as you like." Another drink. "But didn't Lincoln say you were a bottom? Doesn't that mean…" *Drink, drink, drink.*

"Oh God. Stop. I can't talk to you about this, and don't ever say bottom to me again. It sounds weird coming from you."

"Fine, but for the record, I was okay with the conversation. You're the one who was uncomfortable."

His eyes fired up like I'd seen them do so many times. I'd basically just put us in competition without realizing it, a place we were familiar with from growing up. We'd always loved one-upping each other. "Fine. You wanna do this? We'll do it. I like hairy ass, smooth ass, just male ass in general. There are certain things I like and appreciate about both. And just because I'm a bottom and lose my fucking mind when someone is playing with *my* ass, doesn't mean I don't appreciate another man's ass just as much."

Drink, drink, drink. Oh fuck. I drank my beer already?

"Too much?" he asked.

"Nope." My voice came out rough, my throat parched, and yes, I knew it shouldn't be, considering I'd just inhaled a whole beer. "I'll go get those clothes now."

"You do that."

"I will."

"I'll wait right here."

"I'll be right back," I replied…realized how crazy I sounded, and finally actually went.

CHAPTER SIXTEEN

Beau

Beau tries to protect me too much, but I know he loves me. ~ Love, Kenny

I DID MY best to pretend not to notice the way Ash watched me. I'd failed most of the day, but made it a point to try harder after the ass incident. I attempted to keep my distance from him when we were in the pool, tried to swim and relax and do my own thing, but this was Ashton fucking Carmichael we were talking about. He commanded attention even when he didn't try...and most of the time, he tried. It was absolutely impossible to ignore him then. Everything about him was impossible, and he made me do and feel weird things. Like how weird I felt about seeing the picture of him and Linc. I knew it had to have been just the two of them running into each other, but it had made me feel...weird. There was that word again.

When I lounged on a float, he tried to splash me,

then dunk me. He was the biggest fucking kid I'd ever met, but then my gut hurt from laughing so hard, which wasn't uncommon when I was around Ash. It had grated on my nerves in high school, but it didn't anymore.

Then, of course, we had to challenge each other to a game of football in the water because how could we not? It was basically impossible for us not to.

After I'd kicked his ass, we'd grilled steaks for dinner, and he'd started drinking a few more beers. I couldn't help but worry about him when it came to the drinking. It seemed to be a pattern I noticed with him since he'd come home.

We had dinner out back, and when I said, "I should probably hit the road," Ash shook his head.

"Not until we try this new firepit I got. I haven't gotten a chance to use it yet."

So that's what we did. We started a fire and roasted marshmallows like we were kids.

We kept talking, and it got darker and darker, later and later, but Ash didn't make a move to go inside and call an end to the night, so I didn't either.

I wanted to be around him, enjoyed it, probably always had in ways I wouldn't have admitted before. We'd spent the whole day together, and half the time he infuriated me and the other he made me laugh, and as much as I hated to admit it, I soaked up every second of it. That had always been Ash, though, hadn't it? He was that bright star you spotted first at night, this beacon that drew your attention, entranced you and didn't let go. My brain told me I should be angrier that I'd gotten caught up in the power that was Ashton Carmichael, but in that moment, I couldn't find it in me to feel that way.

The fire was going down, the embers fading, yet still we stayed.

I slid my hand across the chair, and a piercing pain ripped down my finger. "Fuck." I jerked my hand away.

"What happened?" Ash worried his full, bottom lip.

"Something cut me." I wrapped a hand around my finger, blood dripping already.

"Come on. Let's go inside and clean it up." He went for the house, and I followed him. Once inside the kitchen, Ash turned on the water, grabbed my wrist, and pulled until my hand was under the faucet. Water and blood mixed as they went down the drain.

"Stay there. I'll be right back."

It was only a moment later that Ash returned with a small first-aid kit. He turned off the water, wrapped a cloth around my finger, and led me to the table. "I can do this myself, you know." Still, I followed his lead. Sat down when he pointed to the chair, watched as he unwrapped my finger and studied it.

"I don't think it needs stitches. It's pretty deep, though."

Then with the gentlest care, he began to put antiseptic on me, bandaged it as though I was mortally wounded. My heart pounded, and I couldn't take my eyes off him, knew I needed to because in that moment, I felt this connection with him that I couldn't explain. Who in the hell was Ashton Carmichael?

"All better." He gave me a sweet grin. Then, as if realizing he still held on to me, he jerked his hand away.

"Thank God you were here."

"Never thought I'd hear you say that. Do you mind repeating it while I record?" he teased.

"Funny guy."

"Thank you."

I rolled my eyes. It was late, after ten, and I'd been there since eight in the morning. It had been a long day, and my eyes were grainy, heavy. "What do I owe you for fixing me up, Dr. Carmichael?" I joked as I leaned forward, not toward him, but with my elbow on the table, resting my head against my good hand. My body was definitely fading. I needed to get home.

"Your hair is all crazy from swimming earlier." From his spot in front of me, Ash ran his fingers through my hair, ruffled it, twisted strands around his fingers, and damn, it felt good. A tingle swept through me, and I closed my eyes, savored it, and he kept going, fingering my hair as if I were his lover.

Ash…this was Ash. That night on the dock slammed into me, the press of his lips and the shock of disappointment when he'd pulled away. The fear in his eyes and the way he'd run, making me feel as though it had been my fault, as though he'd been drunk and that was the only reason he'd done it.

I didn't open my eyes when I said, "Ash…what are you doing? This…this isn't the way a straight man touches another guy."

He jolted backward as though I'd burned him, quicker and with more urgency than he had all those years ago. Finally, I forced my lids open.

"I wasn't… I don't…" His typically happy eyes were wide, this sort of panicked expression in them, and damned if my heart didn't break, if I wasn't beginning to see a battle inside him that he'd maybe been fighting his whole life.

How could I have never seen the depth of it before? I'd spent years angry at him, telling myself I hated him, seething with each new headline or mess he'd gotten himself into. How could I not have seen? "Hey…it's okay. I didn't mean anything by it. I wasn't trying to say anything, but you know you can talk to me, right? Or if you don't feel comfortable with me, Linc would—"

"Whoa, slow your roll, Cranky Campbell." He looked shaken as he hauled himself out of the chair, went for the fridge, grabbed another beer. "I think your imagination is getting away from you." I watched him open the beer, swallow a few drinks, and it felt like my heart was ground into dust, but not for me. For Ash. For the fear in his eyes.

"Ash—"

"Beau."

Don't push, Campbell. You could be wrong…and it's not your place. Even Kenny told me I could be overbearing, and I had no business doing that with Ash. Still, I couldn't stop myself from adding, "I didn't realize I was gay until that night you kissed me. I'm sure I had to have had questions before, but that was the first night I admitted it to myself. I'm not saying you're anything other than what you say you are, but for me—"

"Jesus, Campbell. Lay the fuck off. I touched your goddamned hair. I have no problem with you being gay, but I'm not. Stop projecting your shit onto me. You did it at the graduation party, and I let it go. We're not going there again."

My blood ran cold as I ground my molars together. "Excuse me? I'm not the one who kissed you, and I sure as shit wasn't the one running my fingers through your hair just now."

"It's late." He shook his head, turned his back to me, looking out the window over the sink.

"Ash…"

"Get out, Campbell. You're barking up the wrong tree. I didn't want you then, and I don't want you now."

I paused, waiting for him to apologize, waiting for this to make some kind of fucking sense. My breath hitched when he turned, but he didn't look at me, just kept walking down the hall. When the sound of a door slamming echoed through the house, I did as he said. I left.

"It's SaturGAY, bitches!" Lincoln raised his arms in the air and did a little shimmy as the five of us climbed out of the car and our driver took off.

"Fuck yes!" Rush replied, pulling Linc close and grinding against him. I rolled my eyes at them, and Sawyer laughed. Rush and Linc were going to get themselves into trouble one day.

Rush was great. I respected the hell out of him. It hadn't been easy being the only *out* Supercross racer. The sport wasn't known for being incredibly accepting. And once the season started, he wouldn't be able to attend our Saturgays out because he'd be traveling.

"What's up with you, Beau? You're awfully quiet." Cam wrapped an arm around my shoulders as we walked down the sidewalk, then massaged my neck with his work-roughened fingers.

"And sulky... Why are you sulky, Beau? You're even more grumpy than usual. I know we always drag you out for Saturgay, but I figured since you've been hanging out with Ashton Carmichael so much..." Lincoln grinned at me, and I wanted to strangle my friend.

"You've been with Ashton Carmichael?" both Rush and Cam asked.

"Ugh, Ashton Carmichael," Sawyer added. He hadn't been fond of Ash either, but mostly because Ash had been the typical jock in high school, and Sawyer had...not. But then, Sawyer and I were close despite the fact that we hadn't grown up together, so that counted for something.

"He's not that bad," I told Sawyer.

"I thought you hated him?" Sawyer asked just as Linc said, "Not that bad? He's fucking gorgeous and funny, and you've been with him a whole lot more than you've been with me lately, and he's not that bad? I think my feelings are hurt."

I shook my head as we continued down Fever Street. It was getting busier—the sidewalk getting more crowded, restaurants filling, music and laughter floating out of every establishment.

"I've been busy. I haven't been with Ash very often," I defended myself, even though it was a lie. I'd been with Ash a lot...and I couldn't get our last day out of my head.

The way he'd looked at me...the way he'd touched me...the fire in his eyes when he'd thrown me out.

Get the fuck out of my head, Ash!

Cam pulled away just as Linc jumped onto my back. He wrapped his legs around my waist and his arms around my neck. "It's okay. We'll make up for it tonight!"

And he was right. I needed to. I could be there to support Ash if he needed me. Hell, I wanted to, but the way he'd touched me? The way I'd wanted him to? I had to put an end to that shit real quick, and Saturgay was the perfect night to do it.

CHAPTER SEVENTEEN

Ashton

Ashton Carmichael could go all the way!

MUSIC BLASTED AROUND me as I took my third shot...third? I thought it was my third. Maybe it was my fourth. Who the fuck was counting.

The music made my brain thump, which was sort of welcoming. It helped drown out my thoughts...of Beau...of what I'd said to him last time I saw him...of the feel of his hair and the glint in his eyes and the way he licked his lips and *fuck*. "One more, please," I told the bartender, who nodded at me.

Stupid fucking brain. Why couldn't I make these thoughts go away? Most of the time, I was good at ignoring them, good at pretending they didn't exist, good at reminding myself that they were just thoughts, not actions. I mean, I liked sex. My brain and libido just got sort of twisted up sometimes.

Liar...such a fucking liar.

My eyes were drawn back to Instagram, to Lincoln's page, which I'd psychotically memorized when we met at the grocery store. Saw the pictures, the videos of Beau and his friends as they danced and drank. Why the fuck did Beau mess with my head so much? It was so much easier to pretend when he wasn't around—no, not pretend, because these fleeting moments weren't real. That wasn't really who I was.

The past week had been better. I'd been fine…lonely but fine. It also gave me a chance to work through what had happened the other night. It was the emotions of having him back in my life. Beau might not have felt the same, but he'd always been who I considered my best friend. That and the beer, and *poof*, overly affectionate Ash had made an appearance.

When I refreshed the app, I saw that Lincoln had added to his story.

Don't do it. Don't do it.

Of course I was going to fucking do it.

I clicked on the story, saw Lincoln dancing, laughing. The club was mostly men, which *duh*, I should have thought about the fact that they went to a gay club, and what the hell was Saturgay anyway? That didn't sound like Beau.

As Lincoln panned the phone around in a circle, I

saw him, a flash of Beau, his arms around someone, their bodies moving together as they danced before—"Go back. Turn the phone the other way!" I told video-Lincoln as though he could hear me.

I shook my head, rubbed a hand over my face. When the bartender set the drink in front of me, I swallowed it all, then hit the glass too hard on the counter.

My vision blurred slightly—from alcohol or whatever the fuck was going on in my head, I didn't know.

"Hey, sexy," a soft, confident, very female voice said from beside me.

"Hi." Yes, this was exactly what I needed. I lowered the hat—Beau's hat, which I crazily still wore—but in my head, I already knew it was too late.

"Um...I noticed you from across the room. My friend didn't believe me, but you're Ashton Carmichael, aren't you?"

No, I wanted to say. Because she was standing beside me because of who I was. Most people did. It wasn't about me, it was about football, but still, I knew this was what I needed. This always worked. When I started to feel these things, it had helped in the past. "I sure am, honey," I replied.

She smiled. "Can I buy you a drink?"

"You wanna get out of here with me instead?" I

asked. It was bold, but I was Ashton Carmichael, and hopefully that would help. Bile rose in my throat, but I swallowed it down.

"Yeah, I think I'd like that."

I closed my tab, and we were out the door, kissing and stumbling down the sidewalk. When we got to an alley, she tugged my hand, so I followed her down it. "Eager little thing, aren't you?" I asked, ignoring the twist in my gut.

"I can't believe I'm with you right now. You're so fucking hot," the brunette said. "I don't want to wait, but I can go more than once—here and then wherever we make it next?"

No! I nodded, unable to make words come out. I didn't need to, though. Her mouth was on me again, and we were kissing, her tongue probing me and mine her. We fell against the wall, my hand going down to her ass. Beau's comment from the other night flashed in my head, so I slid my hands up her back, twined them in her long hair, which of course reminded me of my fingers in his short, soft strands and the way they'd been sticking up all over the place.

Get the fuck out of my head!

I kissed her harder. She groaned into my mouth, ran her hand down my chest, my stomach, into my pants.

Come on, come on, come on, I mentally begged my dick to get hard.

"Don't worry, we'll get you there," she replied, rubbing my soft cock with the palm of her hand. I hated myself in that moment, for what I was doing, for what I couldn't do, for being weak, and for the thoughts that had plagued me my whole damn life.

Please just let me get hard.

She kissed her way down my throat, lowered herself, worked my button, and fucking Beau was there again—his laugh and that goddamned smiley face on his bicep.

I looked down at her, tried to see her, but Beau kept being there, the feel of him when we wrestled in the pool.

She pulled me out, this woman who just wanted to pleasure me. Maybe not because of me, more because of who I was, but still, it didn't seem fair to do this to her, to use her the way I'd done too many times. I hoped she could make me feel something else…anything. I just needed to feel.

"I can't," I said, and she immediately stopped.

"What?" She looked up at me.

"I'm sorry. It's not you. I had a lot to drink…there's a lot on my mind, and I just… I can't." I pulled away, tucked my soft cock back in, buttoned and zipped my pants. My head was spinning, my stomach turning.

She began straightening out her dress, looking away.

"I'm sorry. It's not you," I said again. "I'm trying to clean up my image," I lied, and she flinched. "I didn't mean for it to sound like that. Let me walk you back to the bar."

"I'm just going to go home."

"I'm sorry," I told her again.

"I just kissed Ashton Carmichael. I'll be okay." She winked, then turned and walked toward the street. She rounded the corner just as I let go, clutching my stomach as I vomited all over the dirty alley.

I wiped my mouth, then walked the opposite direction until I hit the next main street. I heard music and noticed another bar on the corner. It was a small building, country music playing inside, a totally different atmosphere from where I'd just been. My shot came quickly, and I swallowed it down, ordered another and drank that one too.

I couldn't get hard. There had only been a couple of times in my life that had happened, but usually I was at least able to get myself hard.

In that moment, I hated Beau. I'd spent my whole life never truly sure if he hated me or not, but I hated him. It was his fault. I was able to ignore it when he wasn't around. Every time I couldn't hold it back, every time I fucked up and gave in, it was because of *him*.

I fumbled with my phone, trying to pull it out of my pocket. It dropped to the ground. I almost vomited again when I picked it up. I tossed money on the bar and made my way out again, listening to it ring. When the voice mail picked up, I hung up and called again.

I just made my way into the humid air when I heard, "Ash?" mixed with the thumping bass and a pop song.

"Fuck you!" I screamed at Beau. "Fuck you," I said again, softly, my voice breaking. I turned a corner, kept walking, without any idea where I was going.

"Where are you, Ash?" he asked, his voice filled with kindness…with pity.

"Fuck you," I said again and again and again, and he let me. "I tried, Campbell, I fucking *tried*. Why can't I make it go away?"

"Because it's who you are," he replied, and I realized it was quiet then, that Beau must have left the club.

"No." I shook my head, leaning against a brick building.

"Where are you?" he asked again.

"Going to come and save me? That's what you do, right? You're a hero."

"Don't be a dick."

"Funny you should mention dick, because mine's broken. I couldn't even get hard tonight. She wasn't impressed."

"Not broken, Ash. Maybe it's just fixed now. Maybe it knows what it wants."

"This is weird. We need to stop talking about my cock like this." Fucking Beau. It was always him making me feel comfortable enough to say stupid-ass shit like *my dick is broken*.

"Yeah, well, I just walked out on someone who was quite interested in my cock too, so do me a favor and tell me where you are so I can take you and your weird ass home."

"I thought we were talking about dick?" I asked, unable to believe I was joking at a time like this.

"You said we couldn't talk about it anymore, and stop trying to be funny. It's okay to just be you. You don't always have to try so hard. Not with me."

I didn't, did I? Not with Beau. He was too good a man for that, too honest and real. He always had been, which was why my over-the-top antics had always annoyed him so much. "I don't really know where I am," I admitted. "I'm a little drunk."

"No way! I couldn't tell," he teased.

I looked up at the streetlight. The green light was

fuzzy, but I saw a sign I managed to make out. "Against a brick wall by a light on Bishop Street. There's a furniture store on the corner."

"I know where you are. I'll be right there."

"Wait," jumped out of my mouth before he hung up.

"Yeah?"

"You were with someone? When I called?"

"Yeah, but I'm not anymore. I'll be right there, Ash."

"Okay." I hung up and waited, knowing Beau would come…knowing everything was about to change.

CHAPTER EIGHTEEN

Beau

Beau is magic. He makes everything okay.
~ Love, Kenny

WHAT IN THE fuck was I doing? There hadn't been a doubt in my mind that I was going to go home with the man I'd been dancing with. It had been my plan, what I needed, to fuck Ashton Carmichael out of my damn thoughts.

But that hadn't happened, had it?

He'd called...he'd called, and now I was going running.

I was lucky the plan had been to hook up tonight, because I never had more than one drink if I was going home with someone I didn't know. I liked to be in my right mind when I was letting someone inside me. So I'd been able to go to Sawyer's, who lived close to the bar, and borrow his car since my truck was at home. I didn't figure Ash was in a position to want to be around a driver he didn't know.

"Funny you should mention dick, because mine's broken. I couldn't even get hard tonight. She wasn't impressed."

He'd tried to hook up with someone...he'd tried, and he couldn't perform. I knew how something like that had to affect him—Ash being so damn proud and having used sex to lie to himself...maybe for his whole life.

"Fuck," I groaned as I approached Bishop Street. I saw him sitting on the ground, leaning against the wall, looking down, with his arms on his bent knees. The set of his body screamed sorrow. How long had Ash been feeling this way? How long had he been lying to himself?

I pulled the car up to the side of the road and rolled the window down. "Ashton."

"Sorry, wrong number," he replied without looking up.

"Not sure that works in this situation."

"Ashton who?" he tried again.

"Get in the car, Ash."

"Not sure I can."

Sighing, I got out, walked over, and held my hand out to him. He looked up at me, his hat—my hat—backward on his head, enabling me to see the pain in his eyes, the confusion...the loneliness...the fear.

"Stop wearing your hat like me. You've always tried to be like me."

"Because you created backward caps?" I teased.

"No, but I've always worn mine that way. You didn't start until senior year."

"You remember that?" Jesus, how could he remember something so small? Something like when I started wearing baseball caps a certain way.

"Um…no…?" His brows knitted together as he attempted to lie. "We can pretend it was a lucky guess."

I wrestled with my emotions, wondering what that could mean, because now wasn't the time for me to think about the fact that Ashton Carmichael remembered inconsequential details about me. This was bigger than me. It was about him. "Okay. Lucky guess, then. Take my hand. I'm not carrying your drunk ass to the car."

Okay, so I knew this was fucking crazy, but I swear to God, it was like it happened in slow motion. His fingers twitched, hand slid, arm moved, lifted, and then Ash clasped his hand with mine. His skin was warm, so fucking warm, the pads of his fingers rough, and damned if I didn't feel a jolt of lightning shoot up my arm.

See? Crazy. Why did Ashton always make me so crazy? It didn't matter if he was annoying the shit out of me or just touching my hand. He made me *feel*.

Ignoring it, I pulled him to his feet. Maybe it was the wrong thing to do, but I twined my fingers with his, didn't let go as I made a move to walk to the car. Ash's feet were rooted to the concrete, and when I realized he wasn't going to budge, I stopped, looked back at him. "What?"

"Thank you for coming. I didn't mean to cock block."

"It's fine." I tried to walk again, but he still didn't move.

"Don't pretend like it's nothing. You make sacrifices for people. You're a good man, Beau. Just say 'you're welcome.' I'm not getting into the car until you say 'you're welcome.'"

I chuckled. Leave it to Ash to throw a temper tantrum to get his way when I was trying to help him. But I guess if he was going to throw one, he picked a sweet reason to. "Well...he *was* really hot."

"Hey! I'm really hot."

Yeah, he was, but I wasn't going to sleep with him. "Get in the car, Drunky McDrunkerson, before I leave your ass here."

For once in his life, Ash listened without argument or sarcasm. I helped him into the car and then headed toward his house.

We were quiet the whole drive, Ash with his head against the window. When we pulled up in front of his house, I got out and automatically went to his side to help him. He was already opening the door when I arrived. "I can do it," he said, a slight terseness to his voice.

"Okay."

I'd done my job, gotten him home, and knew I didn't have to go inside, yet I followed him to the porch, waited as he unlocked the door and went inside. There was a tightness in my chest, my thoughts swirling around, battering my brain. I wanted answers. I wanted to know everything. I wanted to be there for him. I wanted to run because somehow I knew that once Ash opened up, nothing would be the same.

"You must think I'm a fucking disaster, huh? I guess I am. I lost my career, and I still can't keep my shit together."

"It's okay if you're attracted to men, Ash. It's okay…"

His eyes blazed with a fury of fire, his hands fisting before he unclenched his right one and shoved it through his hair, clearly having forgotten about his cap. "I need a drink."

"Don't," I told him. That wouldn't help. I had a feeling he'd been using that to help for a long time.

"You're not my daddy, Campbell."

I rolled my eyes, following him to the kitchen. "Grow the fuck up, Ash. You drink when you're uncomfortable…to hide whatever the fuck is going on in that head of yours. Grow up and face it."

He whipped around toward me. "Fuck you! We can't all be as goddamned perfect as you!"

"Do you think it's easy for me? That it was ever fucking easy for me? It wasn't. Nothing has been. My whole goddamn life has been about other people, and fine, that's my choice and I wouldn't change it, but it wasn't my choice to be a gay man, and I learned to be proud about that."

"Did you ever think I don't want to be?" His voice was softer, and when he spoke again, broken. "Did you ever fucking think I don't want to be gay, Beau? I wouldn't have had a career if I'd been gay, and who the fuck am I if I'm not Ashton Carmichael, football player!" He gripped the back of the couch, veins pulsing along the length of his arms. "Who the fuck am I, Beau?"

He took off the hat and threw it, chaos in his movements. My heart ached for him, bled for him.

"I'm tired… I'm so fucking tired." And then he

turned, walked down the hallway and into his room. I didn't know what to do, so I followed. He stood facing the bed, his back to the door, his head down. His spine curled, weighed down by the truth he'd denied his whole life.

"You're the same Ashton Carmichael. You're the one who always beat me at everything, because you're good and you work damn hard. You're the one who makes people laugh. The one who excelled at football and is a better player than anyone I've ever seen." I took a step toward him, then another and another. "You're the guy who played in college and made it to the pros. You're the guy who helped me teach Kenny how to play and who loves my mom's chocolate éclairs. The guy who would do anything to make someone else smile, who makes it impossible to be in a bad mood around you." Another step, and another and another. "The guy who kissed me at the end of a dock and made me admit to myself that I was gay."

He sucked in a sharp breath at that.

"Nothing has changed, Ash. Being gay doesn't change who you are, just who you love. You're a good man, better than I ever let you know you are." Which was the truth. I'd never been truly fair to Ash, had I? If I'd been better to him, maybe he would have felt more comfortable being honest with himself, or me, all those years ago.

"Did my kiss really make you realize you're gay? It was that good?"

I chuckled. Leave it to Ash to focus on that. "Yes, you cocky motherfucker. It was. I was so damn angry at you because of it too."

He turned, faced me, a slight flush on his cheeks, his eyes dewy with unshed tears.

"Maybe you're bisexual," I told him.

"I'm not bi, Campbell. I'm gay. I've spent my whole life trying to be straight…trying to be bi, because at least then I had a choice. I've spent years in denial, telling myself that I *did* find women attractive, that I *didn't* find men attractive, that I didn't crave the feel of a man beneath me, but I did, I always have, and no amount of drinking and fucking women will make it go away."

He ran his hands through his dark hair, fisted it, tugged. "I don't know how to do this, Campbell. I don't know how to be gay." And when his knees weakened and he fell to the ground, I tried to catch him, went with him, wrapped my arms around him, held him as he cried.

"Shh. It's okay. I'm here. I got you, Ash." I ran my fingers through his hair, down his back. Closed my eyes as he clutched the back of my shirt, dug his nails into my skin, pulled himself closer as though he was trying to climb inside me.

I didn't know how long we sat there, how long he cried and how long I held him. Ashton Carmichael...one of my childhood friends, maybe my first real crush, the boy who drove me crazy and challenged me even when he didn't realize it...the guy I'd always thought was the most confident person I knew, and even though I knew it wasn't logical, I felt like I'd failed him.

"I can't believe I just snotted all over you. This better be our secret, Campbell." Ash sat back and leaned against the bed.

"You can trust me."

"I know."

A lone tear fell from his left eye, and I had to fist my hands not to reach out and wipe it away.

"Well, I'm sober now...and tired," he said.

"You should get some sleep." I went to move, to stand, but Ash reached out, his hand tightening around my wrist. "Do you want me to stay?" When he cocked his head, I added, "I'm not trying to get in your pants, Ash."

"Remember? My dick is broken anyway. And I didn't think you were trying. I just appreciate that you didn't make me ask. You've always been able to read me."

I trembled. Fucking Ashton Carmichael. He was going to wreck me, ruin me. I knew it as well as I knew my own name. I probably had always known it.

This time, it was Ash who stood and held out a hand for me. I took it and let him help me up. He went into the bathroom as I took off my shoes. I heard water, assumed he was washing his hands, his face, maybe brushing his teeth. When the door opened, he said, "You can go next." He was still wearing jeans and a tee, so after I took a leak and washed my hands, I kept mine on as well. I went straight for the beanbag chair. It was silly. I could easily sleep on the couch or in one of the other rooms, but I wanted to be close to him in case he needed me. At least that was what I was telling myself.

"Don't be stupid. You can sleep with me."

Aaaaand…he truly was trying to kill me. "That might be a problem, because despite your recent issues, *my* dick is in fully functioning order."

"Fucker." He grinned.

"I'm serious. It's a double bed. Can you upgrade to the master bedroom at some point?"

"Get in the bed, Campbell."

"Yes, sir."

"Hey, my dick just perked up a bit. I guess it *is* working."

I groaned. Did he know what he was doing to me? "You're going to kill me."

"You like me, Cranky Campbell. I think you always have. I was your first crush."

I knew what he was doing. He was trying to turn it into a joke, make light of it all because things were easier for Ash to deal with that way. So I walked over, turned out the light, and crawled into bed with him. He was on top of the blanket, so I did the same. We lay there, quiet, shoulder to shoulder in the dark for an eternity when he said, "You were mine too."

"Your what?"

"First crush."

Yep. He was going to kill me. I was so fucked. "Go to sleep, Ash."

"Guess I'm not the only one who pretends things aren't happening."

"I'm ignoring you," I replied because he was obviously right.

"Then why do you keep replying?"

I opened my mouth...then closed it again. Ashton Carmichael would be the death of me.

"Night, Beau."

"Night, Ash."

"See? Still not ignoring me."

I bit my tongue, kept quiet until his breathing evened out and I knew he was asleep. I wondered what in the hell I was going to do.

CHAPTER NINETEEN

Ashton

I'M GAY.
I'm gay, I'm gay, I'm gay.

No matter how many times I replayed the words in my head, I couldn't believe I was admitting them...couldn't believe I'd said them aloud to Beau. It had been the only time in my life the words had passed my lips, the only time I'd allowed myself to even think them, even though deep down, I'd always known they were true, no matter how much I'd denied it.

I'm gay.

I hadn't been lying when I'd told Beau I didn't want to be gay—at least I never had before. Every time I noticed a man, every time I felt that itch of desire, I told myself it wasn't real, it was a fluke, and most of the time, I was able to ignore it. I got drunk, went out and fucked, and everything was fine. Sometimes the alcohol wasn't needed, but other times it was. I never slipped, never gave in to that desire that lay dormant inside me for as long as I could remember...except with him.

Fucking Cranky Campbell. He was ruining everything. What in the hell was it about him that tied me up in knots?

The bed dipped as he moved. Beau was in my bed. Granted, we were fully dressed, on top of the blankets, and I had no idea how to even make an attempt at anything with a guy, but he was there, beside me. I'd felt his breath on my skin as I slept. Felt his warmth. Maybe sort of wondered if he was hard right then, because my dick was apparently working again.

Holding my breath, I rolled over to my side, faced him, leaned up on my elbow, and looked down at him. The tension he often held in his face was gone as he slept. His lips were soft, this sort of half grin on them. It made me smile as I fought myself not to reach out and trace his mouth with my finger.

His hair was a dark mess. It was mostly straight, just the ends slightly wavy like they always were. My fingers tingled as I remembered what it felt like.

I peeked down at the happy face on his arm, wanted to trace that with my finger too...maybe my tongue. Hmm. What would Beau's skin taste like? How would it feel against mine?

My eyes traveled down his chest, his stomach, his bulge. Fuck, there was a guy with a hard-on in bed with me. What did he look like? Feel like? Smell like? Because yep, I suddenly wondered about the scent of Beau's skin in those intimate places.

I'm gay, I'm gay, I'm gay.

My body had a whole lot easier time accepting it than my brain currently did.

My eyes began to make the journey upward again—stomach, chest, smile—"You fucker! You're awake!"

"What? Me? No!" He opened his eyes when I playfully pushed him. "Okay, maybe, but can you blame me for soaking in the moment…and for giving you time?"

"Time to ogle you?"

"Time for whatever you need."

Ugh. Because of course Beau would be understanding. "It's easier to pretend, to lie to myself, when I'm not around you. It's quite frustrating. If I didn't like you, I'd hate you, which hey, I'm pretty sure you feel the same way. You've spent your life trying to pretend you hate me. That must mean you like me a lot."

I might have been slightly emotionally stunted, because it was much easier to make it all about the *maybe crush* Beau had on me and the fact that I made him realize he was gay than focusing on myself. Oh, and making a joke out of things. Classic avoidance 101. I aced the class.

Beau leaned up on his elbow too, so we were facing each other. I waited for a joke, for him to roll his eyes or call me cocky because that was how we worked. We sniped at each other, were in competition with each other, but I could see by the gentleness in his eyes, that wasn't where he was going to go with this.

"It wasn't easy for me at first, Ash. Try to keep your head from getting too big here, but when you kissed me, everything sort of clicked into place. It was like a light bulb suddenly turned on, and I was like…*ooh, this is why I couldn't love Shan the way she loved me, why I didn't get why sex was so awesome, and oh, why I hated Ashton Carmichael.* I didn't want to admit it. I didn't want to believe it. Hell, I didn't even know anyone who was gay. Fever Falls has grown a lot since then. We didn't have Fever Street back then…well, it was there, but it wasn't as fabulous." He winked at me, and I grinned.

"I had to do a lot of soul searching…and I was scared out of my mind to come out to my mom, friends, people around town. But I did it in my own time and in my own way, and you will too. No one can tell you how or when to come to terms with this. You're calling the play, Ash."

"Sports reference for the win."

"Stop making jokes."

"Did you hook up with anyone after me?" The question just sort of tumbled out.

"Nope. I'm a virgin."

"Smart-ass."

"I waited a few weeks. I know that doesn't sound like long, but I sort of started to get my head around it, and then I wanted to experiment. I told myself I had to do that before I came out. Some of it was probably not incredibly safe—I was going to Atlanta and hooking up with random guys—but I realized I was really fucking gay and I liked it. I met Lincoln right after. We both had fake IDs and were in a gay club. We were attracted to each other, but we weren't compatible sexually. We've been best friends ever since."

There was a twitch of jealousy in my chest, which was absolutely ridiculous. Beau wasn't mine, and Lincoln was his best friend. I wasn't even sure I ever planned to come out.

"I lied to myself...not before the kiss. I can't even fucking believe I did that. It wasn't something I'd ever considered...being attracted to men, but I knew I cared about you, and you were there...so fucking close. Your lips looked so damn good, and I had to know what you tasted like. I just did it. Jesus, it scared the shit out of me, Beau. I blamed you, hated myself, couldn't imagine what I would do if anyone found out. How the fuck could I go to college a gay football player? That was the beginning of the denial."

I closed my eyes because it was easier to continue that way. "Sometimes...I'd let my guard down...I'd look...I'd notice, fuck, I'd *want*, Campbell. God, I fucking wanted so badly—a guy at the gym or a guy at the grocery store. Someone at a club or in a class. Then I'd fucking hate myself for it, would think of my career and hate myself more. Would party hard, fuck more because I wasn't gay if I was fucking women—oftentimes in pairs or more. But it didn't go away." I opened my eyes, ran a hand through my hair. "Fuck, I can't believe I just said all that."

"That right there was the most real you've ever been. Don't hide from me, Ash."

I nodded, feeling weak, raw. Like I was just bare bones and heart and Beau could see it all. I'd never been so stripped down in my life.

"Do you want me to go?" he asked.

"No." What I wanted was to surrender to him, to myself. To let go of all the baggage, football, my fuckups, who I'd always wanted to be, and to just...see what happened. But I didn't know if I could do that. "You gonna let me try and kiss you again, Campbell? I'll do my best not to run this time."

"I'm not so sure that's a good idea. I don't want you to go too fast."

"It's been ten years. I'm not going too fast. And I'm also a whole hell of a lot better than I used to be. You'll like it. I promise."

He chuckled. "There's not a doubt in my head that I'll like it."

"Don't make me beg. I'm not sure my self-confidence can survive it."

"I think your self-confidence can survive anything."

"Campbell…"

"Shut up and kiss me, Ash."

"If you insist."

"Asshole."

"Stop talking, or I can't kiss you. I'm practically a virgin, and you're stressing me out."

He laughed again, and I felt his breath on my face, felt the heat of his body close to mine. "You're impossible. I can't dislike you even when I try. How am I supposed to handle you now?" There was no sarcastic tone to his voice, making me wonder how serious he was. If Beau really worried about what this kiss would mean for our friendship. It seemed as though it affected him in ways I didn't understand.

"This is a lot of buildup for a kiss." I'd slept with a lot of people in my life, a lot, but none of them made me tremble with anticipation the way the thought of kissing Beau did.

"I might fall asleep before you do it."

"Ugh. Fine." I leaned in, brushed my lips against his, felt a zap of electricity course through me. An exaggeration? Probably, but that was what it felt like.

His lips were soft, so fucking soft. Softer than I remembered, but when I leaned closer, kissed harder, I felt his stubble against my skin. The contrast of rough and silky did something to my body, made everything go haywire, like I was functioning on overdrive.

I let my tongue sneak out, trace Beau's lips, sneak into his mouth, and he let me inside. He was holding back, allowing me to lead. I could feel it in his movements, in the tightness of his body, but as my tongue stroked his, he groaned, let out this guttural sound that made my dick hard and my brain soar. "Don't hold back," I told him as I kissed my way down his neck, rubbed my stubbled cheek against his. "Fuck, don't hold back, Campbell."

From there, I basically attacked him. Beau rolled to

his back, opened his legs, and I settled between them. I tightened my hands in his hair, sucked his tongue, nibbled his lip. Beau's large palms ran up and down my back, under my shirt, down to my ass. "This okay?" he asked.

This was fucking incredible. "Don't stop," I told him. As soon as the words left my mouth, he thrust against me, groin to groin, dick to dick, and *fuck*, who the hell knew that rubbing your cock against someone else's felt so damn good? Even with our jeans between us, I felt like I was going to bust my load any second.

His fingers dug into my ass as I rutted against him. I was basically fucking riding him, humping him like a damn dog, and I couldn't find it in myself to care. I wanted him, this, to *feel* Beau in all his masculinity.

I took his mouth again, savored it, the taste of him, scent of him, everything about Beau. In that moment, it didn't matter that Beau was a man or that I was gay, just being with him did. No, actually, that wasn't true. It *did* matter that he was a man, but not in the way I thought it would. Not because it wasn't what I wanted, but because it was what I truly needed. I thrust into him, felt his cock against mine, and it was as if my whole world exploded, as if it was righted. I'd been wrong my entire life, but there with Beau, everything felt right. Not just the sex part, because obviously, it was about more than sex.

We moved against each other, my erection harder and harder by the second. I swallowed his moans and smiled against his lips when he gave me his. His body was hard, his kisses hungry but soft. He pulled me tighter against him, and damn, he felt good.

My balls drew tight as my orgasm slammed into me. I couldn't have held it back if I wanted to, and I hadn't. Beau's body tightened beneath me as he cursed, and it felt really fucking good to have that effect on him, to make him come…to have him come with him.

I dropped my forehead to his, breathed him in as he held me. "I think it's safe to say my dick officially works again. Maybe a little too well." When I'd planned to kiss him, I sure as shit hadn't thought it would make me come.

"Are you okay?" he asked before pressing a kiss to my lips.

"I just came so hard, my brain is mush. I'm fucking fabulous. Oh, that's a gay thing, right? Being fabulous?" I teased.

"Always so fucking funny."

"I'm fine, Campbell." And I was. With Beau, none of that other shit mattered. "Maybe next time we can try that naked. Is that a thing you do? Just rubbing off on each other?"

His laugh vibrated through my chest. "Slow your roll, Ash."

But I didn't want to slow down. I was too fired up. I wanted to *experience*.

CHAPTER TWENTY

Beau

Beau says my smile is contagious. I think his is too.
~ Love, Kenny

So…on a scale of 1-10, I'm guessing I'm at least a 20 when it comes to gay dry-humping, right?

I chuckled, rolling my eyes at Ash's text, then looked over my shoulder to make sure none of the guys were lurking around. The last thing I needed was someone finding out I'd fucked around with Ashton—and not because of me, either, but because of him. He'd trusted me…wanted me…was still trying to figure himself out, and I didn't want to hinder him in any way.

I still couldn't believe it happened. Ashton Carmichael was gay. Not bisexual, not some kid who randomly kissed me when he was drunk. He was a gay man, and he'd been in denial, buried deep in the closet his whole life. I hated that he'd had to live that way, that I hadn't seen it or been able to help him. Would things have been different for him if I'd known? If I could have been there for him?

You're so cocky, I replied.

Ash: Could feel that through my jeans, huh? It's tough being so big.

Me: You're big? I didn't notice...

Ash: Oh, fuck you, Campbell.

Me: Any regrets?

After our mutual orgasm yesterday morning, we'd cleaned up separately. I'd borrowed a pair of shorts, and then I'd been on my way. I'd made up some excuse about shit I had to do, and he'd basically pushed me out of the house, likely having to work through things himself, but I wanted to make sure he was doing okay. Ash would never bring it up himself. He'd joke his way through life if he could.

Ash: Just that I didn't take my pants off so you could see my monster cock.

Me: That I fixed, apparently.

Ash: Who's cocky now?

Me: It's tough being so big. ;)

When he didn't reply right away, I added, **Seriously, Ash. Not trying to coddle you. Trying to be a friend.**

Ash: I know. I'm good. It's you. That helps. Wanna have dinner tonight?

I closed my eyes, leaned my head back against the couch. The fact that it was me helped him. It was strange to think of that, to acknowledge that I could help Ash with anything, that Ash needed someone. He'd always been so confident, larger than life, but that had obviously been a front.

Me: I have to coach Kenny's practice...you wanna go? Then the three of us can have dinner afterward?

Ash: Wow...you must really like me, Campbell.

Me: Who is this? I think I have the wrong number.

Ash: :/

"Pretty sure your face is about to split open, you're smiling so big. You must have either had a good time with someone, or you really want to." I fumbled my phone, hiding the screen as Jace plopped down beside me on one of the fire-station couches. "That good?"

"Sex isn't the only reason to smile."

"It is for the way you just smiled."

Did I still need to continue thinking, *fucking Ash*? He didn't even have to be there to shake my life up. I opened my mouth to reply just as the alarm went off. Jace and I shoved to our feet, everything else forgotten as the team rushed to get our gear, which hung on hooks on the wall, before running to the engine.

My heart slammed against my chest, adrenaline surging through my body the way it always did when I went out on a call. The sound of the sirens echoed through my head, a familiar song I knew by heart.

Smoke billowed in front of us as Langston pulled up at the house, and we jumped out.

"Please!" a woman shouted. "Please save our home!" Flames licked up the side of the house.

"Is there anyone inside?"

She shook her head. "No one. Not even animals."

It was exactly what I needed to hear. I reacted. I'd done this so many times that there wasn't any thought. Ladders were pulled, hoses hooked up. Everyone had a job, and we did it, all with the same goal—to put the fire out as soon as possible.

It was later as I stood under the shower at the station, coming down from the rush of a fire, that I thought about Ash and the fact that I'd left him hanging earlier. I was mentally and physically exhausted, my bones and muscles feeling too heavy as I turned the water off. I wrapped a towel around my waist and went into the locker room to grab my phone.

Sorry about that. We had a call.

My phone rang a second later, Ash's name on the screen. "Hey."

"You fought a fucking fire today?" he asked.

"Um…yeah. That's what I do."

"That's strangely hot and uncomfortably scary at the same time. I mean, I knew about your career, but I didn't think about it until now... You fight fires, Campbell. When people run out, you run in. That's some crazy shit."

My pulse thumped wildly against my skin. I didn't know what it was about that statement that made the reality of Ash and me—if there was an Ash and me...and did I want there to be an Ash and me?—slam home. One night...all it took was one night for me to stumble into *something* with him. Something that would likely end with Ash walking away again. "It's fine, Carmichael. I know what I'm doing. So, do you want me to pick you up for practice, or what?"

"That felt awfully close to a diversion."

"You're imagining things."

"You're speaking to the king of subject change here, but I'll let it go. Yes, you can pick me up. It sounds like you're taking me on a date."

"Pfft, you wish," I teased. "I'll be there in an hour. Then we have to go get Kenny."

"An hour? How am I supposed to get ready that fast? Give a guy some time."

"And you're just admitting you're gay?" I said playfully.

"And *that* sounded suspiciously like a stereotype. I'm ashamed of you."

"You're the one who said *gay dry-humping* earlier. We don't put gay in front of everything, you know."

"Hey! I'm new at this!"

And he was taking it surprisingly well. At least on the surface. "I'm giving you shit. I'll see you in fifty-five minutes."

I went to my locker, put on a pair of boxer trunks and deodorant. After I put on my pants, T-shirt, socks, shoes, and another cap I'd gotten from the station, since Ash stole my other one, I was on my way out of the station and heading for my truck.

I made a quick stop at my house for some equipment I'd forgotten, then headed out to Ash's place. I'd hardly pulled into the driveway before he was coming outside, wearing a pair of shorts and a tee.

I could see the muscles in his calves when he jogged, remembered the feel of his weight on top of me and the taste of him on my tongue. I'd be lying if I didn't admit I wanted more of him. He was too damn tempting for me not to.

"Hey," Ash said as he climbed in.

"Hey."

"I didn't have time to do my hair, so I need this." He again plucked my cap off my head and put it on.

"I know you have hats of your own, and if you don't,

you sure as shit have the money to buy one. Plus, you happen to have my old one. Do you like driving me crazy?"

"First of all, that one's dirty. And second, of course I like driving you crazy. Do you know us? I've spent my life driving you crazy, which is why I'll pretend I don't have a hat and take yours, and you'll pretend you don't love the fact that I give you shit all the time."

Fucking Ashton Carmichael. I needed to get those words tattooed on me.

I ran a hand through my hair, then drove away. We were running a few minutes late, so I called Kenny to have him wait outside for me to swing by and pick him up.

Kenny grinned when he saw Ash in the passenger seat.

"You're coming!" Kenny said when he got inside.

"Yep. I begged and pleaded. What's up, K?" Ash turned around in the seat and held up his hand for a high five. Kenny immediately gave him one. "Ooh. We should come up with our own secret handshake. We'll do that after practice."

"Okay!" Kenny replied. He smiled, and I realized I was smiling too. That I was like all those people I used to roll my eyes at who got blinded by Ash's bright light. He was addicting, enthralling, a force of nature even I couldn't seem to deny.

"What are you smiling at, Campbell?"

"I'm not smiling, and you don't always have to call me by my name, you know? I know who you're talking to."

"I like calling you by your name. I could always use Cranky Campbell if you prefer."

"I can always make you walk if you prefer."

"Fine, you win this time, but don't think I won't get my revenge."

"ABC," Kenny said from the back seat.

"Huh?" I caught eyes with him in the rearview mirror.

"Ashton, Beau, Carmichael, and Campbell. You're ABC."

"Well, shit. If that isn't cute as hell, I don't know what is," Ash replied. "See? We were meant to be best *friends*."

"I thought Linc was your best friend?" Kenny asked.

I glanced over at Ash, who looked away. He almost seemed…hurt, but I knew that couldn't really be the case. "I guess I have two best friends," I replied. A week ago, hell, two days ago, I wouldn't have said that about Ash, but really, it was true. We had history I didn't have with anyone else.

"Oh, then I have two as well—Beau and Ash."

"Good taste." Ash winked at him, then nudged me. "You have good taste too, Campbell."

Yeah…yeah, I thought I did.

CHAPTER TWENTY-ONE

Ashton

LA Avalanche quarterback Ashton Carmichael donates big money to Down syndrome Organization! It's not often we have positive headlines for him off the field.

MY LEG BOUNCED up and down as I sat in my corner while Beau coached. Every few minutes I bit my tongue to keep from yelling something out, from giving advice, or hell, even just in agreement with something Beau said or did. It was killing me. That might sound dramatic, but it was damn near that bad.

I wanted to be out there with him.

I wanted to coach with Beau.

I wanted to play with him again.

Before I knew it, practice was over and everyone was walking away. "Kenny, Adam, come over here. I want to show you something," Beau said to their wide receiver, then stopped and looked my way. I considered batting my eyelashes at him in a silent plea to help him, but apparently I didn't need to because he added, "Wanna help me with something, Carmichael?"

Yes. Fuck yes, I do. "Naw, I'm good."

Adam's eyes went wide, and I shoved to my feet. "I'm kidding. I really want to help." That's all I needed, for them to think I was an asshole.

There were a few whispers from some of the families in the bleachers, but I ignored it. I hoped like hell my helping out wouldn't make headlines. I didn't think it would. Most of the time, they only cared when I did something wrong, and I didn't think the families would want to draw attention to their league that way.

The team stopped and watched too as I jogged over, and when I got to him, Beau rolled his eyes. "What am I going to do with you?"

I could think of a hundred different things I wanted him to do with me, to me, let me try on him, but I was pretty sure they weren't appropriate for me to say. Football was the next best thing to exploring my sexuality with him.

Beau leaned over and whispered, "It's okay to want to participate, ya know?"

"Who are you, and what did you do with Beau Campbell?" But really, I knew what this was. Things had changed between us. Beau saw me as someone who needed help, and he could never stop himself from being there for someone else. I didn't want him to pity me—no, pity wasn't the right word—but I did want him to spend time with me because he wanted to, not because he thought I needed him. I wanted him to offer for me to help him coach because he wanted to coach with me, not because he knew that sitting on the sidelines was killing me, and I had no doubt he'd known.

"I'm the same Beau as always. It's you I can't figure out."

He stared at me and I at him until Kenny cleared his throat. "Beau?" he asked. "Why are you staring at Ash like that?"

He shook his head, his cheeks tinged pink, and replied, "Because he's a dork."

A dork you like, Campbell. But that was okay, because I liked him too.

"Okay, I want you guys to watch me and Ash for a second," he told them, then explained to me what he wanted to do. We ran through a couple of plays together, Beau receiving as I threw to him. The team paid rapt attention. My passion came alive, burst inside me, nearly making me breathless in a way I hadn't felt in a long time. It was as if football was breathing life into me again when it had begun to feel like it strangled me…yet despite the lack of oxygen, it had still been something I'd wanted.

"Did you see how Campbell faked left and went right?" I asked. "I can read him, and that's what you have to learn to do—read each other. Here, why don't you try?" I handed Kenny the ball as Beau spoke to Adam.

We ran the play over and over and over—the four of us. I could see the confidence in them grow, see when Adam knew to fake and Kenny knew the right moment to throw. "Perfect! That was beautiful!"

And it was.

Beau and Adam jogged to us, a grin splitting Beau's face. Jesus, he was…pretty. Sexy, fucking hot, but also pretty in a rugged sort of way. I didn't know if that was normal, if it was okay to think of him that way, but I did.

"You guys did amazing," Beau told them both, and I stupidly wanted to tell him it had been amazing coaching with him. Ugh. I was suddenly incredibly sappy. "I'm going to go grab a drink," he added.

A guy who'd been on the sidelines approached. "You're going to have to excuse me for freaking out a little bit, but I can't help it—Ashton Carmichael's out here coaching my nephew!"

"Just helping. Beau's the coach. We used to play together in high school. I'm just lucky he still lets me play with him." Hopefully, he'd let me play with him in other ways later... "Thank you, though." I held out my hand to the man, and we shook, introducing ourselves.

He spoke to me for a moment, then asked for an autograph, which I gave. Beau had come back by then, and he grinned at me as I signed the paper.

When everyone left, the three of us cleaned up and then went to the truck. "You two wanna grab some pizza before we go home?" Beau asked.

"Is that really a question? It's pizza," I replied, and Kenny laughed.

We headed for the same pizza parlor we'd gone to before. Beau glanced at me and asked, "Want me to get you a beer?"

"Nah, I'm good," I replied, and then said to Kenny, "I'll play Pac-Man with you. Beau can handle the food."

"Gee, thanks," Beau replied just as Kenny said, "Sure!"

Kenny and I went straight for the arcade, where I got us a bunch of tokens. We took turns playing Pac-Man, too many times to count before I asked, "Air hockey?"

"I don't usually play air hockey."

"You don't have to. We can do whatever you want."

"Let's try." Kenny replied, making a strange burst of pride swell inside me.

I added tokens to the machine. The puck came out on Kenny's side. He set it on the table, shot, and *clink*, it went right in.

Holy fuck. I hadn't expected that. "You know this means war, right?"

The puck was warm against my fingers as I set it on the table and...*clink!* "I'm a bit of an air-hockey champion."

"You know this means war, right?" Kenny asked, making me drop my head back and laugh. He was so fucking cool. I loved hanging out with him.

We were neck and neck the whole game. The rest of the points didn't come as easily as the first two, but we traded off each time until we were tied six to six. Not even gonna lie, sweat beaded on my brow a bit as I defended my goal from Kenny and his expert attack. The puck bounced back and forth as we each hit it over and over before I moved in, swiped, missed, and the damn thing went straight in.

"I won! Beau!" Kenny ran toward the arcade door. "I won air hockey! Look, Beau!"

His excitement made me laugh. I felt it in my chest, like it helped fuel my heart.

Beau came through the door, a smile stretched across his face as he looked at the score and then his brother. "You played air hockey?"

"I *won* air hockey," Kenny replied.

"He's good, Cranky Campbell."

"I can't believe he played," Beau replied, then turned to Kenny. "I'm proud of you."

"Do you want to play? I bet I can beat you too," Kenny replied.

I took a step back. "Defend my honor," I teased, then added more money for Beau and Kenny to play while I stood back and watched. I couldn't remember a night I'd had so much fun.

BEAU DIDN'T KILL the engine when he pulled up in front of my house. We'd eaten dinner, then played more games before Beau had taken Kenny home.

"Thanks for tonight," Beau told me. "The coaching, dinner…playing games with him. He likes you. Kenny's a friendly guy, but there's something about you he's connected with. It means a lot to me that you treat him…that you've *always* treated him like…"

"Like the cool-ass guy he is?" I asked.

"Exactly. Not everyone does, and he is, cool I mean."

"Yeah," I replied. "Yeah, he is." Only he wasn't the only Campbell brother who was.

"You're welcome to help me if you want. With the coaching. I'm not sure if that's something you're interested in, but you're good at it. They take to you well, and I could use some help out there. It's hard to get people to volunteer their time—"

"The way you do?" I cut him off.

"I enjoy it."

"Doesn't change the fact that it's a great thing you do and that most people wouldn't. Not sure there's much of anything I'd like more than to help you coach." I'd felt part of something all day—between the coaching and then dinner. I'd felt part of something important, something bigger than myself. And with Kenny…I'd felt like I had a brother.

"Nothing?" he asked, cocking a brow at me.

"Come inside with me, Campbell."

"I'm not sure that's a good idea."

"Come on, don't go all Cranky Campbell on me now. You were doing so well."

"Yeah, well, the problem is—and don't let this go to your head, Carmichael—but I sort of want you. And if I go inside, I'm afraid you'll be too hard to resist, and I'm not sure you're ready."

"Don't I get to be the one to judge that?" I asked.

"Okay…maybe I'm not sure it's the best for me either."

Well, shit. That changed things. "Why?"

"I don't want to admit that."

"Why? Because you like me so much?"

"Ugh. Stop fishing."

"It's okay. I like you too."

"Ash…"

"Beau…" He sighed, and I rubbed a hand over my face before continuing. "I've spent my whole life pretending, lying. Isn't it strange that the only time I can't fake it, the only time I give in and embrace who I am, is when I'm with you? You do something to me. Always have."

And…I was blushing, ladies and gentlemen. *Blushing.* That shit didn't happen very often.

Beau's eyes snapped to mine, his pupils blown large.

"I know, right?" I asked him. "You're kind of addicting. It's very frustrating to the *in-denial* part of me."

"You don't ever have to be ashamed, Ash." He reached out, cupped my cheek, brushed his thumb against my skin. "There's nothing wrong with who you are."

"I'm trying." I closed my eyes. "Trying to work through it. Being with you helps."

"You're going to fucking wreck me, do you know that? When you say shit like that, my whole fucking reality goes up in flames, and I need to keep my head on straight."

"Straight?" I teased.

"Well, maybe not straight, but I need to be smart. It was...tough, when you left. I didn't realize exactly why at the time, but I know now. And I can't help but think you'll do it again, or this will be too much for you."

And by this, I knew he meant being an out-and-proud gay man like he was.

"I'm not rushing you. I'm not saying I'm in love with you and begging you to stay. I'm being honest. Just trying to figure out what to do."

It was on the tip of my tongue to say *me*. Not because I truly wanted Beau to fuck me—I wasn't sure I'd ever be ready for that—but because it was a whole lot easier than being honest the way he was.

"What happens if people find out? I don't want to be the reason you're outed or to make this any harder on you than it already is. Your name is still in the news every day."

"Come inside with me, Campbell. No one will find

out. We'll...we'll take it slow. And I'll be honest. If it's too much, I'll tell you, but right now...Jesus, I want you so fucking much. I've wanted you since I was a goddamned kid, and I'm tired of waiting to have you."

Beau sucked in a sharp breath.

"That honest enough for you?"

"Fucking Ashton Carmichael," he replied, and I smiled, knowing Beau had as hard a time denying me as I had him.

CHAPTER TWENTY-TWO

Beau

I like spending time with Beau and Ash together. They're fun. ~ Love, Kenny

IT SHOULDN'T HAVE been a surprise to me that I was going inside so easily with Ash. I mean, there was the obvious. He was gorgeous, and I wanted him. I really couldn't fucking wait to get on my knees for him, to tease him until he lost his damn mind, to show him how good it could be with a man.

Besides that, there was the truth that Ash had always had some kind of power over me. He made me feel everything more strongly than I did with anyone else—anger, frustration, and yeah, attraction and desire.

I followed him inside. He went straight for the kitchen, but to my surprise, he pulled a bottle of water from the fridge. "You want a drink?"

"No beer?" I asked. It wasn't that I wanted him to have one, it was just typically his MO, and now he'd passed on one twice tonight.

"No. For once I want to be in my right mind when I fuck around with someone. We *are* going to fuck around, right?"

"You've really never touched another man but me?" It blew my mind that not only could he have denied a part of himself for so long, but that he fell into it so easily with me.

"Scout's honor. It's kind of frustrating—both my lack of sexual experience when it comes to men and your *Sweet Beau Campbell* voodoo magic."

A loud laugh jumped out of my mouth. "Voodoo magic, huh?" I asked.

"You never answered my question."

I sobered up real quickly. "Yeah, Ash. We're gonna fuck around. I figured I'd blow you. We could start there."

His hand shot out, and he grabbed the counter as though he needed its support to stay on his feet. "You say that like it's so simple."

"It *is* so simple for me." I stepped closer to him, then didn't stop until I was right in front of Ash. "I love giving head. I'll make you lose your mind. Make you wonder why you waited so long—at least for me."

"Holy shit. Who are you, and what did you do with

the Beau I know? I thought I was supposed to be the overconfident one?"

"No *over* about it," I replied. "This is fun. I like being able to shake you up the way you've always done with me." I clutched his waist, felt his hip bones against my palms, closed the door on all my doubts, fear, and confusion. I wasn't going to pass this up. I was going to enjoy it. "Oh look. I see a bulge."

Ash trembled. "Who's going to wreck whom in this scenario?" he asked breathlessly.

His words shocked my heart, making an electrical current run the length of me. The thought of affecting Ash in any way tied me in knots. He was…well, Ashton fucking Carmichael, and yeah, I knew that was often how I referred to him, but I didn't know how else to explain it. He always felt like he was *more*. More than me, than Fever Falls, than anyone and everything.

I always felt too simple to have much of an effect on him.

"Come on." I nodded toward the hallway. "Let's go so I can taste you." Was it strange that I wanted to suck Ash in his childhood bedroom? The one I'd gone to and spent time in with him?

"You know I'm going to blow my load the second I'm in your mouth, right?" he asked. "And that's not easy for me to admit."

"We'll make it work," I replied, then pulled him along. He took a step forward, and I backward. As if he couldn't handle not being in control anymore, Ash tugged me toward him, put his right hand against my cheek, his left on my neck, and took my mouth.

We stumbled backward into the wall.

"Sorry," he mumbled against my lips.

"You don't have to be sorry. You can be rough with me, Ash."

He smiled against my lips. "I can't believe I'm kissing you."

"You're not. You're talking."

So then he kissed me again. His tongue swept my mouth, expertly pulling moans from me. He pushed against me, rubbed his erection against mine, and whimpered, fucking whimpered. I never thought I'd know the day that Ashton whimpered for me.

I cupped his ass and kissed him deep as I walked, making him move backward this time. Our feet tangled around each other, we almost tripped as he stumbled, and we laughed and kissed our way to his room. He hit the light, and then I pushed him until he fell onto the bed. He kicked out of his shoes as he did so.

"You don't have to blow me if you don't want to.

We can rub off on each other again," he said as I pulled his shorts down. "This time naked, though. I wanna feel your skin."

I couldn't help but chuckle. "It's not a hardship. I *want* to suck your dick. I told you I love it." As I finished my sentence, the cock in question sprang free from the patch of dark, trimmed pubes at his groin. It was a nice dick—long, thick, full of veins, with a heavy, tight sac beneath.

"What about you?" he asked.

"I'll come too."

I trembled, fucking shook as I pulled my shirt over my head, as I took my shoes off, then my pants. I couldn't believe I was there with Ash, that he wanted me so fucking much.

His gasp sent a jolt through me. "Jesus, Campbell. You are so fucking hot. Can I touch you?" Only he didn't wait for me to reply. Ash sat up, reached his hand out slowly, and cupped my balls.

"Oh fuck," we said in unison, then chuckled.

"I'm not sure I like that you're longer than me," Ash admitted.

"I can't believe you just said that. Only you."

"Yeah, but that's why you like me," he replied.

"You're thicker, if that makes you feel better."

He wrapped a hand around me, stroked slowly. The simple touch felt so damn good, my right knee buckled.

"I'm glad it's you...the first guy I experiment with. I'm glad it's you."

The first. Those words slammed into me, though they shouldn't have. Of course I would only be the *first*. What did I expect? This thing between us was just fucking around, and when Ash was ready, he would come out of the closet and hook up with whoever he wanted. "I'm glad it's me too. You'll be even happier when I do it. I wasn't lying when I said I was good."

"You feel good, *Cocky Campbell*." He used Cocky, my name for him. "I think I want to practice sucking you one time too."

My cock jerked as desire shot through me. Precome spilled from my tip.

"Someone likes that." He swiped at my precome, then pulled his finger away, a rope of it stretching between him and my tip.

"You would too. You can explore me later. Let me get on my knees for you, Ash." Unwilling to wait any longer, I dropped to my knees and leaned in as Ash spread his thighs for me. I nuzzled his sac, inhaled his musky scent, rubbed my cheek against the coarse hair of his thighs.

"I thought you were sucking."

"I'll get there," I told him. "You want me to use my tongue on you?" I licked his balls, then looked up at him.

"Oh fuck, Campbell. Do that again." I lapped at him, this time as our eyes held each other. He shuddered, his lids fluttered, then opened again as he looked down at me. I'd never seen Ash so blissed out, his pupils blown wide.

"You want more?"

"You know I do."

"Okay, but I'm not going to let you come right away." I wanted to savor this, wanted it to last, to be good for him. I held the base of his cock, angled it toward me, swirled my tongue around the head. His ass thrust off the bed slightly. He was still watching me as I continued to tongue his glans, licked at the precome leaking from the slit, then pushed forward, took him deep, moving slowly as I showed him just how good at this I was.

Ash's hand came up and tightened in my hair, pulled, his thighs shaking as I swallowed him down, deep throating him.

"Fuck, Beau." His hold on me tightened even more, and he thrust his hips forward. "Shit. I'm sorry."

I pulled off him and smiled. That wouldn't do.

There was no apology in a blowjob. "Why would you be sorry? Enjoy it. Don't hold back. I can take it. I *want* to take it."

"Yeah." He nodded, his face flushed. "Okay. We might have to do this more than once, though, because holy shit, you can deep throat a cock. Can I stand up?"

It was so strange to me, seeing Ash so unsure, so insecure and timid, but obviously so damn full of want. I could see his pulse beating against the base of his throat. "Yes."

I leaned back so Ash could stand. His hands went back in my hair again as I swallowed him, buried my nose in his pubes, his dick down my throat. I flexed my throat muscles, listened to him whimper again. This time it was Ash who started to pull back. He pumped his hips, fucked into my mouth, dropped his head back and looked at the ceiling. "Beau…fuck, Beau," he whispered over and over again.

Every time his body tightened and his breathing picked up, I pulled off him. When he settled down, I went back to work, sometimes me running the show and others him thrusting into my mouth.

It was the third or fourth time I pulled off, preventing him from coming, when he begged, "Please, Campbell… God, you feel so fucking good. I need to come, but I want you to come too."

I gasped when I pulled off him, then spit in my hand and wrapped it around my dick and stroked.

"Shit, now I don't know if I want to watch you or finish my blowjob."

"Really?" I cocked a brow.

"Okay, well, no. I mean, you're hot as fuck, and maybe you can just do that for me sometime, but I really need to come."

I laughed the way only Ash could make me do. I opened my mouth for him, and he slowly pushed his cock inside. "I think this might be the sexiest thing I've ever seen."

I kept jerking myself, felt my balls already tightening, ready to let loose as Ashton thrust between my lips. He pulled my hair, then rubbed my scalp as though trying to soothe the sting. His breathing picked up, his eyes closed again as his thrusts became quicker, more urgent. I hollowed out my cheeks, sucked him.

"Oh fuck. Fuck, fuck, fuck. I'm gonna come, Campbell. Pull off. I'm gonna come."

But I didn't. Why the hell would I do that? His load was my reward, so I went deeper, worked my throat muscles around his thick cock until he pumped his hips again, kept himself buried there, cried out, my name on his lips as he spilled in two long spurts down my throat.

My own orgasm barreled down on me. I pulled off him, worked my cock, held his eyes, his intense stare snared on mine until my vision went blurry, my whole body tingled, and I shot, one spurt hitting the bed, another Ash's leg, and a third the floor.

My eyes darted away, wondering if he would freak out, wondering if this would be the moment he realized just how gay he truly was and ask me to leave, but he didn't. Not Ash. He was maybe the bravest person I knew, outside of my brother, at least.

"Being gay…it's more than sex. Obviously, I get that, but this moment… Christ, Campbell, this moment is one of the realest of my life. The most honest. That sounds dumb. I—" He shook his head.

"No, it doesn't, Ash. I get it because my moment was on the dock with you." It wasn't an admission that had been easy for me to make. My pulse thudded, and my head felt foggy.

He smiled down at me, and I swear he damn near glowed. "I love that I'm responsible for your gayness."

"Dumbass."

"You sucked my dick, Campbell."

"I did…came on your leg too." I swiped at the come on his calf, looked for something to wipe it on.

"Wait," he rushed out. "You tasted me... I want to taste you too. It's only fair."

My stomach flipped, got light. He was going to kill me, ruin me. I held my fingers up to him, and Ash leaned over and sucked them into his mouth. "Thoughts?" I asked him.

"An acquired flavor, maybe? I'll get used to it." He winked, then grabbed my hand and pulled me to my feet. He brushed his thumb against my nipple, let his hands slide down my sides, my waist, touched my flaccid cock. "I used to dream about this...touching a man this way. Feeling a male body against mine. Then I'd go get drunk and find a woman to fuck, tell myself I was just confused. But it wasn't just that. I'd wonder what it was like to just talk with another man I shared something like this with...go to the movies, play football with him. Tackling would be a whole lot more fun that way." He snickered humorlessly. "I was so damn scared, Campbell. I still am. I don't know if I can do this...*how* to do this, but it makes it easier that it's with you. I've always been able to hide it, pretend it didn't exist, except with you. But out there, in the real world, I don't know if I can do it."

"I'm not really into exhibitionism anyway."

"Funny. I'm being serious, though."

"I am too, in a way. Do you think I'm going to push you? Rush you? Expect you to go out there and tell everyone we're...what, boyfriends?"

"Is that what we are?"

What would he say, I wondered, if I told him yes? Did I want that? To try and put a name to what Ash and I were doing? Probably, yes, but that didn't mean he was ready. Or hell, that I was. Not with him. "We're us. We're friends, sort of enemies. We laugh together and tease each other and drive each other crazy. Only now we give each other orgasms too. You don't have to name it anything. Like I said, I'm not rushing you, Ash. This is your life. I would never expect you to come out before you're ready." But I did wonder if he would ever be ready...and I knew he did as well.

"Will you stay the night?"

No...don't do it. Put some space between you. "Yeah."

"Can we stay naked?"

"Obviously. And this is weird, you asking me questions like this." Not because of his honesty—Ash had always been blunt—but because of his lack of experience, because of his vulnerability.

"It's because it's you. Don't know what in the hell it is about you, Cranky Campbell, but you do some kind of something to me." He took my hand. "Come on, let's shower together."

We did just that. We didn't touch while we were in there, but he did watch me the whole time. My dick started to get hard again because Ashton fucking Carmichael had his eyes on me while we were naked in the shower. I dare any man not to get hard in that situation.

We dried off and got into his tiny-ass bed. He climbed on top of me like last time, held himself over me as he rubbed his dick against mine.

"Christ, that looks hot—your cock with mine." There was so much giddy wonder in his voice, mixed with bare-bones honesty.

He lowered his mouth to mine, kissed me slowly, at the same languid pace he rubbed himself against me. We kissed until my jaw hurt, until my balls were full again, until his hot, sticky come shot against my stomach, followed by my second load.

"We're messy again," he teased as he fell on top of me.

"I have a feeling we're going to be able to say that a lot."

And I had a feeling I'd like it more than I should, and miss it terribly when this ultimately came to an end.

CHAPTER TWENTY-THREE

Ashton

The Avalanche are struggling without their bad-boy quarterback, Ashton Carmichael.

WE SPENT THE next two weeks a whole hell of a lot like we spent that one night. I coached with Beau. Afterward Beau, Kenny, and I would go to dinner, but we started switching things up a bit. Sometimes we had pizza, other times Mexican or burgers and fries. I was eating like shit, but Beau and I started jogging in the mornings together too. I'd meet him at the park, or go there with him if we spent the night together, and we'd run before he went to work and I went and ate an éclair with his mom.

It was...weirdly comfortable, domesticated, and for the first time in years, I felt like I had family. Kenny was great, and Beau's mom treated me like she did Beau and Kenny. Being around them, especially Beau, felt different than being with anyone else. As far back as I could remember, even before I played professional football, it always felt like people wanted something from me. They let me get away with shit I shouldn't have gotten away with or treated me like I was something special. I knew I'd taken advantage of that at times and knew part of it came not only from the way I played, but from the confidence I feigned. Beau hadn't let me get away with shit in high school, and he still didn't now. He... Fuck, it felt like he *saw* me, the real me, when no one else took the time to look.

Beau spent most of his nights in my bed. The day after he gave me that first blowjob, I'd ordered new furniture for my parents' old room. We now stayed in the master room with a king-size bed, even though I was plastered all over him most of the time. I was obsessed with his body, with the way he felt, the masculinity of him and feeling him against me. There were days when I just touched him everywhere, looked at him, learned his body. I hadn't stuck anything inside him yet, but I wanted to. Fuck, did I want to.

I'd also never had so many blowjobs in my life. We ended most days with my dick in Beau's mouth; either that, or rubbing off on each other. Everything about him was addictive, and when it was just us, it was easy to pretend I was out, that I felt comfortable in my skin.

I glanced at the kitchen clock, saw it was later than it usually was when I heard from Beau. He'd worked today, but we didn't have practice or a game. My stomach was growling, though, and I was definitely ready to get some food, so I called him up, and when he answered I asked, "What are you bringing me for dinner? I'm hungry, Cranky Campbell."

"All you want me for is to bring you dinner, huh?" he asked playfully.

"Well, duh. You sort of spoil me, and I like it."

He laughed. "It might be late tonight. I was about to call you. I just got off the phone with Linc. He's feeling neglected. I promised him dinner at Fever Pitch tonight."

Well, shit. Now *I* was feeling neglected, and yeah, I knew that was fucking crazy. Beau and I were together every damn day, and obviously, we had to have a life outside of each other, but I kind of liked my private life with him.

"You wanna go?" he asked.

"What? No. That's stupid. Not going out with you guys, being all butt-hurt and crashing your bestie night."

"It cracks me up to hear you say things like *bestie night*."

"I would only say that to you." There were a lot of

things I only felt comfortable doing or saying around Beau, which again, was crazy. Did I think the word *bestie* was too gay to say in front of others? That made it sound like there was something wrong with being gay, and there wasn't. I actually quite liked being gay when I was doing it with Beau. It was the whole outside-world thing that stressed me out.

"You wouldn't be crashing it. Linc would love having you there, but being honest, he would likely start to wonder *why* you were there. I don't mind, but…"

Me. He knew I would mind. "Go have fun with your friend. I'll see what Wyatt is up to. And stop being weird. You never coddle me."

"Nope, not me. I don't bring you dinner every night we don't go out with Kenny…or end each evening with your dick in my mouth."

"Hey! I told you I'd try it with you, but you said you liked sucking my dick. I mean, it's a good dick, Campbell. It's a different kind of coddling than you usually do."

I didn't have to see him to know he rolled his eyes at me. "I don't know how I put up with you," he replied playfully. "And it *is* a good dick. I do like sucking it."

"Like or love?"

"I'm going now."

"Wait! Campbell. I mean, *like* is just okay. I'm not sure I'm comfortable with just being okay. You should love sucking my cock."

"I'm hanging up now."

And since it was Beau, he of course really did hang up on me. The thing was, I was pretty sure I'd more than like sucking Beau off. I'd love it.

Fucking Beau.

I went to the kitchen and scoured the fridge and pantry. I truly didn't have anything to eat, and I shouldn't sit in the house all night. Wyatt had been one of my best friends in high school. I shouldn't dread calling him, and I hated that I did. It was like I thought he'd take one look at me and know I thought about sucking Beau's dick. But then, I'd felt weird with him before the whole dick-sucking thing too.

Taking a deep breath, I made the call, and he was quick to agree to dinner. I wasn't going anywhere on Fever Street, so we met up at a bar Wyatt liked.

"Hey, man. How's it going?" he asked when I arrived, and I adjusted the cap on my head before replying.

"Not bad. How about yourself?"

"Is that Beau's hat?"

Oh shit. How in the fuck did he know I was wearing Beau's baseball cap? Okay, dumb question. Surely it had to do with the whole *Fever Falls Fire Department* logo on it. "Um...yeah...I..."

"You're coaching with him, right?"

I let out a heavy breath. That was the most logical excuse. I probably should have thought about it myself. "I am. It's great. Everyone has been great about keeping it under wraps, not wanting the publicity. Kenny and the other guys, they love to play so much. It's a pure love of the game too. It's not about winning or popularity. They're just proud to be out there. It's refreshing."

And it was. It was my favorite part of working with them.

"It's nice of you to do it, but man, I'd go a little crazy without the wanting-to-win part. The Ashton I remember would too."

He was right about that, but things were different now. "I can see why you'd say that but...I can't explain it. You should come and watch them play sometime. It's an incredible experience."

His brows pulled together as though he hadn't expected me to say that. It was a far cry from professional football, and I wondered briefly if I should like it as much as I did.

He said, "Yeah, maybe I will."

I wanted him to, I realized. It wasn't that Wyatt was

a bad guy. He was a good person, but I just didn't know how to be myself around him; if he would accept who I was, if he truly saw me as Ash his old friend or if he saw me as Ashton Carmichael, quarterback for the Avalanche.

We had a good conversation after that. I drank my sweet tea while he had a beer, and we laughed over old times and crazy shit we used to do. It wasn't long into the evening before I felt glad I'd come.

"Do you remember Shannon?" he asked.

"Beau's high school girlfriend?" Which was weird as shit to say or think. The thought of Beau with a woman didn't compute. Not the Beau I knew now.

"Yeah. She's good friends with Holly. We're having her over for dinner next week, and Holly was wondering if maybe you wanted to come too."

No…no, I didn't. No good could come of this. "Are you trying to set me up with her?"

Wyatt held his hands up and laughed. "No, it's Holly, I swear. I just promised I'd ask. I'll tell her you said no, but this way I don't get in trouble for not asking." He winked.

What would he say if I told him I couldn't be interested in Shannon? In any woman? What if I told him it was Beau I wanted? "Look at you, Wyatt the matchmaker," I teased, hoping to play it off and change the subject.

"Holy shit! Are you Ashton Carmichael?" a guy said from over my shoulder.

"Fuck!" another guy said.

And just like that, the calm of my evening was over.

Cranky Campbell: Linc insisted on Netflix after dinner. Apparently, he's having issues with a guy he hooked up with who wants more.

I felt for Lincoln, I did, but I also wanted to strangle him because I'd been hoping Beau would come over after dinner. Lincoln was used to fucking around with guys. I was new to it, damn it. Couldn't he figure it out on his own?

I didn't say that, of course. Instead, I texted back: **Eh. You're getting a little too clingy anyway. I need a break from you.**

Cranky Campbell: Whatever you have to tell yourself. I know you'll miss me.

I would. Damn him.

Me: Ugh, I hate you.

Cranky Campbell: ;)

Now I was bored as shit and knew Beau wouldn't be coming over.

So…I paced around, thought about how much it sucked that Beau wouldn't be coming all over my stomach tonight, or me on his, it really didn't matter which. If he wasn't swallowing my load, I really liked when we came together, our bodies sticky, his jizz all over me and mine on him.

It wasn't long before I realized there wasn't one single part of me that wanted to be alone tonight.

But then…there had been something I'd been thinking about…

No time like the present, right?

I stripped, grabbed my laptop, climbed into bed, and found some gay porn. The urge had been increasing in me the past two weeks…to see two men together. Beau was always so confident in bed. I'd spent my life pretending I was confident there, but I truly wanted to be with Beau.

Okay…I could do this. I wanted to do this. I mean, it would help when Beau and I took it to the next level. The last thing I wanted was to always feel like he had to walk me through everything.

After signing up, I scrolled through the videos: twinks…I wasn't sure that was my thing…guys in business suits, app hookups, delivery guys, blah, blah, blah…firefighters? My cock twitched. I sat forward.

Okay, I could get down with that.

As though someone could see me, I looked around the room as the video started to play. A guy walked into a locker room, wearing the yellow firefighter pants without a shirt. Ridiculously, I wondered if Beau ever walked around like that, because it was hot as fuck.

He stripped out of his gear, then went to the shower, where there was another man. They kept looking over at each other, which yeah, I admit was a little cheesy, but the looking led to touching, which led to sucking cock, which wasn't cheesy at all.

I wrapped my hand around my own dick, pumped it up and down, riveted by the scene in front of me.

And then…oh shit. I leaned in, watched as they moved to a bench in the locker room. The fireman bent over it, the other guy spreading his ass cheeks wide, then diving in, licking and sucking, making the fireman writhe and whimper. His eyes rolled back in his head. There was hair in his crack, but the other guy didn't seem to mind. He told him how good he tasted, how tight he was, pushed his tongue in…and I licked my lips and stroked faster.

I gripped my balls, thought about Beau, about eating him out that way, about my tongue in that most intimate place on him. Would he call out my name?

What would he taste like…feel like…

I wanted to devour him, to pleasure him, to make him fly the way he did with his mouth on my cock. I'd suck him too, wanted to know what it felt like to have his dick on my tongue, but it was when my balls tightened and I shot my load all over the keyboard, probably fucking up my computer and not giving a shit, that I realized how much I wanted inside him, wanted to experience everything with Beau Campbell.

CHAPTER TWENTY-FOUR

Beau

I wonder if Beau has ever been in love.
~ Love, Kenny

"Beau?" Kenny said the moment I picked up the phone. I was on my way out the door to head to Ash's, but instead sat down to talk to my brother.

"Hey, you. What are you up to?"

"I want to cook dinner for you tonight. Can you come?"

Ash and I were going to do some work in his yard and then planned to grill. A stab of disappointment cut through me, which I immediately felt guilty for. This was Kenny. I never felt disappointment in spending time with him. That wasn't going to change just because I liked hanging out and fucking around with Ash. "You know I can't pass up dinner with you and Mom."

But then another thought stumbled through my brain...of me leaving Ash at home, alone, while I went to spend time with my family, and I asked, "Do you mind if Ashton comes? I don't know if he'll be able to, but—"

"Yes! He's the best."

"Hey now. I wouldn't go that far," I teased, and Kenny laughed.

"You're always the best-best, Beau."

"Well, I wouldn't go that far either, Kenny, but thanks."

We spoke for a little while longer before getting off the phone. When I arrived at Ash's, I knocked, which was quickly followed by, "Getcha' ass in here, Campbell."

Chuckling, I walked inside. It was midmorning, and Ash stood by the coffeepot in a pair of jeans and nothing else. They hugged his ass just right, while still riding low enough on his hips that when he turned to me and grinned, I saw his hip bones, and that sexy-ass V-shape I liked to trail my tongue over.

I walked to him, paused, then traced a finger down the valley I'd just been admiring. It was still fucking crazy to me that I could touch Ash that way, but I damn sure planned to enjoy it. "Your cum gutters are sexy."

"Excuse me, my what?"

I chuckled. "Cum gutters. I'll have to jerk off in them next time we fuck around."

"Jesus, Campbell. Everything you say gets me fired up...get it? Fired up...you're a firefighter..."

I shook my head and smiled. "I don't get it. Can you explain it to me?"

"Asshole." He looked away, toward the coffeepot.

"Wanna go to dinner at Mom's tonight?"

Ash's eyes darted to mine. "No shit?"

His response landed in my chest. Was it really that surprising that I'd ask him to eat dinner at my mom's house? I wondered how often people had ever done things like that for Ash, and if they did, if there was always some ulterior motive. He was always too shocked that I just wanted to spend time with him. "Yeah, of course. Kenny's cooking. He's pretty good. It won't be anything fancy."

"I don't want anything fancy."

"I guess it works, then." I went to step away, but Ash reached out. This time it was his hands on my hips, holding me in place. He rubbed his thumbs against my skin, beneath my shirt.

"I like it when you're nice to me."

My lips pulled into a frown. "Was I really not nice to you? I know I was...irritable, but did I ever hurt you?" I would hate myself for it if I did. I knew I hadn't always been fair to Ash, and yeah, I gave him shit, but...

"No, you didn't hurt me. You always made me feel confused, which means I tried harder, which means you pulled away more...and it was a mess. I would have run if you'd been anything different than you were. I did run after graduation, but...you're extra nice to me now. You suck my dick and eat my come. You let me coach with you and invite me to your mom's house for a non-fancy dinner."

Leaning in, I chuckled against his lips, pressing a quick kiss there. "I like being nice to you, Ash."

"Ooh! I love chocolate cake. Can I help you make it?" Ash asked Kenny, basically bouncing on the balls of his feet like a child. He held the same excitement about the smallest things, similar to how Kenny did. I envied people like them, people who looked for the joy in every life situation. Ash had been blessed in his life. Not everyone got to do what they loved. But he'd suffered too—losing football, his parents, and denying who he was. He didn't let those things get him down, though. Was there ever a time in my life that I just looked forward to baking a cake? I couldn't say there was.

Kenny's glee at Ash's question took over, and he

began rambling too quickly for anyone to understand him.

"Slow down, Kenny. Take a couple deep breaths, and then reply again," Mom told him.

He did as she asked, then said, "Yes, please. I'd love for you to help."

"Let's do it," Ash replied.

The two of them then forgot Mom and I were around as they got busy.

"You're the captain, and I'm your wingman. Lemme know what you want me to do," Ash told Kenny, and I swear to Christ, my damn heart swelled.

Kenny directed as they got busy on their cake. I leaned against the opposite counter, watching them, with Mom beside me. Every so often Ash would look over his shoulder at me and wink or grin. I returned each gesture with a playful smile, when really my throat was too fucking tight to breathe.

Ashton Carmichael was in my mom's kitchen, making a cake with my brother…my brother who clearly loved the hell out of him. Afterward, I'd go home with him, spend the night in his bed. And it was…it was everything.

"You look happy," Mom whispered in my ear as they mixed the cake.

There wasn't a question in my mind that Mom would know, that she'd see something was going on. I'd had to prepare myself for that before bringing Ash over today. Still, I knew what this was. I knew Ash was experimenting, being honest with who he was, and that it likely wouldn't go anywhere other than that.

"I can't really talk to you about it," I replied. Sharing that I was happy with Ash would be outing him, and regardless of what she knew, or thought she knew, it wasn't my place to do that.

"I understand. Moms know all. And I approve."

As much as I appreciated what she said, I had to be honest with her. "Don't get your hopes up, okay? Things aren't always what they seem." Yes, Ash and I had fun together, and we were…something, but I didn't want her to think there would be more. Ash being in the closet complicated things. Our lives being so different complicated things. He was happy in Fever Falls at the moment, but I wasn't foolish enough to think he'd want to stay there. After he licked his wounds, he would realize the world was open for him. He could have or do anything he wanted. In some ways, nothing had changed. I would always be second in everything related to Ash.

"Wanna lick my spoon?" Ash turned to me, wagging

his eyebrows...and his face paled. It was as if he'd just noticed what he'd said in front of my family. Fear burned in his eyes as they darted to Kenny and then my mom. I'd be lying if I didn't admit the sting of disappointment I felt, even though I knew the score.

Kenny didn't notice a thing as he picked up the pan and went for the oven.

"Here, let me open it for you, Kenny," Mom told him, and I knew she was pretending not to notice Ash's obvious insecurity.

I walked over, plucked the spoon from his hand, and licked some chocolate off. "I'd love to lick your spoon." After a quick glance to see Kenny and Mom had their backs to us, I leaned in and whispered, "It's okay. You can be yourself here. And if you're not ready, that's fine too. Not everyone knows you're full of sexual innuendo."

"Well, shit. I must not be very good at it, then," Ash replied, his voice holding a slight waver.

"Can you repeat that after I take my phone out? I'd love to have on camera your admission to not being good at something. Even if it is a lie."

"Good save, Campbell."

"Eh, gotta keep your head big, Carmichael. I like it that way."

His eyes darted down, and I could have sworn there

was a tinge of pink to his cheeks. I still wasn't used to vulnerable Ash.

"Can we play catch, Beau? I wanna practice," Kenny asked once the cake was in the oven.

"What about the half-cooked dinner and cake?" Mom crossed her arms.

Three pairs of eyes turned her way, and I had no doubt Ash and Kenny were silently pleading with her the same way I was.

"Please, Mrs. Campbell?" Ash asked, and Mom laughed, shaking her head.

"Just a bunch of kids, you are. Go on. I'll finish the food."

We made a beeline for the backyard, as though we were twelve and being set free to play until the streetlights came on.

Ash and I spent an hour playing ball with Kenny. There were times I just sat back and watched Ash with Kenny, in wonder. Saw Ash in his element, with a football in his hand, but saw a different side of him too. The teacher, the coach, the pure love he had of the game itself. Saw Kenny soak it up in ways he didn't even do with me. Ash was a natural, and Kenny seemed to want to soak up every bit of knowledge he had.

It again reminded me of that day in the park when

we were in high school—of teaching Kenny to catch. Until Ash came back, I hadn't thought about that in years, hadn't let myself because I'd wanted to ignore anything about Ash that made me feel emotions other than annoyance. But it had been there even then.

"You bird-watching over there or what, Campbell?" Ash asked, pulling me from my musings.

"I thought you were supposed to be funny?" I teased.

Ash clutched at his chest. "Why you always breaking my heart? My humor is my armor, ya know?"

Yeah, yeah, I did.

Before I realized what was happening, Ash tossed me the ball. My instincts made me catch it, and then he was going for me, tackling me to the ground. We wrestled around, me trying to hold the ball and Ash trying to get it from me. Then the ball was gone and it was just us, rolling around, trying to one-up each other because that's who Ash and I were. It was always a competition.

I managed to roll over on top of him, Ash on his back, my groin between his legs. We were breathing heavily, and there was grass in his hair. "I win," I whispered as I held him down.

"You sure about that, Campbell?" he replied.

Heat rolled through me, head to toe. "Oh, I see what you're trying to do here. I can work with this." My dick began to fill as I savored the feel of him beneath me.

Just as I went to lean down and take his mouth, Kenny said, "Don't give up now, Ash!"

It snapped me out of the trance Ash always put me under. He said I had some kind of voodoo magic, but I didn't. It was all him, the fucker.

I rolled off him and onto my stomach because, yeah, the boner was still there. He cocked a brow and laughed. Then I was laughing and Kenny was asking what was so funny.

"Your brother's face," Ash teased, shoving off the ground.

"Ha-ha. Very funny."

"Come on, K-man. Let's go into the house so Beau can come to terms with the fact that I won."

"But Beau was winning," Kenny replied.

"He gave in because he's scared of me." Ash laughed, put his arm around Kenny's shoulders, and the two of them went inside. Little did Ash know he was right—I was scared of him and what he made me feel.

CHAPTER TWENTY-FIVE

Ashton

Ashton Carmichael used to play like he was in love with the game, and Ashton in love was a beautiful thing to witness!

I ADJUSTED BEAU'S cap on my head. He glanced at me from the driver's seat of his truck, but then his eyes went quickly back to the road. Today had been... Hell, I didn't really have the words to describe what today meant to me. It had been like I had family for the first time in too long. In some ways, it was even different from my adoptive parents. I loved them, don't get me wrong. There hadn't been a part of me that hadn't, but I'd also known I'd been living Dad's dream for him. He'd wanted football, and at first I'd wanted it because I wanted to make him proud. Luckily, I fell in love with it. Beau loved football too, but it was different. His friendship—and Kenny's and his mom's—wasn't forged from my play on the field.

"Am I ever going to get my hat back?" Beau asked, breaking the silence.

"Now come on, Campbell. You know me better than that. I always get what I want."

"And you want my cap?"

I turned to him even though it was too dark to truly see him, and replied, "I want your cap."

That wasn't all I wanted from Beau. But considering I was *me*, I wasn't sure how deep my want went or if I could handle the answer, so I didn't add that I really just wanted him.

"So damn spoiled."

"We've gone over this before."

"Kenny loves you," he added.

My eyes were drawn to the darkness outside the window, the headlights showing me a group of deer in the field as we drove out to my house.

"I've never seen him connect with someone as strongly as he does with you."

My heart went wild, like the roar of the crowd in a packed stadium. "Well, I'm hard not to love."

"Be serious."

"I am. Seriously, have you known anyone who didn't love me? And don't roll your eyes at me."

"You can't even see me." There was a chuckle in his

voice.

"I don't have to see you to know you, remember?"

"It's okay to be vulnerable. You only are when it comes to sex with me."

Because of course he had to mention that. I already hated the fact that I felt so out of step when it came to fucking around with him. "I liked you better when you were Cranky Campbell."

"I can be cranky with you. I'm just about there already. Keep ignoring the seriousness of the situation, and I'll be good and irritable. No one can bring it out of me like you."

Which I had to admit, I fucking loved.

"Ticktock, Avoidance Ash."

So I liked things on my terms. Big deal. "I'm not avoiding." He turned toward me just as another car drove by, enabling me to see his cocked brow. "Okay, so I'm avoiding. It's weird. Most of the time, I love the attention."

"But it's hard when it's real. That's how you know when it's important—when it's tough. You're real good at playing the part, but I know you, Ash."

He did. There wasn't anyone in the world who knew me like Beau. Even when we were kids, I always felt like he somehow saw through me. I groaned, turned the hat forward, and leaned my head against the seat. "I love your brother. It feels good that he looks up to me. I'm scared to fuck it up, though, man. Or that I don't deserve it. And then there's your mom. She treats me like she does you and Kenny. Like..."

"Family?" Beau finished for me.

"I know it's stupid." How could they feel like I was family?

"No, it's not." Beau reached over and put his hand on my thigh. I set mine on top of his, rubbed my fingers against his rough skin, felt a lump that I knew was a prominent vein he had there, brushed my thumb over his knuckles. "They've both fallen for you. You might be stuck with us now."

"What about you? Have you fallen for me?" The questions just sort of fell from my tongue, like I didn't have any say in the matter. Beau groaned, a sound I was familiar with. "I sense some avoidance coming from you in five...four...three...two..."

"Funny."

"I've already gotten you to admit you like me. I'm totally going to make you admit you're falling for me too."

"Aren't they the same thing?" Beau asked.

"No, a hundred percent different, but you just answered me. Don't worry, Campbell. I'm basically irresistible."

"You're a pain in my ass."

"Not yet, and when we get there, I'll be careful not to hurt you."

A laugh jumped out of Beau's mouth, so deep and hardy that he almost choked. Obviously, that made me laugh too, and that was basically how we spent the rest of the ride home. Thank fuck for that because there was a part of me that wanted to tell him this was the best night I'd had in years, that he made me feel a part of something. That I was falling for him, or hell, maybe I'd already taken a fucking nosedive off the cliff, without my damn parachute, and I wasn't sure I'd survive the fall.

But instead we laughed, and then I dragged him into my house and we showered together. There was something else on my mind, of course, because I'd watched gay porn last night and realized I wanted my tongue in his ass. That was sort of a big deal.

And a whole hell of a lot easier to say than the whole freefalling-off-a-cliff-for-him thing. So when we went back to my room, both smelling like the ocean from the new soap I bought, I said, "Funny story…I watched some gay porn last night. Blew my load all over my laptop. You might owe me a new keyboard."

Beau whipped around to face me, his eyes damn near bugging out of his head. He seemed to get a hold of himself, so instead of mentioning the fact that I watched porn, he said, "Why do I owe you a laptop?"

"Because it was firefighter porn, which means I was thinking about you. Hence it being your fault. I'll send you the bill."

He laughed a deep, happy sound that radiated into my chest. Fucking Beau Campbell. He stepped closer to me, then closer again, the color of his eyes darkening and sparking with lust. "You watched firefighter porn without me?"

"Yes. I might need you to wear those yellow pants and suspenders for me sometime—with nothing else, by the way. Fucking hell, Campbell, it's sexy."

"Turnout pants?" Beau grinned, flicked my towel open, and yep, my no longer broken cock was already hard as steel.

"Did the firefighter get on his knees?" Beau asked as he began to lower himself.

My dick screamed at me, like silently yelled, *Stop! What the fuck are you doing? We love head!* but I ignored it, grabbed his arm, and didn't let him move. "No...well, I mean yes, but that's not where I'm going with this." Because I wanted to taste him...and I wanted to do something for Beau. Everything about us felt lopsided, like he gave and I took, and I didn't want that with him.

This time it was me who opened his towel, my eyes on his chest, then down to the hard rod between his legs. It jerked as though he felt my stare like a caress, and yeah, I wanted that in my mouth too. "I'm basically planning on devouring you. I want you in my mouth, Campbell. Wanna know what it's like to suck you...then I thought..." The words stuck in my mouth like glue. Why the fuck couldn't I say it? This was me.

Instead I reached around him, cupped his ass, teased his crack with my finger.

"You wanna eat my ass?"

For some reason, his bluntness surprised me, making me blink a few times. "Yeah, I do."

"You're not going to hear me argue with that."

Before I could respond, Beau's mouth went down on mine. His tongue seduced my lips, and I opened for him, craved him, wanted him inside. He pushed me backward onto the bed, in a way no one had ever done to me except for him, and it made my cock throb.

He buried his face in my neck, sucked the skin there, rubbed his stubble against me.

"Christ, touching you melts my damn brain," I said huskily as I grabbed his ass, pulling him tighter against me. As good as Beau felt on top of me—his weight and his muscle—I wanted this to be about him. Okay, and maybe about me too, but in a different way than it typically was. I wanted him to feel good, and I wanted to be the one to do it. I wanted to know his body, his taste, experience him in ways unique to us.

He thrust against me, our cocks moving together. Before my brain went any more haywire, I flipped us, put myself on top. "Be good and let me suck your dick."

"In what universe would I argue with that?"

"Well, you do like to make things difficult…"

"Are you putting my dick in your mouth, or what?" Beau winked, and damned if both the wink and his question didn't get me harder.

I kissed my way down his chest, licked his nipples. Beau felt so fucking good beneath me, against me, with me. Since I'd told him I was going to devour him, that was exactly what I did. I ran my tongue along every dip, every groove, every muscle. Anything I could taste, I did, until I got to his cock, tall against his belly.

The tip was wet, a pearl of precome at the slit. "I'm assuming I'll be really good at this, but try not to come too soon. I want to taste your ass too."

I leaned in, but Beau cupped my cheek, angled my head toward him. "It's okay to be nervous or unsure. You don't have to hide it. This is a big deal."

A heavy breath escaped my lungs. Even when I didn't know what I needed, somehow Beau did. I wanted this, but it was hard. I hated that it was, that I couldn't jump right in to being a gay sex king and had to start at sucking dick 101. "Thank you. I…" Without finishing, I looked down, opened my mouth.

"Look at me when you do it, Ash. See how much pleasure you give me."

And again, that somehow was exactly what I needed. I was lying between Beau's hairy thighs, looking into his eyes as I angled his dick toward my mouth and licked it. I started at the base, working my way up before swirling my tongue around the head.

Yes. Yes, yes, yes, yes. I sucked him, savored him. Memorized the feel of every vein. I couldn't go deep, but just tasting him wasn't enough, so I pulled off, rooted my nose around in his pubic hair, inhaled his scent.

"Ash…" Beau said huskily, rubbing his hand over my head. I wanted more of that, more of my name on Beau's tongue, more groans and soft noises of pleasure, so I took him into my mouth again. Alternated between licking his balls and sucking his cock, while wondering what was so scary about this. I wanted it, wanted Beau.

He pumped his hips slightly, not too much, like I

would do for him, and I had to admit, my ego sort of wanted to tell him to let loose on me. My gag reflex won out.

When his hand tightened in my hair, I knew he was close, so I pulled off. "What's the best way to do this?"

"You can keep sucking my cock if you want."

"I love your dick—not like, *love*—but I…I really want your hole, Campbell."

His hand shot out and grabbed his balls.

"Holy shit, did that almost make you come?"

"It was hot as fuck, Ash."

I moved out of the way while Beau turned over, got on his knees, and bent over, resting on his forearms with his ass in the air.

Kneeling behind him, I spread his cheeks, took in the light dusting of hair in his crack, the tight hole I wanted to ravish. "Christ," I whispered, rubbing my thumb against it. He clenched, and I did it again. "It's a pretty fucking hole, Campbell." I wasn't sure if it was the right thing to say. Could I call his asshole pretty? But it felt like it to me.

"Jesus, you fucking wreck me."

That put us on equal footing because Beau did the same for me.

Leaning in, I brushed my tongue against his tight

ring of muscle. When he moved against me, I did it again and again and again. Beau whimpered, pushed back against me as if he was trying to ride my face. "Fuck yes. That feels good. Give me more, Ash."

His words fueled me. Using my hands, I spread his cheeks farther, pushed deeper, was pretty sure that his ass was the best place on earth to be. If it was this good with my tongue, what would it ever be like if I got to fuck him?

He tasted like musk and soap. I loved the feel of him against my skin. My cock ached, and each time Beau made a sound in pleasure, it throbbed again.

"Finger me," he said as he pushed back.

Well, okay. I wasn't going to argue with that. I sucked my first finger, got it as wet as I could, rubbed it against him. His hole swallowed it up as I slowly pushed the digit inside. "Fuck, you're tight." I'd had anal with women before, but it was different with Beau, *more* with Beau, and we were talking about a fucking finger.

"Yesss. Slide it in and out."

I'd never had my ass played with. A few girls tried to slip a finger back there, but I never let them, tried to tell myself I didn't wonder about it because wondering felt like the first admission to the things I'd been trying to hide.

Beau had no qualms about enjoying it, though. He owned his pleasure, begged for more, took control, and offered it at times too. I wanted my tongue in him again, so I did my best to lean in, lick at his rim while fingerfucking him at the same time. When my finger rubbed against a spongy spot, his body jolted.

"Fuck, right there. Rub that right there."

I'd heard having your prostate played with felt good, but even if I hadn't, I would have known it from Beau's reactions. Every time I slid my finger in, I teased that spot. His breathing got more intense—quick, short, panting breaths. His pleasure made my cock leak.

Suddenly, his movements became jerky, his hole clenched, and he threw his head back and shouted my name. It was as if it was the first time I'd heard it, like he was calling me a king. Beau collapsed onto the bed, his orgasm some kind of beacon for mine.

"Jerk off on me."

"Yeah, okay. Don't have to tell me twice." I wrapped a fist around my cock, pulled it, dropped my head back as my balls tightened and the world exploded, never to be the same. I opened my eyes, looked just in time to see my first long spurt land on Beau's ass, slip in his crack. It was probably the sexiest thing I'd ever seen, and I cried out as I shot again, this one hitting his lower back.

I fell on his back, sweat and my come making us stick together. "How'd I do?" I asked when my breathing got closer to normal.

"I might not ever want you to stop."

I smiled against his ass, then kissed it. I didn't think I'd ever want to stop either.

CHAPTER TWENTY-SIX

Beau

Beau thinks Ash is awesome. I think he's awesome too. ~ Love, Kenny

"OH, HEY. I'M not sure if you remember me. I'm Lincoln."

I rolled my eyes at my best friend, who sat in a booth at Blazes, a diner across the street from the firehouse. I'd finished my jog with Ash, who'd headed home afterward, and since I'd still had a little bit of time before I had to get to the station, I'd called Linc to have breakfast. We gave each other shit, but I missed him. Linc was typically the one I spent most of my time with. Now I was always with Ash, and I didn't know how to be with Lincoln and Ash at the same time. Not when no one could know what we were to each other...not when I still didn't know what we were to each other besides friends who fucked around.

"Lincoln who?" I asked with a smile before sitting

across from him. My eyes darted toward the second cup of coffee beside him.

"Rush is in the bathroom. I was with him."

"Oh fuck. Not again."

"We were lonely. Not everyone is like you."

Rush and Lincoln had a habit of fucking like rabbits when they were feeling lonesome, and well, horny, only they weren't in the mood for Grindr. Technically, I wouldn't give a shit because I didn't make a habit of sticking my nose where it didn't belong, but I had a feeling Rush cared about Linc in ways Linc didn't care about him. Rush would never admit it, and Linc didn't see it, but there was no denying the way Rush looked at him. "I don't want him to get hurt, is all. And it would fuck up the group."

"Oh, you mean the group you never hang out with anymore. And what about me? I have feelings too."

I opened my mouth to call Lincoln on the fact that Rush truly was just a good friend with a dick to him, but that I wasn't sure Rush felt the same. Unfortunately, he came out of the hallway and nodded at me. "You have a hickey on your neck."

My hand shot toward my throat. Holy fuck. Ash had given me a hickey and I hadn't noticed?

"Oh shit. How did I miss a hickey?" Lincoln leaned

forward, trying to see.

"You didn't, but I know you were wondering if Beau was hooking up with someone we didn't know about. Now you have your answer. If he wasn't, he wouldn't have looked like he was about to vomit." Rush winked at me, the bastard.

"Grindr trick," I replied.

"Nice try. You hate Grindr," Rush added.

My eyes shot to Linc. Why in the hell would he have mentioned the fact that he thought I was hooking up when he knew that if I was, it was with Ash, and he was in the closet? I hadn't spelled it out for him, of course, but Linc had to know. "So did you two have fun last night?" I asked, cocking a brow at them.

"Yeah," Rush replied with a shrug.

Lincoln bit his bottom lip, looked at me, and I could see the apology there, that it had been an accident. And he was also likely feeling guilty for fucking Rush again.

"I thought you went home with that guy you met at the club a while back." Lincoln was trying to cover for me, but the truth was, Rush likely didn't give a shit if I was fucking anyone. It wasn't his style. He'd only said something for Linc, which was the shit that made me feel like he had feelings for him.

"Coffee?" the waitress asked, effectively putting an

end to a conversation I was pretty sure both Lincoln and I wanted to be over.

"Yes, please," I replied.

We ordered after that and then chatted about everything other than fucking because we all had shit we wanted to keep to ourselves at the moment. Rush had his arm around the back of the booth, around Lincoln, and I could see the guilt swimming in Linc's eyes because of it. We needed to make time to talk—or I guessed I did. Linc obviously had some shit going on that I'd been too busy to notice, and despite his outgoing personality and his large group of friends, he didn't typically talk when he felt like that, except to me.

When breakfast was over, the three of us said goodbye outside. Rush left first, ruffling Lincoln's hair in a weird way I didn't quite understand. The moment he walked around the corner and out of view, Linc said, "Fuck, I'm sorry. I didn't say much. We went out without you last night, and I might have drunk a little too much, complained you would rather fuck someone than hang out with us, and then took Rush home with me."

"Jesus, Linc." I ran a hand through my hair, wishing I had my damn cap. It was apparently lost to Ash for good now.

"He doesn't know it's…you know who."

"You don't even know who it is. I never confirmed anything." Plus, after our conversation about me always being with Ash, I was pretty sure Rush knew. Not that he would ever say anything. I trusted Rush.

"This is what happens when I'm needy! You should know me by now!"

I shook my head, then pulled him into a hug. "Don't make me admit it."

"I might need you to admit it," he replied, looking up at me and fluttering his lashes. Linc and I had a strange relationship. We were nothing alike, but we needed each other, we understood each other. I wasn't sure he let anyone else really get him. In some ways, he was like Ash. They both had that strong exterior, both hid behind their sarcasm so no one dug deeper. I apparently was a digger and hadn't realized it.

"I love you. You're my best friend. I just…" How in the fuck did I finish this sentence? I just what? Wanted to be with Ash every moment I could? That sounded needy as hell and not like me.

"You're mesmerized by his magic dick?" Linc teased.

"I don't know who you're talking about, and I haven't fucked him."

Linc pulled back, mischief sparking in his eyes. "Oh,

Beau, I'm disappointed in you. Do you need some pointers?"

"Fuck off."

"I love you too."

"I know you do." I kissed his forehead. "I need to get to work."

I waited until Lincoln walked away, and then I jogged across the street to the station, my conversation with him still fresh in my mind. There was something going on between Ash and me. That much was obvious because…fuck, even then I missed him, wanted to spend time with him. I'd never had that with anyone, this desire to be in their presence the way I did with him.

I liked having him in our kitchen, with my family. I loved the bond he formed with my brother. And I was also beginning to feel like his house was mine; I wanted to be there all the time, because it both reminded me of when we were kids and still felt fresh and new—like us. It was unnerving and exciting and sort of felt like someone else was trapped in my body. What had Ash done to me?

We got a few calls throughout the day. An older woman had fallen and broken her wrist, and we got there before the EMTs and made sure the situation was stable. Then there was a false alarm on a house fire. Nothing too exciting.

It was an hour before the end of my shift. Ash and I were texting about the game that night, and Jace was sitting on the same couch as me, talking to whatever girl he was with at the time, when we got a call for a warehouse fire on Old Mills Road. The area was abandoned, and apparently the flames were spreading quickly.

My adrenaline started pumping, transporting me to another world, that place I went when I was heading into the flames.

We were dressed and in the engine in no time flat, the sirens loud, fueling the spike of courage and determination we needed to do what we did.

As always in a situation like this, Mom was there, in my head…joined by Kenny…Lincoln…and now Ash. All the people I had to make it home to.

I shook those thoughts. They were okay. We would be okay. This was what we did.

Flames danced in the distance, a large billow of smoke, and I felt the familiar stab of guilt that I was letting Kenny down tonight. I wouldn't be able to coach…but Ash could. I didn't like depending on anyone else, even other assistant coaches, but this was…this was Ashton Carmichael.

Fire. Won't be at the game. Can you let Mom and Kenny know, Coach? You got this.

The reply was almost instantaneous. **Be careful. I kind of like you. Get yourself home safe. I'll take care of everything else.**

In that moment, I knew I was one hundred percent gone for Ashton Carmichael.

CHAPTER TWENTY-SEVEN

Ashton

Let's see how well Ashton Carmichael can perform under pressure!

FIRES WERE SCARY as shit.

My nerves were on edge from the second Beau texted me earlier in the day. I played it off well when what I really wanted to say was, *Can you just come home, please? 'K, thanks, bye.*

Obviously, this was what he did. He always had, and I wasn't freaking out like this every day, but I'd heard the tremor in his voice when we'd talked about his job, the knowledge of just how dangerous it was. How was I supposed to deal with this all the time? And wait...all the time? Apparently, I was getting a little ahead of myself too.

Trying to ignore those thoughts, I called his mom and offered to pick Kenny up and take him with me. I went to Campbell's Confections, and she told me she'd meet us at the game; then Kenny came out and got in the car with me.

The last thing I wanted was to overreact and stress him out, but who the fuck knew—Kenny seemed to have his shit together more than most people I knew. Maybe was more settled about Beau running toward fires than I was. I just wanted to kidnap Beau.

From the passenger seat, Kenny asked, "Is Beau your boyfriend?" prompting me to swerve into the other lane, get honked at, and almost kill my maybe boyfriend's brother. I was doing awesome.

"Huh?" I answered with, my hands suddenly sweaty and my heart running a marathon. Now I had to worry about Beau *and* figure out how in the fuck to answer this.

"Do you love Beau? I love Lori."

My throat swelled. Shit, I couldn't breathe. I suddenly couldn't fucking breathe. Love? How did we get from boyfriends to love? And was this something everyone assumed? That we were boyfriends in love?

Oh God. I was going to puke.

Not that I didn't want to be Beau's boyfriend, because let's be honest, I really fucking did. And we maybe already were, and we'd kind of talked about it, but it was different talking to Beau than anyone else. That didn't change the fact that I didn't know what the fuck to do. I wasn't ready for anyone to know. What if everyone knew?

I settled on, "Who's Lori?" as I gripped the steering wheel and held back the urge to vomit while running the car off the road with the brother of my boyfriend, whom I might be in love with, in it. Beau was going to kill me. He was going to have to fight a big-ass fire and then put out the extra energy to kill me.

"She's from the center…she's pretty. Do you think Beau is pretty?"

I swallowed hard. Beau was sexy as hell. He got my dick hard in no time flat, and yeah, he was beautiful, but I was pretty sure I wasn't supposed to say all that to Kenny.

"Does Lori know how you feel?" I asked.

"Yes. I'm going to ask Beau to take us on a date."

My heart melted right there on the damn spot. I wanted to take Beau on a date with Lori and Kenny.

But I wouldn't…not yet. Even just thinking about it made me dizzy. It was one thing when it was just me and Beau, but I didn't know how to do this with other people. Christ, what would my old teammates say? I'd been the talk of the league for years, and I didn't want that anymore.

"Is Beau your boyfriend?"

"No," jumped out of my mouth before I could think about it. Bile burned my throat. It felt wrong…it was wrong, but then, I wasn't out. I didn't know what was expected of me. Beau would understand, wouldn't he?

"Oh." Kenny looked down at his lap, and I knew I'd disappointed him along with myself. "You make him happy. Beau's a hero. He should be happy."

I pulled into the parking lot of the gymnasium and turned off the car. My throat was still tight, my chest heavy, but that fear was still there, a powerful weight that wouldn't release me. "Beau *is* a hero. He's the best man I know, and he does deserve to be happy. He's…very important to me." He was maybe everything to me. My probably boyfriend that I was likely in love with. But I didn't know how to publicly be in love with Beau.

"People think I don't understand, but I do. I wouldn't be afraid if I loved someone. I love Lori."

Then, without another word, Kenny got out of the car. Me? I sat there and heard what he said…wished it was that easy. Was it? Was loving Beau really that easy?

The game was a fucking disaster. I coached for shit. We lost…fucking lost, and it was the night I coached. I couldn't concentrate on the game—just Beau, me, the fucking fire, what Kenny said.

After the game the gym became a madhouse. Visitors from the other team bombarded me—Ashton, can you sign…any chance you'll come out of retirement…would you like to go out after… I was dizzy by the end of it, my head spinning. I'd let Kenny and the team down, fans, myself.

And fuck, where was Beau? I still hadn't heard from him, and neither had his mom.

I hid out until everyone had left, went home, took a shower, and drank a fucking beer. I didn't know why tonight shook me up so much. It was maybe a hundred people at the game. I'd been in stadiums with thousands.

Would it go public now? Would I wake up to articles talking about how I coached Kenny's team? Would reporters come out?

"Is Beau your boyfriend?"

Aaaaand, time for another beer. Which I drank. Then looked at my phone. Then drank another. Then told myself to chill the fuck out.

Before I knew it, Beau was there, and I was glad I didn't lock up. My room was dark, and his fingers were brushing against my face. I didn't know what time it was, when or how in the hell I fell asleep. I just knew he was fucking *there*, and I needed him.

"Sorry to wake you. Should I not have come over? I

just..."

"Come here." I wrapped my arms around him and pulled him on top of me. His weight was a welcome relief, a comfort I needed.

Yes...yes, he is my boyfriend.

My tongue dipped into his mouth, my nails dug into his hips, his cock hard against mine.

Yes...yes, he is my boyfriend.

"We lost the game. Fuck, I can't believe we lost the game," I said between kisses. I was angry at myself, felt like I let him down, in more ways than one. "My head was all fucked up. I was worried about you and..." *Kenny asked if we were boyfriends.*

"Hey." Beau pushed up onto his hands, his arms boxing me in. "Who cares about the game? It happens."

"My ego cares about the game just a little bit." I was an ex-professional-player. I should have been able to keep my head in it better.

"I'm fine, Ash," he said as though he had a direct link to my insides. "I'm fine."

"We both know you're hot, so stop rubbing it in."

"Stop avoiding."

"I want you," I admitted. "Can I have you, Campbell?" I cupped his ass through his jeans, my need on my tongue.

Yes, yes, he is my boyfriend.

Though that didn't really feel like a strong enough word, did it?

"You want inside me?" Beau asked, burying his face in my neck, licking my collarbone. "I've been dying to have you in my ass."

"What a coincidence. I've been dying to be there. Maybe we should get naked?"

"You think?" Beau went to pull away, but I grabbed ahold of him.

"You fought a fire today."

"You've said that to me before. I fight a lot of them. It's what I do."

"It…scares me…the thought of losing you." I'd lost too much—my biological parents had walked away, my adoptive parents died…football…

"I'm not going anywhere. I promise. I mean, you're Ashton fucking Carmichael." He winked at me.

"You gonna shut up so I can fuck you, or what? This is sort of a big deal, Campbell. I'm about to make love to a man for the first time." It didn't escape my attention that I said *make love*. I'd never made love in my life. I'd never done anything that resembled something real, except with Beau. Luckily, he either didn't catch it or knew not to call me on it.

"I'm not the one always talking; that's you."

I pulled him down, and we kissed and laughed. We rolled over, still kissing and laughing, and fuck, there was no one in the world I liked laughing with more than Beau Campbell.

It was rushed after that as we tugged at each other's clothes, throwing them around the room. I gasped when I had him naked, at the large bandage on his right pec, and yeah, maybe also because Beau naked was a beautiful thing.

"I'm fine," he said again. "Something hit me, is all." Then he was kissing his way down my body, nuzzling my heavy balls, rubbing his scruff against my sensitive dick, kissing and licking me.

"If my cock goes in your mouth, I'm blowing my load. I can tell you that right now."

"I'm that good, huh?" he teased.

"How did you become the cocky one?"

"Just love your dick." He licked it from base to head, and I literally almost fucking died.

"You'll love it in your ass too. Christ, I want inside you something fierce."

Beau rolled off me, onto his back, and spread his legs. "Then I guess you better come and get me."

Well…when he put it like that…

My hands trembled as I reached over and grabbed the lube and a condom from the drawer. I'd ordered them online, hoping this moment would be coming soon. I clicked on the bedside lamp, which bathed the room in a soft light. I knelt between Beau's muscular, spread thighs.

"You're really going to let me in there?" I brushed a finger over his tight ring of muscle.

"I'm going to fucking *love* you in there."

My dick spurted against my stomach. Fuck, he was so damn sexy. I'd never been turned on the way Beau got me going. "I guess you're right. I *am* pretty good at this."

"Stop stalling, Ash. Lemme feel you. It's been a while for me, so you're gonna have to do some stretching first."

After tossing the condom on the bed, I pumped lube onto my fingers. Beau held himself open for me, waiting for me, and fuck, I couldn't wait to give it to him.

It wasn't the first time I fingered him; still, I reveled in how tight he was, how fucking hot.

"You can give me two fingers. I fucking want it."

"You're killing me, Campbell." I pushed two fingers inside, and we let out heavy breaths in unison. I pushed my fingers in, played with his prostate the way he'd taught me to do. I was learning his body through his instruction, and though part of me was insecure because of that, the other part fucking loved it. This was something special between Beau and me that I'd never have with anyone else.

He pushed against me, rode my fingers. I was in awe of his pleasure, the fact that he could take part of me inside him, own it, claim it, fucking love it.

"If you don't get inside me soon, I think I might die."

That was enough encouragement for me.

I ripped open the condom wrapper and rolled it down my length. I lubed up my cock just as Beau rolled over. He was sort of on his side and stomach, his top leg bent and his bottom straight, giving me access to his ass. Kneeling with one leg behind him and one between his, I angled my cock toward him. "Fuck, I can't believe this is happening." None of it...Beau...me...Beau and I together.

I pushed between his cheeks, watched as my crown breached his rim. "Fuck...oh fuck..." He was tight...so fucking tight and hot, and holy shit, I couldn't take my eyes off him. Off his body opening up and taking me inside. "Goddamn it...you're so fucking sexy, Campbell." His hole spread as I pushed farther and farther inside. His body fit me like a glove, like he was made for me.

"More. You feel so good. Give me more, Ash."

We were both trembling, both sweating as I worked my way inside. When I was buried inside him, my eyes rolled back. I couldn't move. I knew if I did, I'd blow my load. "I can't believe I'm inside you." It felt like everything had led up to this moment, since that kiss on the dock, maybe even before. They'd all been stepping stones to get me here, to get *us* here.

He used his top arm to pull me down, to kiss me until I couldn't fucking breathe. When I pulled away, he asked, "Are you fucking me or not?"

I was. I so fucking was. Pushing up onto my knees again, I used my hand to spread his cheeks, watched his body let me go as I pulled out, accept me as I shoved inside him again. I took him slow, nearly fucking died in the process, but I wanted this to last.

His nails dug into my arm, and I suddenly wanted to kiss the smiley-face scar on his arm. It was a silly thing to think in that moment, but I couldn't help it.

My body felt alive, nerve endings going crazy, sparking wildfires through every inch of me. Beau begged for more, made sexy sounds in the back of his throat every time I slammed home.

"I'm not gonna last," I admitted. My balls were heavy, filled with come, my orgasm burning through me as it waited to explode.

"Me neither. Fuck, me neither."

I pulled out, rolled him. Hefting his legs over my shoulders, I pushed inside again. Beau spit in his hand, wrapped it around his cock. Just seeing it made lust shoot through me, rain down on me.

He jerked himself, eyes locked on mine as I continued to pound into him. "Come first," I begged because I really fucking needed to please him.

"Right there, right fucking there."

He tilted his head back, opened his mouth, showed me his pleasure. I bit my lip, fucked harder into him as his body quaked, tightened, his load shooting out on his lip, on the bandage on his chest.

"Fuck... Goddamn, you're beautiful," I gritted out before my own orgasm barreled into me, washed over me as my body felt like it came apart, just shattered, my come filling the condom inside him...inside my boyfriend.

CHAPTER TWENTY-EIGHT

Beau

Mom says Beau is afraid of more things than he realizes, but it's all heart kind of stuff.
~ Love, Kenny

SECONDS TURNED TO minutes, minutes to an hour as we lay there in the dark. The moment felt heavy, loaded. Part of it was from me, because sex with Ash had felt…different. Less like fucking and more like something I'd never experienced before.

If the night was big for me, I knew it had to be even more so for Ash. So I held him, kissed the top of his head, wrapped my arms tighter around him, letting him work out whatever was in that complicated head of his.

"I found my biological mom," he finally said against my chest, his breath warm around my nipple.

"Holy shit. What? When?" I hadn't known that was something he'd wanted to do. I couldn't imagine how I would feel in that situation. I didn't think anyone could unless they lived it.

"Years ago. I was in college. I was…curious. There was that part of me that wanted to know why…why they hadn't wanted me. It wasn't that I didn't love my parents. I did—I do. They gave me a great life, and I know they loved me, but I…I don't know. I wanted to know what I did wrong."

"You didn't do anything wrong, Ash. You were a baby."

"Logically I knew that, but emotionally was a different story. I used to tell myself all these reasons they gave me up, but the truth wasn't nearly as pretty or exciting as the lies I'd told myself."

I tugged at him until Ash climbed on top of me, settled between my legs, his chest against my groin. I fingered his short hair, rubbed his cheek, let him know I was there.

"There was no real reason. No one was sick. She hadn't been too young. She hadn't not had the money. She'd just…not wanted me. She hadn't loved my father. I'd been an accident, and so she let me go so she could live her life."

My heart ached, broke for him. I couldn't imagine what that felt like, especially for someone like Ash. Someone who was so bold, noble, and strong…someone who didn't want anyone to know he needed love, while desperately yearning for it. "That's her loss, baby. Not yours."

"You called me baby." I could hear the smile in his words.

"Yeah, I know. That was weird. I've never called anyone that before."

"Now I feel special."

"You are," I admitted.

He tensed up briefly against me before leaning down and peppering kisses against my stomach. "Well, shucks. Aren't you sweet?"

I laughed, and Ash nibbled my stomach. It was eye-opening to see someone in a different light and realize that all those bits and pieces you thought made up who they were, were more your issues than theirs. I guessed that's what happened when you judged people, when you decided who they were without all the answers. I'd made assumptions about Ash over the years, but I would never do that again. I knew who he was, and that person was incredible. "Oh God. I *am* sweet. So glad you can't hear what just went through my head."

"Tell me."

"No."

"Please?" He stuck his tongue in my navel.

"Maybe after you finish your story."

"Damn it."

"You can't get one by me, Ash. Not anymore."

He sighed, played with my happy trail. "Guess who found me when I started playing pro ball?"

My stomach dropped, and my hands clenched.

"Guess who suddenly wanted a relationship with me then?"

"Fuck." I cupped his cheek, brushed my thumb back and forth over his face. "That says more about her than it does you. She doesn't deserve you in her life."

"The last incident before my retirement?"

My gut tightened, and I wondered if he felt it, if he knew that the thought of him with someone else made me see red.

"It was blackmail."

"Huh?" I asked. "Did you...did you really have sex with them?" I wasn't judging him for it. I'd had my fair share of fun, sometimes with more than one other person, but I wanted to know.

"Yes. Of course I did. I hate myself for the way I've used women, Campbell, but most of them? Most of them used me too. They didn't want to be with me because they liked me; they wanted to be with me because I was Ashton Carmichael. Bridget...we'd been dating. I liked her. I didn't desire her or love her, but I liked her enough that I thought I would feel okay in my life if we stayed together. Bridget liked to have fun, and the foursome was her idea—not that she'd had to try to talk me into it. I think some stupid part of me thought that proved my masculinity or something."

I sighed, and he brushed his finger along my bandage. I kissed the top of his head. "I'm here, Ash. Keep going. I'm not going to judge you."

"I know you won't...not you. So, we drank a lot. I...I had to take Viagra off and on too. I needed it with women, sometimes."

Ash buried his face in my stomach, and my heart broke for him.

"So we had sex. I hadn't known about the pictures. She told me about them. I paid her for them—and the fucked-up part was I would have given her money regardless. I don't give a shit about that. Still, she leaked them. She'd gotten what she wanted from me. She wasn't the first."

My blood ran cold. My whole body went rigid, tense with anger and pain for Ash. "Jesus, baby. I'm so fucking sorry. You didn't deserve that. Why didn't you say anything? Why didn't you tell people?"

"Would it have mattered?" he asked. And then, more

quietly, added, "I love football. I want football. I *still* want it. Who am I if I'm not a football player? But part of me, part of me was relieved."

I squeezed him tighter, held him. Wanted my body to melt into his. I would do anything to protect him, to take care of him, to make sure no one hurt or used him again. "I will never use you. I don't give a shit about football. I only care about you."

"You're one of the only people in my life with whom I never felt like you wanted something from me."

I didn't want *just something* from Ash...I wanted *him*. I always had. "That's kind of a lie because I want you... I've always wanted to be a part of your world, your life, but I just didn't understand it."

"That's different."

"Is it?" I asked.

"Yes, because I've always felt the same about you. It's like...like it was always there between us. We might not have known it, but it was."

He was right. I knew it down to the marrow of my bones. "I'm falling in love with you, Ash," I admitted, despite the tightness in my throat, the thump of my heart, and the spinning in my head. "I know it's soon and you're not out. I'm not trying to put pressure on you. I've just...never had something I wanted as much as you, something I was willing to fight for." I hadn't even been willing to fight for football. My whole life I'd told myself it was because I had a family to take care of, but I was sure it was really fear. I wouldn't make that same mistake with Ash.

"Holy shit. We're in *love*, Campbell." He leaped up and straddled my hips. "Do you know what this means?"

"No…?"

"Me neither, but it sounded good."

Laughing, I cupped his face with both hands, pulled him closer, and took his mouth. It was a kiss filled with desire, with years of want and denial. "You said *we're* in love, Carmichael."

"I did? That's weird."

"Fucker."

He was quiet for a moment, then said, "Kenny asked tonight if I was your boyfriend, and I told him I wasn't."

It was both like a punch to the gut and something I understood. I waited for him to continue, and when he didn't, replied with, "So?"

"I lied because I was scared. I want to be committed to you, but I'm so fucking scared. I know it's stupid, that I need to get over myself, but what if I can't? What if I can't do this?"

"Cut yourself some slack. You're just getting comfortable in your skin. I'm not pressuring you."

"What if it never happens?"

"It will."

"What if it doesn't?"

"I don't think there's anything you can't do, Ashton Carmichael. Come on, you know that."

I sat up, and his arms went around my neck, his legs around my waist. "Well…I *am* really fucking good."

"You are, but I won't ever admit that again."

"What about just once a week? Or at least once a month. I'm sure we can come to some kind of agreement."

"Nope. Never."

"You're killing me here, Campbell. We're teammates. We gotta work together."

"What will you do for me?" I asked him.

He answered with his lips against mine, kissing me, then sliding off me, sucking my cock between his lips until stars danced behind my eyes and I came in his mouth.

"I'm already getting used to the taste. I think I kind of like it."

When we collapsed onto the bed again together, both of us breathing hard, I said, "Okay, we might be able to come to an agreement."

Then we laughed, held each other, and went to sleep.

CHAPTER TWENTY-NINE

Ashton

Ashton MVP Carmichael brought his team all the way!

OKAY, SO IT was embarrassing to admit, but I wanted to spend all my time with Beau.

When he wasn't working, we were together. From practice to games to jogging together. I met him for lunch sometimes. We'd eat at a restaurant called Blazes across from the firehouse. People saw us together, of course, but I told myself they would think we were just two buddies hanging out. I wasn't sure if I believed it. I was starting to feel more relaxed, safer.

When I stopped by the fire station, I couldn't help but notice his work buddy Jace. I remembered him from the first time I'd come when he'd asked for my autograph. Jace was hot. He and Beau seemed to get along well. He was a whole lot more like Beau than I was—serious and responsible, and did I mention hot? It took me a while to realize I was jealous...jealous of some guy who worked with Beau, even though I didn't even know if he liked men or not. The sudden insecure streak was pissing me off, but this was Beau, and I was in love with him, so I just wanted him to be *mine, mine, mine.*

So one day I'd found a way to bring Jace up, and found out he was straight. Not that it should have mattered. Being in love had short-circuited my brain.

Kenny and I hung out a few more times just the two of us. I went to dinner again at Beau's mom's. I felt like shit that I was forcing him to lie, to hide who we were, but I just couldn't get past the fear. It wasn't as if I thought his family would turn me away, that they would look at me differently. Beau hung the stars in their eyes, but no amount of logic could overpower cutting myself open like that, giving them access to who I truly was inside.

I only seemed to be able to do that with Beau.

It was a Sunday night, and Beau and I were at Fever Pitch. We'd been coming here for dinner more often. It had always been Beau's favorite place, and I realized I liked the atmosphere too. Even though anyone who looked at Beau and me would only see a couple of friends sharing a meal and maybe a beer, it almost felt like we could be more ourselves there. That we were like any other couple, and that I wasn't forcing him to hide. Yeah, Fever Pitch was in what Lincoln called *the gayborhood*, but it wasn't as if the only people who went there were part of the LGBTQ community.

Across the booth, Beau took a sip of his beer. We'd ordered our drinks but not our food yet since Lincoln was on his way to meet us. Beau had told me that Lincoln had been giving him shit for not hanging out anymore. The last thing I wanted was to take Beau away from his friends, so I'd told him he should invite him to dinner.

"I remember the first night we saw you here. It was love at first sight for Linc. He was flirting shamelessly, and you couldn't quit guzzling down beers to save your life," Beau said softly.

"Story of my life." He frowned, and I continued. "Come on, don't pretend you didn't notice alcohol was my Band-Aid." I'd used it to get through too many sexual encounters to name…to try and hide my attraction to men…and to Beau.

"I noticed."

"I know."

"Is it something you struggle with? Something we should worry about?"

I liked the *we* in that sentence more than I cared to

admit. Fucking Beau. He had me all tied up. "No. I'm not an alcoholic. How often do I drink right now? I could go months without drinking, but I enjoy sharing a beer with you. I used it before, yes, and sometimes drugs too, but I was never an addict."

Beau grinned at me, but before he could reply, I heard, "The party's started. I've arrived," from Lincoln as he sat down in the booth beside Beau. He leaned over and kissed Beau's cheek, and even though it was innocent—full of friendship and support and history—a stab of jealousy pierced my gut. I wanted to be able to kiss Beau in public. What the fuck was wrong with me that I couldn't?

"Y'all look good. Especially you over there, Mister Sexy Football Stud." Lincoln winked at me.

"Linc…" Beau warned.

"Hey! Leave the man alone. He speaks the truth!" I told Beau.

"Oh, sugar, I think we're meant to be," Lincoln told me, and Beau rolled his eyes.

"I don't think I'm going to enjoy hanging out with both of you at the same time." Beau took a drink.

"Can't handle us, huh, Campbell?" Beau sure as shit could handle me. I quite liked how he handled me.

"Don't let him fool you. Beau pretends to be a stick-in-the-mud, but really, he loves this shit. He doesn't know what he'd do without me." Lincoln grunted when Beau elbowed him in the side.

"I pretend to be a stick-in-the-mud? Fuck you very much. I just act like a grown-up."

"Which translates into what?" Lincoln fluttered his lashes at Beau. "B-O-R-I-N-G. But we know it's just an act. There's a wild man in there just trying to burst free."

"Oh, Jesus Christ," Beau replied.

"Oh my God. There was this party for Beau's twenty-first birthday, and he might or might not have gotten a little bit too drunk. He was dancing on the tables, singing at the top of his lungs—"

"Wait, wait, wait," I cut Lincoln off. "Dancing on tables and singing. That sounds familiar, Campbell. I believe that's something you'd give me shit about." I knew how he'd looked at me the night of our graduation party—the frustration and annoyance that had been in his eyes...but I'd felt something else in his stare too. Something that seared my soul, made me want to run, while at the same time, made the need to be closer to him flare to life even more. It had been what made me go looking for him that night. It had been what made me kiss him.

"I don't know what you're talking about," Beau

answered.

"Oh, yeah, sure you don't," I said, then to Lincoln, "Continue please."

"He'd been wild as hell that night. Then, of course, he turned back into straight-man-trapped-in-a-gay-man's-body Beau, made everyone shut up so he could turn on the TV and watch the end of a college football game. And then he got all emo, took two guys in the bedroom, and had his first threesome—oh. Oops…"

It was as if my heart stopped, like I was in a hospital and they put the paddles on my chest, shocking me forward, and I jerked toward the table.

Beau had stopped partying on his birthday to watch me play football…

Then he'd slept with two men.

I didn't like the fucking part, but the other? The other made my heart swell.

"You know you're judgmental as shit," Beau told Lincoln, effectively preventing a conversation about the other revelations from happening. Not that I knew what to say anyway. I was distracted by the fact that Beau had fucked two men after watching me play ball. Not that I hadn't had my own threesomes.

Beau added, "Gay men can like sports. It's not a straight or gay thing."

"I know. It was a joke. Not a very good one, obviously."

"Well, no one has ever said you had a good sense of humor," Beau replied, and Lincoln gasped.

They playfully tossed jabs back and forth to each other before Beau launched into a funny story about Lincoln, then Lincoln another about Beau. We ordered dinner and ate. I was caught between enjoying seeing them together, seeing Beau with a close friend, watching him let go and laugh, and the J word again that was a weird-as-fuck feeling for me. I didn't do jealousy.

They were telling a story about Lincoln in nursing school when my cell rang. My pulse jumped, wrapping against my skin, when I saw a familiar California phone number. "I'm...going to step outside and take this real quick," I told them.

Beau frowned at me as though he was worried something was wrong. I did my best to give him a reassuring smile. My finger lingered over the screen as I walked away. "Hey, hold on just a second."

"Still think the sun rises and sets on you, I see," my agent, Andrea, replied.

"Ha-ha." When I got outside, I leaned against Fever Pitch. "Okay, I'm here."

"How are the sticks treating you? Helping you get

your head on straight?"

No, not straight...but my head is clearer than it's ever been... "It's not the sticks, and I'm doing fine. You?"

"Good," she replied. "You keeping in shape? Staying out of trouble? The only headlines I'm seeing are the initial ones with you popping up in your hometown and the latest about coaching the special-education team. Good call."

My heart leaped into my throat. I should have known that would happen eventually. I couldn't believe it stayed quiet as long as it did, that I'd missed the headline or that reporters hadn't come calling. "I'm not doing it for my reputation, Andrea. I'm doing it because I want to." Because I loved doing it.

"Does the reason really matter?" she asked bluntly. "What matters is that it *is* helping your image. And there have been some talks...the Tigers' quarterback's contract is up after this season. They don't have the money to keep him. He doesn't want to stay, and they're looking to rebuild their team. You'll draw a crowd...especially coming out of retirement."

The phone damn near tumbled out of my hand. Blood rushed through my ears. I might be able to play... I might be able to go back... I could prove them all wrong about me.

But did I want to?

"Carmichael, you there?" she asked.

I cleared my throat. "Yeah, I'm here. I also see what you're saying. They can afford me because I'll be cheap, right? I'm a liability."

"An ex-liability who has been spending his time off out of trouble and coaching those with developmental disabilities."

"Don't." I could hear the venom in my words. "Don't use that. You don't get to use that like it's a marketing strategy. I won't tolerate it." It was probably one of the realest, most pure things I'd done in my life. I would never let her use Kenny or his team that way.

"Sorry. I didn't mean to offend you, but you know how the business works, Ashton. At least you used to."

"Yeah, yeah, I know." And it made me sick to my stomach.

"Keep your nose clean, okay? Don't draw any negative attention to yourself. Keep in shape, and we'll talk soon. I can't make you any promises. There are a lot of months between now and then, but this could be big for you. Don't fuck it up."

With that, she hung up. I dropped my head back, took a few deep breaths.

I might have a team. I might be able to play again.

I would lose Beau.

"Hey." Beau's voice startled me, made my eyes snap open. "You're white as a ghost. Are you okay?"

Don't draw any negative attention to yourself. Don't fuck it up.

He reached for me, put a hand on my hip, and reflex had me jerking away. He yanked his hand back. "Shit, I'm sorry. I wasn't thinking about being in public. I just wanted to make sure you're okay."

"Yeah, I'm okay. I'm just not feeling great. I think I need to head home."

"Oh." The corners of his eyes crinkled, and it was so damn cute, I wanted to kiss it. "I can have Linc take me to my place."

"Will you come home with me?" I asked, my voice full of vulnerability. "I know you're hanging out with Lincoln, but…" But I needed him. I wanted him. "Never mind. I'm being ridiculous."

"Yeah, of course I'll come with you. I just wasn't sure you wanted me to."

"I want you," I whispered. I always wanted Beau.

I waited outside while Beau went in to pay and made up an excuse to tell Lincoln. We were walking to the car when he asked, "Who was that on the phone?"

"Just an old friend," I replied. Why stress him out

with the possibility of a move to Texas if it might not happen? Which obviously was just me trying to make myself feel better.

I drove us home, and we showered together. When we were in bed and I was buried inside Beau, all I could think of was how right it felt, how much I would miss him if I left…but I was also unsure whether I was strong enough to stay.

CHAPTER THIRTY

Beau

I always wanted to be just like Beau. ~ Love, Kenny

"How do I look?" Kenny asked as we stood in front of the full-length mirror in his bedroom, me straightening his collar. I'd be lying if I didn't admit my stomach was in knots. Yes, Kenny was twenty years old, but I was about to take him on his first date. I was scared to death I'd fuck it up, or she would hurt him. There wasn't anything in the world more important to me than protecting Kenny.

But he was a grown man. Of course he would want to start dating.

"You look great," I finally replied just as Ash said, "It's stiff for a first date."

I tossed him a glance and threw my hands up in frustration. Ash ignored me, pushing off Kenny's bed and heading to the closet. "I'm not saying you don't look good. You're handsome as hell. Better-looking than this guy." He pointed at me, making Kenny laugh. "I just... We're going bowling. I've never seen you in a collared shirt like that. This girl, she likes you for who you are. She'd have to be crazy not to, so I think you should go more relaxed."

I watched Ash as he poked around in Kenny's closet. A moment later he pulled out a blue Henley. "This'll go well with your eyes." He walked over and handed it to Kenny, and my damn heart had crawled up into my throat. "I can't tell you how many times girls have told me how much they like my eyes when I wear colors that make them pop. You wear this, and she'll be putty in your hands."

"Huh?" Kenny asked.

"She'll think you look real nice," I cut Ash off, but really it just gave me something to focus on. I'd known I'd fallen for Ash already, but in that moment, it was like watching him hold my heart in his hand. He was caring for my brother, and there were no words for what that did to me.

"What he said." Ash winked at me.

Kenny tugged off the shirt I'd chosen and pulled Ash's choice on. Ash ran his hands down Kenny's chest, straightening his shirt out, then pushed his fingers through Kenny's hair, mussing it up. "Girls dig messy hair."

"Have you had lots of girlfriends, Ash?" Kenny asked, and it felt like the question sucked the air straight out of my lungs. It was a silly response. There was nothing wrong with Ash having been with women before me. Again, he very well could have been bi…but it was the fact that he didn't identify that way. That he knew himself to be a gay man who had only been with women because he'd felt like he had no choice. He'd been lying to himself.

It made me ache for him. It made me hurt for the women too.

"Umm." Ash scratched his head, looking away from Kenny. It was obvious he hadn't expected the question. "I wouldn't say a lot…"

"Do you have a girlfriend now? Does she care that you're always with Beau?"

My throat burned with the taste of bile as I turned, walked over to the window, and looked out.

"Um…no. I don't have a girlfriend, and I would never let anyone tell me how much time I could spend with Beau. He's my best friend."

It was unbelievable how sometimes words could both build you up and tear you down. This was Ashton fucking Carmichael, saying I meant something to him, that he would put me first, but at the same time, he was denying an intimate part of us. It wasn't something new to me. I'd known the score, and I hadn't been lying when I said I wouldn't rush him. Everyone had the right to come out in their own way and time, but that didn't mean it didn't hurt. This was my family. We were safe here.

"Your brother is stuck with me," Ash added, and I could tell by his voice that he'd turned to face me, spoken to my back.

So I took a couple of deep breaths and turned back around. "There's no exchange policy?" I teased.

"Oh, come on, Campbell. You know I'm priceless."

"I wouldn't go that far." But truthfully I would. Ash had the power to entrance people, to make them feel special, for them to sit back in awe of him.

"I'm crushed."

"Ugh. Fine. You're priceless. Whatever." I rolled my eyes playfully and earned a laugh from Kenny.

"You make Beau smile more than he used to," Kenny told him. I shoved my hands in my pockets. So much for the bro-code.

"Do I now? That's very interesting."

"Asshole." I shook my head.

"Eh. I guess he makes me smile more too," Ash replied, and damn it all to hell if I didn't smile again.

THE NIGHT GOT more interesting from there. Lori's parents damn near shot through the roof when they realized Ashton Carmichael was accompanying their daughter on her date with Kenny. Being a firefighter was a cool job, but it didn't hold a candle to ex-pro football player.

It took us nearly an hour to get out of their house. Thankfully, they hadn't asked *why* Ash had come along, so we didn't have to lie.

The four of us went to dinner first. Kenny and Lori were sweet as hell. It amazed me seeing my brother and all he'd accomplished. He'd never let his disability hold him down, whether it was school, college, sports—life.

He was a whole lot braver than me...than anyone else I knew.

After dinner I drove us over to the bowling alley. Billiards was our first stop. We decided to play teams—Ash and Kenny against Lori and me. She was a fucking pool shark and could have beaten anyone there without my help.

"Good game!" Kenny wrapped his arms around her

in a tight hug. I stood back as Ash caught my eye and winked. The fucker had my baseball cap on, but so far it had helped with no one recognizing him. Or hell, maybe they just didn't give a shit.

He walked over, put his cue up, then brushed his fingers with mine before jerking back. "Nice game, Campbell."

I shrugged. "I didn't do much."

"I'm sorry," he added softly before looking over his shoulder.

I didn't need him to tell me what he was sorry for, which of course made guilt thicken my blood. "You don't have to be sorry. We're good."

But there was a part of me that wanted more, that wanted everything with him, and when Ash's eyes darted away, when he shoved his hands in his pockets, I knew it was eating him alive more than it was me. "Ash...we're good. You're good."

We went from billiards to bowling. The heaviness of some parts of the evening lifted, and we laughed. There was nothing in the world like laughing with Ash.

For a little while, I pretended that things were different, that I could claim him as mine, and I thought maybe Ash was doing the same.

CHAPTER THIRTY-ONE

Ashton

*Ashton Carmichael plays with a whole lot of heart,
only I'm not sure if he always realizes it.*

IT HAD BEEN a few days since our double date under the guise of two dudes playing chauffeurs. It wasn't my proudest moment, lying to Kenny for the second time. The whole night I'd wondered what it would be like to reach out and hold Beau's hand the way Kenny held Lori's. To claim Beau as my own. What was the worst that could happen? Some asshole might talk shit, but if they were that kind of person, why did I care in the first place?

But then I thought about football…the shit I'd heard in locker rooms, the lies I'd had to tell myself for years…the possibility of getting my career back and proving everyone wrong about me, that I wasn't some fuckup who put dumb shit ahead of my career. That I took football seriously. That I was worthy.

Of course that scared me deeper into the closet again. I wanted to prove everyone wrong, even if it was only for one more season before I left on my own terms. But did getting football back mean losing Beau?

Lori's parents hadn't asked a word. No one had taken a second glance at us all night. Maybe we could do this. Maybe Beau and I could keep going the way we were. I could go back for a year, prove the headlines about me wrong, and then live openly with Beau.

Okay, so maybe I was imagining a nonexistent fairy tale where two men rode off into the sunset together, but still.

Grumbling at myself, I went into my old room, which I'd turned into exercise space, and worked out. I'd jogged with Beau that morning, but ever since the phone call from my agent, I'd been hitting it extra hard.

When I felt like my muscles might give out on me, I showered, then headed to a meeting I'd scheduled. My brain turned to mush while I talked and signed papers for two hours, which obviously meant I needed a chocolate éclair. I mean, I worked out twice already. I deserved it.

"Hey, Beth," I said to Beau's mom as she put baked goods into the glass case by the register.

"Hey, you." She leaned over the counter and kissed

my cheek, the way she would have with Kenny or Beau.

I closed my eyes, savored the feel of her. This woman who treated me like her son...who loved her boys and accepted them.

"Beau's working, right?" she asked while handing me my treat. She just might have been one of my favorite people in the world.

"Yeah, he is. Where's Kenny?"

"He'll be here in a minute. He's walking down from the college." Fever Falls Community College was a few miles up the street, which made it convenient for them. A couple of customers came in, and she told me, "You can sit down for a bit."

I did while waiting for her to finish, studying the pinks and browns she'd decorated with. A few minutes later the bakery was empty again, and she sat with me at the small, circular table.

I felt her eyes on me as I finished eating. For some reason, I couldn't make myself look at her, afraid of what I'd see, of what I might show her. There was a heaviness to the moment that felt different from any of the other times I'd been with her.

"I know it might sound strange, but I'd like to thank you."

I wiped my fingers on a napkin and frowned.

"Thank me?" She had nothing to thank me for.

"Yeah. You've brought a light into my boys' lives—both of them—that had been missing. Kenny has always had Beau. That's never been a question, but...well, I'm sure it's different having your brother than someone you don't feel *has* to be there. You make Kenny feel special, like he belongs to something outside of his family or events that are all tied back to having Down syndrome. Football, the center, his friendships are all in his life because of that. And you're not. You're there because you just want to be, and I'm not sure if you know how special that is."

My tongue felt like it swelled, preventing me from speaking. It was one thing to hear something like that from Beau, but to hear it from his mom? There were no words to describe what that meant to me. I opened my mouth to try and find some, but she shook her head, stopping me.

"Let me finish first because I feel like this part might be even harder for you than the other. I don't know if you see just what you've done for Beau. It's hard to put into words really. Well, I guess I could take a page of your book and say Beau's always been a bit of a Cranky Campbell."

I couldn't help but smile at that.

"I mean, he has his career that he loves. He has me and Kenny, his friends, and football, but nothing that was really just *his*, if that makes sense. Something or someone he wanted just for himself because it made him happy. This friendship with you is something Beau wants for himself, something that makes him happy on a different level, and I'll never be able to thank you enough for that."

I shifted, uncomfortable in my skin, with the praise. I appreciated what she said, but I didn't want to be thanked for being Beau's friend. I didn't deserve that kind of praise. "You don't have anything to thank me for. I spend time with them both because they make me feel good too. Kenny's smile could light up the whole damn world, and Beau…" I closed my eyes, took a couple of deep breaths. "I…I think you know we're more than just friends." It was the first time in my life I'd admitted anything like that, except to Beau.

"I thought maybe you were, but I wasn't going to pry. It's your business—yours and Beau's."

"I'm in love with him, but I don't…" My eyes started to water, right fucking there in the middle of the bakery. "Shit. Why is this so hard?"

Beth got up, locked the door, closed the blinds, and flipped the OPEN side around.

She knelt in front of me. "You don't have to say anything you don't want to say."

But I did, I wanted to. Wanted to let the words free, at least to someone. To family. "I don't know why this is so fucking hard for me." I wiped my eyes on the back of my hand. "I'm in love with him, but I can't... I'm not..."

"Hey." She clasped my chin softly, angling my head so I looked at her. "I'll tell you the same thing I told Beau when he came out to me. I love you. You're perfect the way you are. If anyone doesn't understand that, fuck them. You have nothing to be ashamed of, but this is also your show, your life. You decide when and how, okay?"

I wrapped my arms around her, pulled her to me, fisted my hands in her shirt, and just breathed...breathed in a way I was only able to do around Beau, because it was in those moments that I was completely free.

We held each other until I stopped crying, until I wiped my eyes and made a joke so she'd laugh. We stood, nodded at each other before she hugged me again, and just like that, I knew I was one hundred percent accepted by her, but that she wouldn't mention it again unless I let her know it was okay.

I excused myself to the bathroom while she opened the bakery back up. I splashed water on my face, smiled at myself in the mirror, the weight on my shoulders feeling lighter than it had in years.

I'd told someone other than Beau, and it had been okay.

This sort of high took me over, swam in my bones, built me up. I'd told someone, and it had been…incredible.

A smile still curved my lips when I came out of the restroom. When I saw Kenny, my body became lighter, felt like I was floating, like I was invincible. I wanted to let him in, to share with him who I was the way I'd done with Beth.

"Ash!" He damn near glowed when he saw me.

I hugged him, and the three of us chatted for a few minutes before I nodded outside. "You wanna go for a walk with me, or what?" I asked.

"Yeah. I'd love to!"

We walked down the street and around the corner toward the park. When we passed the firehouse, I thought of Beau. One of the engines was gone. Was he on it? Was he off risking his life and being a hero while I sat here thinking it was a big deal to tell his accepting family I was gay? It felt like such a small thing when I compared it to something like that. I knew it wasn't—not really. It was cutting yourself open in one of the most intimate ways.

"So...I have something to admit to you," I told Kenny as we went into the park, heading straight for the picnic table Beau and I shared more than once.

Kenny frowned. "Is everything okay?"

"Yeah, K-man. It's good. It's just...well, I lied to you about something, and I'm feeling terrible about it."

"It's okay, Ash. I'm sure you had a good reason."

His unwavering support and forgiveness warmed my soul. "I wouldn't say that quite yet. You don't know what I did, and I have a habit of fucking up big-time." I'd done it a lot over the years.

"I trust you."

Reaching over, I wrapped an arm around Kenny and pulled him in for a half hug. We sat at the table, my knee bouncing up and down like crazy before I forced myself to look at him, to own the truth, and said, "Remember when you asked me if Beau was my boyfriend?"

He frowned again, dimples deepening in his face. "Yeah."

"Well, when I said no to you...I lied. Beau is..." My boyfriend, my lover. None of them carried enough meat to them. They didn't feel strong enough. "We're together, and I love him."

"Okay... That makes me happy. I want you and

Beau to be together. I want you for a brother. But I don't understand why you would lie about it."

No, he wouldn't, because he was so open, so honest. I could learn a lot from him. "It's tough to explain. Things aren't always simple."

"But you love him. Why can't that be simple?"

I ran a hand over my face, unsure of how to answer. "It should be. I wish it was. But this is new for me, and I'm still trying to work through it."

"But you love Beau and he loves you?" Kenny asked.

"Yeah, I think so. I know how I feel." Beau had said he felt the same.

"Then I still don't understand why it's not that simple."

A million different replies ran through my head, but they were all excuses. In the end, all I could give him was the truth. "I don't either, K-man. But I'm trying, and until then, I need you to do me a favor and keep it a secret. I didn't want to lie to you about it anymore. It's not fair to you or Beau, but I'm not...I'm not ready for anyone else to know."

"When will you be?"

"I'm not sure."

"Okay." Kenny grinned. "I can keep a secret. And I have a new brother!" His joy radiated from him, blinding me. I tried to keep up, but I couldn't. If somehow we could contain Kenny's passion for the world, everything would be okay.

Right then, everything felt better than okay—it felt perfect.

"Can you keep one more secret for me? I had a meeting today I want to tell you about," I asked him, and when he nodded, I leaned forward and told him.

CHAPTER THIRTY-TWO

Beau

Beau is in love! ~ Love, Kenny

MY HANDS TIGHTENED on the steering wheel. My stomach rolled over and over, and for a moment, I thought I might have to pull over and vomit.

I'd just finished my shower after work when I'd gotten the call, and since then it felt as if I lived in some sort of parallel dimension. Like I was floating, flying, dizzy, and yeah, strangely sick too.

I was going to fucking kill him.

Jesus, I fucking loved him.

I hardly had the truck parked in his driveway before I jumped out, engine off but keys inside. I never knocked anymore, and he never locked the door, so after skipping stairs to get onto the porch, I shoved the door open and stepped inside.

Ash sat on the gray couch, his hair wet as though he'd just gotten out of the shower, wearing a pair of jeans and a tee and my damn hat backward on his head. His legs were spread, the television remote on his lap. He looked up at me, his blue eyes snagging on mine…and grinned.

"You bought a fucking football field for me, Ash."

"Who says it was me? From what I heard, it was an anonymous sale."

I took a step closer, then another and another. "You bought a football field for me, Ash." My heart pounded in my ears, making everything sound like an echo.

"So? I also came out to Kenny and your mom today too. They know you're head over heels for me."

I knew he expected me to make some kind of comment about him being the one who was crazy about me, but I didn't. I couldn't because what he said was true. Not because he'd bought the field, but because he was Ash…my Ash, and he probably always had been. "You're right…I am. You really told them?"

Another step, then another and another.

"I did." He nodded. "And it wasn't so hard. They were okay with it. That may sound stupid, because they love you and I know they're not bigots, but—"

"It doesn't sound stupid. It sounds human." Whether we wanted to admit it or not, we all wanted to be accepted, to be loved for who we were. And everyone was scared of not being just that.

Suddenly, I could breathe. It was as if I was caught up in a whirlwind of Ash...this beautiful fucking man who seemed to have all the confidence in the world, but was sweet and vulnerable. And yeah, sexy as hell, but what really got me was his heart. "Why would you do that? It wasn't cheap. I can pay you back, but—"

"Shut up, Campbell. I don't want your money."

"What do you want?" He didn't speak until I stood right in front of him, between his spread thighs.

"You."

"You had me before this. You've always had me, you fucker. From the moment you kissed me on that dock, you've had me."

"Things might not always be easy with me. There might be...obstacles." Ash leaned forward and ran his hands up the back of my thighs until they rested on my ass.

"I don't want easy."

"What do you want?" he asked, the same question I'd asked him.

"You. I feel you down to my bones, Ash." I went to my knees, and we kissed. Ash's hand cupped my cheek, his other sliding down to my neck as I tangled my hands in his hair.

I was burning from the inside out. My heart and brain felt chaotic, wild with love and lust and need, but also calm, at ease, because he was there and he soothed me. Ash wanted me, had chosen me. He loved me.

Our teeth clashed, tongues tangled, hands grabbed and clutched and pulled. When I couldn't take it anymore, I sat back, ass on my heels, and ripped my shirt over my head. I took care of his next, pulling my hat off him with it before tossing them both. "Lean back," I told him.

Ash did, sank into the plush fabric as I worked open his button and zipper. He lifted his hips, and I took off his pants and boxer trunks. His cock was swollen, leaking on his stomach. His balls heavy and tight. When I leaned in and nuzzled them, inhaled his scent, Ash groaned while fisting my hair.

"Christ, what you fucking do to me," Ash said as he sank lower. I took the head of his cock into my mouth, sucked him, nursed his crown before taking him deep. His hips moved, undulated, his ass hanging off the edge of the couch.

I let my fingers dance over his hip bones, over his thighs, down beneath his balls, until I teased his crack, testing the water.

Ash's hand tightened in my hair. He tugged at it

until his cock slipped out of my mouth and I looked up at him…and he nodded, so damn much vulnerability in his eyes that burrowed inside me, bonded us together on a deeper level.

"You sure?" I asked. "I don't need it."

"Not your cock…I'm not ready for that, but your finger, yes. I wanna try it with you."

"Can I eat you out first? It's fan-fucking-tastic. I know you'll like it."

"Of course you can. What kind of guy do you think I am? If you're going to finger-fuck me, you better lick me first."

I chuckled. Fucking Ash. "Turn over. Kneel on the floor with one leg on the couch."

Scooting back, I got out of his way, shoving the coffee table away too. Ash took a deep breath…then just went for it.

"I checked it out in the mirror, and it's a good hole, Campbell. You'll like it, but this is still weird as fuck. I've never had someone look at my asshole before."

My dick throbbed. "You looked at your hole with a mirror? Did you finger yourself?"

"Nope, saved that for you. Treat me well."

"I think that might be one of the sweetest things you've ever said to me."

"Really?" He looked over his shoulder at me and cocked his brows.

"The way to a man's heart is through your asshole."

"Just mine?"

"For me."

I ran my hand over the curve of his ass. Goose bumps pebbled over his skin. "Don't be nervous," I whispered as I used my thumbs to spread his cheeks, and looked at the tight, pink ring between them. "Fuck, baby. So goddamn pretty. I might become addicted to it."

I leaned forward, and before Ash could reply, flicked my tongue over his hole. "Just what I thought. Addicting."

"Do it again."

I rasped my tongue over him again. He tasted like soap and musk, heady and rich, going straight to my brain. The more I licked and probed, the more relaxed he became. Soon, Ash was whimpering, pushing back against my face, and riding the couch.

"Fuck, that feels good. Why in the hell didn't anyone tell me?"

"It'll get even better." I sucked my finger, got it nice and wet, then pushed at his rim. Slowly, his body opened for me, sucked me in, and I watched, mesmerized. I took my time, let him adjust, savored every sound, every groan and sigh and whisper of my name.

I added my tongue, licking him and working his ass with my finger at the same time. I felt his body relax around me, could see the difference in how he writhed beneath me. "Looks like I might owe you a new couch too. Gonna make you come all over it."

"Fuck, I could. I so fucking could."

Leaning over him, my chest to his back, finger still up his ass, I whispered, "But I want you inside me. Do you want inside me, Ash?"

"Fuck yes." Then we were pulling away frantically. Ash reached for my pants, but I pushed him down on the couch.

"Stay."

"Bossy motherfucker, aren't you?"

"I can be." I stripped as I went to the bedroom, grabbed the lube and a condom. He was stroking his cock when I got back to the living room. "Save that for my ass."

"I'm ready for you."

I didn't know why I wanted him to fuck me on the couch, why I wanted to ride him there.

Standing beside him, I ripped open the condom wrapper, rolled it down his erection, then lubed his rod and my hole.

"Fuck, that's hot, seeing you get yourself ready for me."

"I'm glad you like it." I winked, threw a leg over him, and straddled his lap. I pushed up on my knees, then grabbed his cock, angled it at my hole...and sank down. I drove us both crazy—a slow, sweet torture as I took my time. I closed my eyes at the stretch, rocked into it, savored the feel of Ash's blunt nails as they dug into my hips.

"Fuck. You are so goddamn hot and tight."

Picking up the pace, I rose and lowered myself, over and over and over again, treasuring the feel of Ash inside me. "You fill me so fucking good."

When I leaned over and kissed him, riding his dick, Ash whimpered into my mouth. I couldn't help but smile against his lips. I fucking loved driving Ashton Carmichael out of his mind.

"Goddamn, you're good at this." He wrapped his arms around me, and I squeezed, concentrated on tightening myself around him even more, still unable to believe this was us, that we'd made it to this place. Ashton fucking Carmichael was mine, and I loved him.

His hands slid down my body until he grabbed my ass, digging his nails into me there too and working with me to ride him.

My balls tightened, my vision went blurry, and it felt like my whole body was oversensitive. "Fuck, you're hitting me right where I want you."

His dick continued to hit me just right until my body tensed, white-hot sparks exploding in my gut. "Fuck, I'm gonna come."

He reached for my cock, but I swatted him away, wanted him to see what he did to me, that he could make me blow my load all over him with just his dick in my ass.

I slammed down on him, lifted and sat again. An electrical storm went off behind my eyelids. I bucked against him as my orgasm damn near blew me apart. When I opened my eyes and saw my come hanging from his lip, I shot a second time, landing on his chest and neck, while our eyes held.

When Ash licked his lip? It was all fucking over for me, and I crumbled, broke into a million pieces that all had his name on them.

"Beau… Christ, I want to stay inside you for the rest of my life, but I also might die if I don't come."

"Then do it."

I leaned in, bit his neck as I felt his whole body go rigid beneath me. His cock jerked in my hole, and he groaned before whispering my name over and over again. His voice cracked, emotion seeping through the fissures in his words.

Ash's arms tightened around me, his face against my chest. "Fuck, Campbell...this is the way it's supposed to be, isn't it? Me and you?"

"Yeah." I kissed his forehead, his temple. "It is. Just us."

"You got me all choked up and shit," he said with a chuckle.

There was a throw slung over the back of the couch. I grabbed it and laid it on the cushions, and the two of us went down on top of it. His cock fell out, softening, come probably leaking all over him and the blanket, but we didn't care. "You bought me a fucking football field, Ash." I pushed his hair off his forehead.

"It's not a big deal. I wanted you to have one to coach on."

"Us," I replied.

"Us, what?"

"Wanted us to have one to coach on. Together."

He closed his eyes, didn't speak, and then buried his face in my neck. I held him while he silently worked through all the things going on in his head and whatever it was he was keeping from me.

CHAPTER THIRTY-THREE

Ashton

Ashton Carmichael takes a lot of flak for some of his recent off-field antics, but there's a solid guy behind the bravado.

"HEY, BUDDY. HOW'S it going?" Wyatt asked when I answered his call.

"Pretty good, man. What's up?" It was Saturday. It had been a couple of weeks since I'd purchased the field for Beau and his team. Things had been...well, sort of a whirlwind since then. The sale had been organized through my lawyer and was anonymous, which really made the town talk. They'd all been trying to figure out who had purchased the land and the reasons behind it. I didn't know why, but I hadn't expected the talk.

Beau did what he did and played it off well, claiming he didn't know who bought it, that he was just honored someone had.

We weren't stupid, though. We knew people were

tossing around my name, especially considering I coached with him. The more I thought about it, the more I wasn't sure why I had done it anonymously anyway. Why the fuck couldn't I buy a damn football field for a team I was coaching?

Because I'd wanted it in Beau's name. I'd wanted it to be *his*, and I was afraid that would come with too many questions.

"You there?" Wyatt asked, making me realize he'd been speaking to me while I was daydreaming.

"Sorry, you're just boring," I teased, and Wyatt laughed.

"You've always been a sarcastic motherfucker. Anyway, Holly's out of town tonight. She's visiting her parents. I thought maybe you'd want to grab a beer or something?"

"I can't, actually. Beau and I are…working on some remodeling around my house." *Liar…I'm such a fucking liar.* Why in the hell was this so goddamned hard for me?

"You need any help?" Wyatt asked.

Fuck. I should have seen that one coming. I didn't even know if Beau and I had plans that night, but I figured we did since we were always together. I wanted to be with him. Cheesy or not, I always wanted to be with him. We were in that gooey honeymoon phase I teased many of my friends about in the past. "Shit. It's Saturday, right? I forgot, we're going to his mom's for dinner tonight."

So if anyone couldn't tell, I was now the biggest liar in liar town.

"Okay… Well, what about Thanksgiving next week? I wasn't sure if you had plans, but Holly and I were thinking you might want to come over. We have quite the feast. Shannon and a few other people will be there."

Fuck. I obviously had plans with Beau on Thanksgiving. When I didn't reply, Wyatt sighed. "Ash…you know you're my friend, right? Nothing else matters. If there's something you want to share with me, you can. It won't change anything."

My heart began to thud, and my palms got sweaty. He knew. Of course he fucking knew. How could he not? Everyone probably fucking knew. We were together all the damn time.

I took a couple of deep breaths. The urge to hang up the phone was there. My conversation with my agent echoed, together with the ringing in my ears.

It was a ridiculous response. Logically, I knew that, but I didn't know how to get around the way it made me feel.

"I…" He'd said it was okay… Beth knew…Kenny

knew... I wanted people to know Beau was mine. I sort of wanted to be growly about Beau belonging to me. I wanted people to know I belonged to him too. This was Wyatt. He'd been my best friend. I should be able to do this.

"Beau is welcome too, ya know? Or not... I don't want to assume, but everyone sees you guys together all the time, and—"

"Yes," I blurted out.

"Yes what?"

"What you're thinking...about us. Yes." My legs gave out, and I collapsed onto the couch, my knee bobbing up and down like crazy.

"Cool. I don't give a shit who you fuck, Carmichael. I'm not going to pretend I'm not shocked, but I guess it sort of makes sense. You guys always seemed to be in on something no one else was."

I smiled at him thinking that about us and breathed a sigh of relief. He didn't care. Wyatt didn't care. "Not everyone is like that."

"Then those people don't matter."

His words were true. I knew that in theory, but yeah, that emotional stuff still had me a bit fucked up. "There might be a team interested in me next year. I don't know for sure, but...this could complicate things. No one knows. You can't say anything." Just saying those words had lifted some of the weight off my chest. It felt good to speak them—both about Beau and the team.

"Holy shit. That's fantastic. Will make things difficult with you and Beau, though. What does he say?"

Another silence from me.

"You fucking dumbshit. He doesn't know?"

"I'm going to tell him. I just didn't want to do it until I knew it was a real possibility…and until I knew what I would do."

"What do you mean, what you would do? You would give up pro-ball for him?" There was such shock in his voice that I felt it in my soul. This was football—professional football. It had always been the most important thing in my world. It was who I was.

"I don't… Fuck, I don't know." When I heard a door slam, I pushed off the couch. "Listen, I gotta go. Beau is here. I'm going to tell him, okay? And thank you…for being okay with this."

"Jesus, did you really think I wouldn't be?"

I was still adjusting to being okay with it myself. "I gotta go, Wy. I'll talk to you soon and…I appreciate the invite for Thanksgiving, but we'll be at Beth's."

"You're welcome, man."

We hung up just as Beau came inside.

"What's—"

"I told Wyatt," I interrupted him. "About us." A sort of high, giddy feeling washed through me at the admission. It had been...surprisingly easy to say. Strangely, much easier than when I'd told Beth or Kenny. It was as if the bubble Beau and I lived in together was expanding, fitting more people inside. Maybe it could stretch around my whole life, even football.

"How did it go?" Beau asked, concern in his eyes.

"He knew before I told him." Everyone likely did. "And...he didn't care."

Beau smiled, wrapped an arm around me, and gave me a hug. "No, I didn't think he would. But I'm proud of you."

The crazy thing was, I was proud of me as well. "I guess that means we should celebrate tonight. What do you want to do?"

He tensed up briefly and pulled back. "It's Saturgay... We're going to Fever. I missed the last one. Linc will kick my ass if I'm not there."

Well, shit. I'd forgotten about Saturgay when I'd told Wyatt I couldn't go out.

"I could stay home. I—"

"No, that's fucking dumb. You're not staying home,

Campbell."

"You could go with us... The guys won't say anything. Wear my cap. Most people there won't even recognize you, but if they did, they wouldn't say anything. They won't out you."

I opened my mouth to tell him I couldn't go, that I'd just stay home, but then...fuck, I wanted to go. I wanted that experience with Beau. I wanted to experience it myself. After all these years, I deserved to go to a gay bar with my boyfriend, didn't I? "Let's do it."

"You don't have to," he said, but the ear-to-ear smile on his face told me he liked the idea.

"I want to." I hadn't realized how badly I did, but I fucking *wanted* it. To be a normal couple, out with Beau.

He grabbed me, pulled me close, grinded against me a little, making my dick take notice. "Fuck, I love you."

"I love you too, Cranky Campbell."

"I'm not cranky anymore, remember?"

"Guess you just needed me."

He rolled his eyes, pushing me down onto the couch. We celebrated with a blowjob. It wasn't necessary, but hey, he liked sucking my dick, and I sure as hell liked being in his mouth. I wasn't going to deny either of us the pleasure of the experience.

Afterward we cooked shitty dinner together and ate.

We showered and dressed. I wore a hoodie, jeans, and Beau's hat—forward, as if any of it made a difference. He didn't mention it, though, because that wasn't Beau.

I sure as shit admired him in the jeans that hugged his ass and a black button-up shirt with the sleeves rolled up to his elbows.

We were silent for most of the drive to Fever. When we parked in a lot down the street, Beau killed the engine. "You nervous?" he asked.

"Yeah…and I fucking hate that I am. It makes me feel weak."

"You're not weak, Ash. This is something deeply personal. We all deal and accept and come to terms in our own way. There are no rules to being gay or coming out or how you realize it or accept it. Life would be a whole lot easier if there were. It's real easy for those outside of a situation to judge what a person should do, how they should feel or how they should handle it. Your story is yours. No one else's. No one has your experiences, and no one needs to understand it but you…and maybe me."

I chuckled, and he reached out and brushed his thumb against my cheek. "You're here, with me. That's all I care about. Me and you, Ash."

"Me and you, Campbell."

"I told Linc we'll be here. He's telling the guys. They don't know all the details, but no one will question you. Straight men can go to gay bars."

I looked over at him, the dome light dancing along his features. "Do straight guys want to eat their boyfriend's ass after going to a gay club?"

He smiled, which made me smile because I loved seeing him happy.

"No, but I hope you do."

"I do."

For a moment, I almost leaned forward and kissed him, but I made myself stop.

"This is your night, Ash. You lead and I'll follow."

THE NIGHT WENT by in stages.

The loud beat of the bass vibrating my chest. Seeing men dancing and kissing and just...*being*. The nerves. The jealousy. Then the nerves again.

Seeing Lincoln, Sawyer, and Camden. Meeting Rush. Holy fuck, Beau had gorgeous friends. Not as sexy as Beau was, but if I wasn't so confident, I might be slightly worried.

Lincoln knew. There wasn't a doubt in my mind

about that, but then I figured he'd known for a while. The other three...they must have figured it out, but they were still looking at me confused, like they couldn't make sense of me. Welcome to the fucking club. I was twenty-eight and couldn't understand myself either.

Rush came around first. He apparently liked football. We also talked some about dirt bikes and Supercross. He promised to take me riding sometime. I didn't know if he did it because he wanted to hang out with me or because of Beau, but I appreciated it. Rush was in professional sports...and he was out. If he could do it, why couldn't I?

There was a part of me that considered drinking one of everything to help myself relax, but I didn't need that, I didn't want it. Tonight was supposed to be about me...me and Beau.

We were in a back corner. It took me a few minutes to notice Beau, Lincoln, Rush, Sawyer, and Camden were almost in a circle around me, like they were protecting me...like they had my back.

The more we talked and laughed, the more I liked them. The more I enjoyed their company, the more I loosened up. Eventually, I wasn't in a gay bar listening to pop music with my boyfriend's friends. I was just in a bar, having fun with my boyfriend and our friends.

And it felt good...it felt right. I wanted to hold on to it with both hands, squeeze it tight, live it.

Beau stumbled forward when a guy accidentally ran into him. He had white-blond hair, eyeliner, and a gorgeous smile. "Sorry...oh...hey." He grinned up at Beau, and I recognized the smile. "That was an accident, but I can't say I'm sorry for it. Holy shit, you're sexy."

Beau laughed it off, apparently not sensing the rapid beat of my heart. The guy was just...so fucking free. He saw Beau, wanted him, and went for it. Beau would never have to hide with a guy like that.

"Thanks, but I have a boyfriend." Beau winked at him.

"He can join too," Blondy replied.

"Why don't you come dance with me? I'm better-looking than he is anyway," Camden told him. The guy obviously wasn't picky, and shrugged, disappearing through the crowd with Camden.

I couldn't say exactly what it was that made me do it—jealousy, pride, the fact that I'd told three people and it had gone well all three times, or just plain want, but I reached out, hooked my finger through the belt loop of Beau's jeans, and tugged him toward me.

"What are you doing?"

"Shh," I replied. I leaned against the wall, and he

stood between my legs. He was technically blocking me from prying eyes, but I still felt a surge of adrenaline at touching him like this in public. "I'm holding my boyfriend."

"I think I just swooned," Lincoln said.

"You don't have to do this, Ash. You don't owe me anything."

No, I didn't owe him anything, but I owed it to myself...and I wanted this. Wanted him. *I'm safe here*, I told myself before pushing the cap up on my head so I could kiss him more easily. I nodded, and Beau grinned, reading exactly what I wanted.

"Yeah?"

"Yeah."

He leaned forward and pressed a soft kiss to my lips. It went zero to sixty in no time flat. I felt fucking invincible—like I was flying.

I held on to his hips, and Beau rubbed against me, deepening the kiss. His tongue swept my mouth, and fuck, there was nothing in the world as good as feeling Beau against me.

"Fuck, Ash. Sort of feel like banging on my chest here," Beau said into my neck. "Like I can stand on the bar and scream to everyone that you're mine."

"That might draw attention."

"Can I kiss you again?"

"I'm already trying to figure out what's taking you so long."

His mouth came down hard and fast on mine. The kiss was filled with urgent hunger and need. I suddenly wished we weren't in a bar anymore so I could get on my knees for him. There had never been a time I thought I would feel okay with wanting that, with doing it, but I was. I so fucking was.

Just when I lowered my hands to his ass, a light flashed from the other side of my closed eyes.

"What the fuck?" Lincoln said.

"Give me that shit," Rush added. And I knew, I fucking knew without opening my eyes, what was happening. Beau jerked away from me.

There was a group of men, all standing around with cameras and phones aimed at me, at us, taking photos, recording. Not guys I would have seen here any other night, but reporters.

Rush grabbed one of them, pulled the camera from his hands. All hell broke loose after that—people looking, taking their own pictures, because they knew something was going on. Shoving their way closer.

"Let's go," Beau said, but I was already moving with him through the people. I looked back to see Rush,

Sawyer, Lincoln, and Camden trying to head people off.

It didn't matter, though. I knew it fucking didn't. Bile rose in my throat, and my vision swam, but I didn't know if it was because I'd been caught, or because of my reaction to it. It shouldn't matter. Why the fuck did it matter?

The second I burst from the door of the club and onto the sidewalk, there were more cameras, mics shoved in my face.

"Ashton Carmichael, are you gay?"

"What were you doing in a gay bar?"

"Do you have a boyfriend?"

"Have you been hiding him your whole career?"

"Does this have anything to do with why you left football?"

"What about the purchase of the field?"

"Get the fuck out of his face!" Beau growled as we pushed our way through the crowd.

We ran to his truck, were silent the whole drive. My stomach clenched, was so damn tight, I knew I could lose it any second. My head throbbed, my heart too. They knew...everyone knew. It would be all over the news in no time.

"Shit, I'm sorry. I'm so fucking sorry, Ash," Beau said when we pulled up at my house.

Before I could reply, my phone started to ring. It was my agent. "I can't...I can't do this right now."

The call ended, and then the phone began ringing again immediately.

"Yeah, whatever you need." Beau reached for me, but I shoved the door open and got out of the truck.

My phone didn't stop, and suddenly it was all I could hear—my phone, my agent, the questions, twisting in a powerful cyclone in my brain.

"Ash?" Beau asked.

"I just... I need some space. I need to figure this out."

Without another word, I walked away. I hardly made it to the toilet before I emptied my stomach, vomiting until there was nothing left.

I fell against the bathroom wall just as my phone started ringing again.

I didn't get a chance to say anything before I heard, "What the fuck were you thinking?"

I was thinking that for once I could be me, that maybe, just maybe, that would be enough...and now it was all over.

CHAPTER THIRTY-FOUR

Beau

Beau says I can accomplish anything. He makes me believe it. ~ Love, Kenny

ASHTON CARMICHAEL'S SECRET GAY LOVER!

DOES ASHTON CARMICHAEL PLAY FOR THE *OTHER* TEAM?

FOOTBALL'S EX-BAD-BOY SWITCHING TO GAY ORGIES?

PLAY-ACTION ASS—I MEAN *PASS*

I SLAMMED MY laptop closed, tired of all the headlines. Sharp pains stabbed my chest when I breathed, and it took everything in me not to throw the computer across the room.

It had been five days since we'd gotten caught at the bar. Five days of my phone ringing like crazy, reporters camped out at my house, at Mom's house.

Five days since I'd heard from Ash.

Fucking Ashton Carmichael. That was the worst. I

could deal with the other shit. I didn't give a fuck what people said about me. I did care what they said about my family, or the harassment they'd been subjected to, and I cared about the fact that Ash had run away. Not just from the situation, but from *me*.

"Fuck." I leaned forward, elbows on my desk, my hands fisted in my hair. My stomach had been in knots for five days. They'd even had to give me time off because my personal shit was bleeding into the job.

It wasn't every day shit like this happened in Fever Falls.

My phone buzzed beside me, making my pulse kick into high speed. My hand jerked forward, fumbling the damn thing, a silent, quite infuriating prayer bouncing around in my head—*please be Ash, please be Ash.*

Kenny: There's no one with cameras at the school today.

Me: Good. Still wait for me to pick you up. I don't want you walking.

Kenny: I'm an adult, Beau. I can take care of myself.

I sighed. Yeah, yeah, he was. Kenny could probably take care of himself better than I could. I didn't see him getting himself into situations like this. Still, I couldn't help but reply with: **Please?**

Kenny: Okay.

Kenny: Have you heard from Ash yet?

My gut clenched tighter, like there was a giant fist around me, squeezing the life out of me.

Me: I'll see you soon.

As I set the phone on the desk, the slide of a key in the lock came from behind me. I didn't turn as it twisted, as the door opened, as someone stepped inside and then closed and locked it again.

"I guess they're starting to see how boring you are. It's clear out there. Not a camera in sight," Linc said as he crossed the room.

"If I'm so boring, why do you always want to be around me? I can't seem to shake you."

"Pity," he replied. "I feel sorry for you, plain and simple." He leaned against my desk, crossed his arms and sighed. "And I might sort of love you. You're my best friend."

"Thanks, Linc. I love you too."

He stepped forward, wrapped his arm around me, and kissed my head. "I'm sorry, sweetie. Men suck."

"I feel like shit…like it's my fault. I just…" I guessed part of me didn't really see that it would be a big deal. So he was gay…who cared? Not that I didn't respect him and understand he hadn't been ready to come out, but the cameras? The headlines? I hadn't seen that coming, and it reminded me that Ash was part of a completely different world than I was.

No one gave a shit in Fever Falls. Outside of here, people cared.

"Why would you feel guilty? You didn't force him to put his dick in your ass. You certainly didn't force him to like it so much...or to fall madly in love with you, or to go to the bar with us. He was there because he loves you and wanted to be with you...and maybe because you're hot and he knew all the guys there would see it." Linc winked, and I rolled my eyes at him.

"I miss him." I shrugged. "And I feel responsible because he was with me. I should have...I don't know, protected him more."

"You aren't responsible for everyone you love in the world. I know you like to pretend you are. Hell, I know I like to pretend you're responsible for me sometimes...but you're not. You're not a superhero."

"Take that back." I smiled, even though I didn't really feel it. Or maybe I did. My friendship with Lincoln always helped, even when he drove me up the damn wall.

"Okay, so you're kind of a superhero, but Ashton is also a grown-ass man who isn't acting like it right now. I get that he's hurt, but does he not think you're hurt too? And he can't fucking let you know where he is? I'm going to kick his ass next time I see him...or you know, have Rush do it for me. Ashton's bigger than me, and those muscles...fuck, those muscles."

Closing my eyes, I dropped my head back, as though that somehow gave me answers. I *was* hurt, worried, and pissed...because I was there. Whatever way the chips fell, I was there, and I would deal with it, while Ash had run away and hidden...and obviously didn't care enough about me to even let me know he was okay.

A FROWN TUGGED at my lips when I saw the group of men in front of the college. The temperature in my body spiked, shot to dangerous levels as I jogged toward them. When I saw a familiar head of perfectly behaved darkbrown hair standing in the center of them, my whole fucking world blew apart. I didn't realize I'd sped up, run faster, and suddenly I was there, shoving one of the reporters away from Kenny. "Leave him the fuck alone!" I shouted, with cameras in my face.

"We're not doing anything wrong; just asking a few questions. Isn't that right, Kenny?" one of the men said. Kenny was speaking so fast, I couldn't understand him, his words all tangled together. "He was telling us about your boyfriend, Ashton Carmichael. How long have the two of you been hiding your relationship? Did you allow all the sexual escapades over the years to keep up the facade?"

"Leave us the fuck alone," I said again as I wrapped my arm around Kenny, trying to walk away.

I hadn't made it but a few feet when I heard, "What about the suggestion that this is all some kind of ploy? Out-of-control football player tormented by being gay? Went to his hometown, coached a special-needs team, donated a football field? You have to admit, it's genius. He cleaned up his act, making himself look like he was a victim of toxic masculinity in football, while he's donating to good causes, settling down with his stable boyfriend and coaching a special-needs team with him? Ashton is a whole lot harder for a team to turn away now, without the league blowing up for being homophobic."

White-hot rage sliced through me.

No. No, no, no, no.

Ash wouldn't do that.

"Fuck off. You don't know him if you think that." It was a stupid thing to say, but I couldn't help myself. I wasn't going to let them twist who Ash was that way. I sure as shit wasn't going to let Kenny feel like Ash had been using him.

"His agent has been talking to the Tigers about him for weeks. Did you know that?" the man asked.

My foot caught on the edge of the sidewalk, and I nearly tripped. My grip on Kenny tightened.

"B-B-B-Beau?" Kenny looked at me, and I shook my head.

"Don't say anything. Don't believe them." We were walking again, but they continued to follow.

"Are you going to stay loyal to him now that you know he could have been using you both for his image?" the reporter, who wore a shirt which read *Glitz & Glam*, said again, and I couldn't say what came over me. Anger short-circuited my brain. My head throbbed. I was pissed at the reporters, the situation…Ash.

Could Ash have been using me?

"He didn't tell you, did he? You didn't know about Texas?"

Before I could stop myself, I'd balled my right hand into a fist and swung. It connected with warm flesh, and he stumbled backward.

Cameras went off, not just from the fucking pricks who'd cornered Kenny, but students from campus. Phones were aimed at me, recording.

Kenny was crying.

"Stay the hell away from us," I ordered, wrapping my arm around Kenny and going for my truck.

Once I got my brother safely into the passenger seat, I jumped to the driver side and fled. A safe distance away, I jerked my truck to the side of the road. "Fuck!" I yelled, banging my open hands against the steering wheel over and over and over again. My hearing was fuzzy, my eyes blurry as rage overtook me.

It wasn't until I heard a soft, "B-B-Beau?" from beside me that I allowed myself to be brought back to reality again. Jesus, what in the hell was I doing? I didn't lose my shit like that, especially around Kenny.

"Shit," I cursed. "I'm sorry, Kenny. I just…"

"I didn't…I didn't…I didn't tell them anything," he replied, fiddling with the corner of his journal.

"No. I'm not mad at you. And even if you did tell them something, that's alright. You don't have to lie for us, okay? I'm not mad at you. I'm never mad at you."

He closed his eyes, took some steadying breaths, and I was so damn proud of him for collecting himself so he could go on.

Kenny nodded and looked down. "Are you mad at Ash?" His speech wasn't as clear as it usually was, but it was better than it had been a few moments ago.

Yes. Actually, I wanted to kill Ash. "That's hard to

explain. Things are complicated."

"Do you think what that guy said was true?"

"No," automatically slipped from between my lips. "He would never do that to you. Are you kidding me? Ash loves hanging out with you. You're his K-man, remember?"

"Is Ash still your boyfriend?"

That question was a whole lot harder to answer. I closed my eyes, took a deep breath. The Tigers were interested in him. There wasn't a part of me that didn't believe that. It was what he'd been hiding from me. Why wouldn't he have told me if it wasn't because he planned to go…and leave me behind.

My gut cramped. My head swam. I didn't know what to think…to say, to *feel*.

"I don't know. Life is…difficult sometimes."

"Don't…don't do that. Don't talk to me like I'm a kid," he replied.

So I didn't. I let my eyes meet his, thought about what had happened and the fact that there were numerous missed calls from me on Ash's phone he hadn't returned. I thought about how we'd spent the last five days…about the team. About what the reporters had said. "No, Kenny. Ash isn't my boyfriend anymore."

CHAPTER THIRTY-FIVE

Ashton

Controversy continues around Ashton Carmichael.

I DIDN'T TURN around at the sound of footsteps behind me, just continued to sit at the end of the dock, my bare feet in the water, making circles.

"Still pouting?" Wyatt asked.

"I appreciate you letting me stay here, but please don't try and understand this. You can't understand it, Wyatt." I didn't know what made me come to his parents' lake house, the one we had the graduation party at, and where I'd kissed Beau what seemed like an eternity ago. And even though it had only been a week, it felt like a lifetime since I'd touched him at all. Since I'd held him, kissed him, laughed with him. Fuck, I loved laughing with my Cranky Campbell.

"You're right. I can't understand. I'm still around to talk if you need me. And if you don't want to talk to me, there's a certain boyfriend of yours that will likely understand."

My heart ached at the mention of Beau. I missed him in my bones, hated myself for walking away from him, but there was just so much shit in my head, I didn't know how to sort through it all. And I knew if I saw him, if I talked to him, all that would matter was how much I wanted him. How I fucking *ached* for him and always had. That was what got us in this situation. There was no doubt in how I felt about Beau, but if I didn't learn to be okay with it, all I would do was continue to hurt both of us.

"Have you seen him?" I asked.

"No. Reporters are still hanging around, though."

"Fuck," I cursed quietly. While I was hiding away, I was leaving Beau to deal with that shit alone. "I need to call him, see him."

"Well, that would likely be easier if you hadn't broken your damn phone."

"Andrea wouldn't stop calling." And I hadn't memorized Beau's number.

"You probably need to talk to her too, Ash," Wyatt scolded.

Yeah…there was a whole lot I needed to do. Most of it started inside myself. "I don't know what's wrong with me…what I'm going to do."

"You don't have to keep yourself locked away from the world to figure that out. You do that with the people who love you. Campbell…he loves you, Ash, and I sure as shit know your dumb ass loves him. Talk to him. Figure it out together."

How did I figure it out with him when I wasn't sure if I deserved him? Or if I could be what he needed me to be? "I'll figure it out, Wy. Thanks."

He sighed. "I brought my laptop over. It's in the kitchen. You might want to take a look at it."

The dock creaked as Wyatt walked away. I closed my eyes, remembered that day ten years ago, the feel of Beau's lips against mine. It'd been like I'd been living in a fog, this muted, clouded world, and hadn't known it. The moment our lips touched, when I felt him, my world had cleared, had been bright and real for the first time. And when I'd run away from him then, I'd gone back to a blurry, foggy existence.

Ten years later and I hadn't grown much, had I? I was still running from who I was…still running from Beau Campbell.

As soon as I heard the wheels of Wyatt's car on the gravel, I shoved to my feet. My heart thudded in my throat as I made my way to the house. If Wyatt brought his laptop, it was important that I saw what was going on. A million possibilities ran through my head, and when I got inside, and Googled my name, bile rose in my throat. It was worse than I could have imagined.

"No...no, no, no, no." My hands fisted. I bit my lip, tasting blood as I looked at the headlines.

> THE HEARTBREAK OF ASHTON CARMICHAEL—THE COST OF BEING GAY AND HIDING YOUR SEXUALITY IN PROFESSIONAL SPORTS
>
> FOOTBALL'S BAD BOY WASN'T REALLY SO BAD AFTER ALL
>
> ASHTON CARMICHAEL'S SECRETS—YEARS OF PAIN, HIS HIDDEN GAY LOVER, AND HIS TICKET BACK TO PROFESSIONAL SPORTS
>
> ASHTON CARMICHAEL—FROM PARTIES AND ORGIES TO COACHING THE DEVELOPMENTALLY DISABLED. HEART OF GOLD OR PLOY TO GET BACK INTO OUR GOOD GRACES?

The last one made my blood run cold. My molars ground together. Beneath the headline was a photograph of Beau punching someone...and a scared and confused Kenny watching.

"Oh, fuck, Campbell. What did I let happen?"

My eyes scanned the article, reading about my life with Beau, with Kenny. The coaching, the field, the possibilities in Texas, and how the journalist thought

Beau and Kenny were a publicity stunt. That Kenny was just a way to make myself look good...that Beau was a way for me to try and get back on a team.

It was as if it didn't compute. Did they really think I would do that? Did they care?

When I saw Andrea's name, my vision blurred. I swiped at my eyes and realized I'd wiped away tears. They'd gone after Kenny...Beau had gotten into a fight.

I'd let it happen.

They'd cheapened the love I had for him, tried to turn it into something ugly when it was the only real thing I'd ever had.

What did you do to stop them? Would they have been able to do that if you'd spoken up?

I squeezed my eyes shut but didn't try to ignore the thoughts swimming around in my head. I didn't get that luxury, not when I'd left Beau to deal with this shit on his own.

Zeroing in on where I left off in the article, I found Andrea's name. Each word I read made my blood pressure spike more intensely. I knew what she was going for with this article, what my promo team was probably pushing her to do, what I'd allowed her to do by ignoring her and then throwing my phone against the wall in anger. She was trying to spin this in my favor, using my sexuality and homophobia as an excuse for some of my off-field antics. And while in some ways what she said was true, it made anger and shame rain down on me.

This was my life, my story, my truth... I should have been the one telling it.

I deserved that, didn't I? After all this fucking time, I deserved to say the words—all of them. I deserved to be happy. I deserved to figure out what I wanted, and to make it happen.

Because the only thing I did know was that I wanted Beau, and I wasn't willing to give him up again. Not without a fight.

CHAPTER THIRTY-SIX

Beau

Ash needed to fight for Beau, but Beau needs to fight for Ash, too. ~ Love, Kenny

MY HAND ACHED when on reflex I used it to push open the door of Campbell's Confections. It was closing time, so I turned the sign over behind me as Mom looked up at me from one of the glass cases she was arranging.

"How'd it go?" she asked, and I shrugged, plopping down in one of the pale-pink chairs.

"Fine. Chief just said that once the doc clears me for my hand, I need to get my ass back to work." Because of course I had to fuck up my hand punching an asshole reporter in the face. At least he wasn't pressing charges. That would have been... I didn't want to think about what could have happened.

Mom sighed, walked over, and cupped my cheek. "I hate seeing this face so sad. I hate it when the best man

I've ever known is hurting."

Shaking my head, I leaned back so her hand fell away. "I'm not the best man you've ever known, Ma."

"So, what? You're in my head now? Don't tell me how I feel. That's not you."

I shrugged, crossing my arms and pouting because my boyfriend ran away from me, I'd damn near broken my hand, and I deserved to pout, damn it.

Mom sat on the opposite side of the small, round table, both of us leaning against the wall. "When your father left…I was ready. It was okay, ya know? We were fighting a lot. I knew he couldn't be what we needed him to be. I knew we would be better off without him. I didn't worry about me at all. I didn't worry about Kenny either, but you? You I worried about."

"Gee, thanks. This isn't helping me feel better. Did you really think I couldn't handle it?"

"What? No, that's not what I meant. I just… You have such a strong sense of loyalty, Beau, that I knew it would be harder for you to deal with, because leaving wasn't something you'd ever do. You could have gone off to college, you could have played college football, but you didn't. It's my biggest regret, if I'm being honest—not pushing you to go. I was selfish, and I'm sorry about that—"

"What? No, you have no reason to feel bad. I made my decision, and nothing you could have said would have changed my mind. I like my life. I'm happy." Kind of. I did like my life, but I hadn't realized what it was like to truly be happy until I had Ash. Ugh, and of course everything had to go back to Ash again.

"No, I get it, and that's where I'm going next. You've never made waves, Beau. You were always a good boy who did what was expected of you. You never got in trouble, you made sacrifices for other people. You never fought for something you truly wanted. You just…accept whatever comes your way. Don't you think it's time to fight for your happiness?"

A warm spark flared to life in my chest, but I quickly tried to stamp it down. "He's the one who ran away. I've called and texted him. What else am I supposed to do? And should I really fight for someone who isn't willing to fight for me?"

"Nope," she replied. "You should never accept less than what you deserve. Never. And if Ashton can't give you that, then you walk away. But I know you. Even if this hadn't happened, you would have let him go. If he went to Texas and asked you to go with him, no matter how much you might have wanted to, you wouldn't have gone. I'm not saying that Ash deserves you. I don't know if he does, but it's time you made some waves. Fight for what you want, say how you feel. Don't write off your happiness because you think it's easier for Ash, or me, or Kenny. It's not your job to carry everyone you love on your shoulders."

My eyes darted toward the ground. She was right. I knew she was. No matter what happened with Ash, I knew I would regret not saying my piece. "Even if I wanted to talk to him, I couldn't. I don't know where he is."

"I have a feeling you could figure it out if you wanted to." She stood up, walked over, and kissed my forehead. "I love you, and I'm proud of you. Don't let that fire burn out of your eyes."

I opened my mouth to reply, but before I could, the door swung open. Kenny stumbled inside, babbling and breathing heavily. Fear cascaded down my spine as I pushed to my feet and went to him.

"Hey, what is it? What happened?" I rubbed his back, tried to get him to settle down as Mom brushed the hair off his forehead. If someone had cornered him again…said something to him… He was supposed to be with Lori and her family. Mom had asked them not to leave him alone.

He kept rambling, his words mangled and coming

out too quickly to understand. My heart was in my throat, my pulse pounding until Kenny shoved his phone at me. "Look, look, look," he said over and over again.

I brushed my finger over the screen to open his phone, and when I did, an Instagram post popped up. Ashton Carmichael's Instagram post. When I saw the photo attached, my knees went weak. They nearly collapsed beneath me as I made my way back to the chair and fell into it.

It was a photo of us...back in high school. It was taken from behind, at a distance. I doubted anyone would know it was me. The sun was setting, and we were on the football field, walking toward the end zone. We were silhouettes, shadows against the sunset, Ash with his arm around my shoulders and me with a football in my hand.

I didn't remember the day, or knew the photo existed, much less who took it. But Ash had it...he'd had it all these years. You could see the corners were bent, the paper faded, aged as though it had been held a lot, not as though it had been in an album and never looked at again. It was as if this photo had lived, if that made sense.

Finally, when I could tear my eyes away from us, from Ash and me, I began to read his post.

Hold tight, folks, because you're about to see a side of me you've never witnessed. I mean, it's still a pretty amazing side because it's me. ;)

I've been lucky in my life. I'd be foolish not to see that. I might have been born to a mother who didn't want me, but she gave me to people who did. They chose me, cherished me, loved me. I had a comfortable upbringing, with a father who liked nothing more than to throw a football with me in the front yard. And from the start, I was good. Later, he would tell me I was born to play football, and I believed him. I took that message with me my whole life. We practiced daily. I was always on a team, and they went to every one of my games.

It was in high school that things began to change for me. Not football, of course. It was my heart, my soul, what I was born to do, but that's when I began to realize I was different than my friends.

The last thing in the world I wanted was to be different. I didn't have the confidence to stand out. I was real good at playing the part, feigning strength I'm not sure I've ever had. I made it my goal in life not to be different, to pretend those feelings didn't exist. I saw my worth in football and what people thought about me. I spent my life trying to live up to that image, and being different...being gay threatened that. I couldn't be gay if I was born to play football.

So I spent my life telling myself I wasn't. Doing any and everything I could to deny who I was.

Except with him. It was so damn hard to lie to myself when it came to him.

Even when he didn't know it, he did something to me. Made me feel like I was more than football, made me want things I didn't think I could ever want. I drove him fucking crazy, and I loved that, because he didn't take my shit. He saw through the facade, those walls I built up around myself, and I don't think he realized he did it.

He made me want to tear them down, but I couldn't, so I ran.

I've spent the last ten years running, lying, telling myself football was the most important thing because I was born for it. Because I shared it with my father.

What would I be if I lost that? Who was I without football?

Those ten years ate away at me, eroded my soul. I was drowning and didn't know it, dying a slow, painful death while pretending I was on top of the world.

Everything I did was my choice. I made a lot of mistakes. I'm not a victim, not really. I don't want pity or for excuses to be made about me for things I've done, but the lies were getting harder to keep. I was sinking deeper and deeper...to the point that I lost what I thought defined me. I lost football.

And then he came back into my life. He fired up my soul, my world, in ways I didn't believe possible. He still didn't let me get away with shit, he called me out, challenged me, enabled me to challenge myself. He made me want to be different if different meant I had him.

I thought I could skate the line, have him and keep lying to the world. There was a part of me that still craved acceptance, that needed to be liked, to prove myself.

That needed football.

So I ran away again. I not only ran from him, I ran from myself, and I can't do that anymore.

I'm a gay man. I've always been a gay man.

A gay man who lives and breathes football.

A gay man who needs more than just football.

I didn't know how to have both, or if I wanted both. But I know what I want now. I want my truth. I want to be different. I want to be happy. I want to be free.

And yeah, I want him too, and damn it, Cranky, you better still want me too (I mean, really, duh. It's me, remember?).

When I had him, I still had football. No one can take that away from me, even if I'm not playing professionally. Football is still mine, it's ours, and there's nothing in the world like sharing it with him.

This is my story, and I wanted to be the one to tell it, so that's what I'm doing.

I'm Ashton Carmichael, ex-football-player for the Avalanche, and I'm in love with a man. From that one moment we shared ten years ago, maybe even before then, I was in love with him. ABC is what K-man called us, and he was right. If that's not destiny, I don't know what is.

I like who I am. I'm proud of it, and really, what matters besides that?

My hands were shaking. Kenny's cell fell from them.

Ash…fucking Ash. I was right all along. He was going to wreck me, and I wanted it. Wanted him.

"I gotta go." I picked up Kenny's phone and gave it back to him. "I…"

"Go get him, Beau!" Kenny said.

Mom smiled. "Make waves."

I planned on it.

CHAPTER THIRTY-SEVEN

Ashton

Tied game, in overtime. Does Ashton Carmichael have what it takes to pull it off?

HE WASN'T GOING to come. Christ, he wasn't going to come.

Still, I didn't move, didn't get up from my spot on the dock, and waited for him. I'd wait forever for Beau Campbell, I thought. I was the one who kept us waiting before. It was now my turn.

My stomach twisted nervously when I heard tires on the gravel. My palms started to sweat even though it wasn't hot, because this was Beau, and I wanted him so fucking much. More than anything.

If it was Wyatt, I was going to fucking kill him.

"Playing hide-and-seek by yourself?" Beau asked, and I smiled. It was what I'd said to him as I'd walked onto this same dock toward him that night long ago.

Beau touched my shoulder. "I'll play. I found you.

Freeze."

"You mixed up hide-and-seek and freeze tag," I told him. "But I miss you too much to care about the details."

"You took my line," he replied.

I scooted over as Beau sat on the edge of the dock with me, just like we'd sat ten years before. "You came out…on Instagram. It was mushy as hell."

A laugh rumbled in my chest, falling from my mouth. "Holy shit, it was mushy. See what you do to me, Cranky Campbell?"

"Do I make you feel like you can't breathe without me?" he asked.

"Oh, look at you. I publicly declared my love for you, and you're still reaching for compliments. Isn't that my job?"

"Answer the question, Ash."

"Yeah, you do."

"Do I make you feel like you can do anything if I'm by your side?"

"Yep."

"Like you weren't really complete without me?"

"Uh-huh." He was really playing this up, wasn't he?

"Like you'd do anything to be with me? Even if it meant a long-distance relationship or me moving to Texas with you or wherever the hell your career might take you because losing me isn't an option?"

I whipped my head around so I faced him.

"If that's how you feel about me, then we're damn lucky because that's how I feel about you too."

"You would move away with me? You wouldn't even move away for *you*." Goddamn it, I kind of wanted to cry. Fucking Beau.

"Being with you *is* for me. I haven't cared enough about anything in my life that I had to fight for it...except you, Ash. You're worth fighting for...I'm worth it. Being with you makes me happy, and I'm not willing to lose that. You're obnoxious and cocky. Needy for attention. Oh, and a hat thief. Did I mention you're a hat thief? But I love you...I love you so damn much it hurts. You fire up my soul, Ash."

"Holy shit, Campbell. I'm not sure I can follow that up." My heart was beating so damn hard, it nearly burst out of my chest. How did I get so lucky?

"Wow, did you just admit I'm better than you?" he asked with a smile.

I reached over, ran my fingers over his bandaged hand. "We're both pretty damn good. Together, the best. You're cranky, and perfect. But I love you...I love you so damn much it hurts. You fire up my soul, Campbell."

"Copycat." He winked.

Again, I fingered the bandage. He'd punched someone because of me. "I'm sorry for leaving you. You deserved better. I should have been there with you."

"You're here now," he replied, and I was. I was right where I always wanted to be. If he'd have me, I'd never leave his side again.

"I told Andrea I don't want to go back. I don't care who offered. We have a team here—you and me. I want to stay with you, coach with you. This is where I belong." There was so much I wanted to do. Coach Kenny, be with Beau...maybe find a way to work with LGBTQ high school athletes. Help pave the way for them so their road would be easier than mine.

He closed his eyes, dropped his forehead against mine, and breathed me in. I wrapped my arms around him, inhaled, and did the same.

"I belong to you too," he replied.

"We're getting mushy again."

"It'll be our secret," Beau added. "Now don't you think you should kiss me again? We get a do-over. We can make this one end the way the first one should have."

I really liked the sound of that. I pressed my lips to his. Beau opened and let me inside. Just like the first time we sat in this same spot and kissed, the world righted itself. Fireworks went off in my stomach.

I was free.

When we pulled away, it was on our terms. I stood, held my hand out, and helped Beau up. "Come home with me, Campbell. I miss being naked with you."

He laughed, and I felt it in my chest. There was nothing like Beau's laugh. "Well, I did fix your dick and all."

"Asshole."

"You love it."

I loved him.

"Let's go home, Ash."

And we did just that. Together.

EPILOGUE

Beau
Six Months Later

I feel like we live in a fairy tale! We all lived happily ever after. - Love, Kenny

"ARE YOU GOING to play with my hole, or what?" Ash asked, making a laugh shoot up my throat and jump from my lips. You'd think he wouldn't be able to shock me anymore, but he could. He basically did it every day.

He wiggled his ass at me, making me shake my head at him. We were naked, in bed. We'd woken up, taken a shower, and then somehow ended up back in bed together, where he made love to me for hours on end. There was nothing like the feeling of Ash inside me. Sometimes I still couldn't believe he was mine. That we made it from those two boys who were in competition with each other, to the guys at the end of that dock that night, to where we were now—living together, coaching together, loving each other. Life was funny like that sometimes. You never knew what would happen.

"For someone who doesn't like to bottom much, you sure like my fingers or my tongue in your ass," I teased him. Not that I was complaining. I loved that Ash liked a part of me, any part of me, inside him.

"It's not that I don't like it. I'm still getting used to it. I have a tight hole, Campbell. You said so yourself."

Ash had bottomed a few times over the months, but it wasn't something he wanted often. He was mostly a top and that was that, just the same as I preferred to bottom.

"But I still like to feel you…know you get that part of me no one has ever had."

Okay, so my heart might have melted a little bit. How could it not when Ash said things like that to me? "I don't even know where to start. That was sweet, Ash." I leaned in and rubbed my nose into his neck. "You're so fucking sweet to me…and I also have to make sure I say that I have a tight hole too. *You* said so yourself. But I love playing with yours, and it would be okay with me if I never got to fuck you again. I just want you. That's all."

"Oh my God. Stop being so sappy, and finger me before we have to go."

We laughed like we always did when we were together. I didn't remind him that he started the sappiness. I had more important things to do. So I slid down the bed, used my tongue on him, savored the feel of him writhing and moaning beneath me, then used my fingers to bring him to orgasm.

After, I licked him clean, kissed his stomach, his chest, his lips. "Come on. We have to go to Mom's."

"Hurry. Get off me. I don't wanna be late. I'm stoked for K-man to see what I got him for his birthday."

I rolled off Ash and watched as he climbed out of bed and walked naked toward the bathroom. We'd decided I would move in with him, and now the place was a mishmash of his things and mine. I was renting out my house. Part of me wanted to sell it, but then I thought maybe I could keep it. Maybe there would be a time when Kenny might be able to use it as his own. It was close to Mom's.

Once Ash's tight ass disappeared into the bathroom, I got out of bed and went with him. "What did you get him?" I asked.

"I already told you, I'm not telling. You'll see when Kenny does."

We got into the shower again because one couldn't go to their mom's house for a birthday party smelling like sex and come.

After we got dressed, Ash donning a Fever Falls Fire Department cap, we went out to my truck and drove to Mom's. There were already a few cars in the driveway and on the street when we arrived. Just as we got out of the truck, Linc pulled up behind us, so we waited for him.

"Hey, sweetie." He gave me a hug and a kiss on the cheek, then turned his attention to Ash. "Hey, sexy. You ready to give me a try yet?" Linc reserved a wink for Ash, and I rolled my eyes. He was forever flirting with Ash, but I knew it was all in fun. Lincoln would never hurt me, and I also knew that it was his way of trying to feel involved with us. I'd learned things about my friend that I hadn't realized were there, just by being with Ash.

Linc talked a big game...but he needed me, needed to feel he wouldn't lose his place in my life. I didn't know what made him need me, and he sure as shit wouldn't ever lose me, but it was just a part of who he was.

"No, but I can put a feeler out for any other closeted football players, if that's what you're looking for," Ash teased, leaning in and hugging Lincoln too.

"Sigh, he must really like you if he's still turning me down," Lincoln told me.

"I guess he must."

We went inside. The house was decorated from top to bottom—pun not intended. Kenny stood by the table, pouring punch in a glass. He handed it to his girlfriend, Lori, before his eyes landed on us.

"Ash! Beau!" He grabbed Lori's free hand because he was a gentleman like that, and the two of them came over.

"What about me?" Lincoln asked.

"It's good to see you too, Lincoln," Kenny told him.

I nudged Linc. "Don't worry. He likes Ash more than me too."

"Hey, K-man. Happy birthday." Ash gave Kenny a tight hug, and then it was my turn. We said our hellos to Lori as well, the five of us chatting until Mom came into the room.

"Hey, boys." She kissed Lincoln, who said hello, and then she went to Ash.

"Hey, Ma," he told her, and they hugged before she and I did the same.

I loved watching Ash with our family. I knew he'd always wanted a big one, and even though it was only me, Kenny, and Mom, he had a bit of an extended family with Linc and the guys, and of course Wyatt and his family. I just wished his parents were alive to see it.

The house began to fill with people—from school,

the football team, the center. We laughed, played games, and celebrated Kenny.

It was three when Ash was looking out the window like he was expecting something.

"What did you do?" I asked him.

"Nothing." He feigned innocence just as a large delivery truck pulled up. "K-man! Your gift is here!"

We all crowded outside just as they began to pull out a full-sized Pac-Man arcade game, followed by an air-hockey table, which Kenny now played religiously too. When Ashton Carmichael introduced you to something, you couldn't help but fall in love with it, just like people couldn't help but fall in love with him.

"Ashton! Where are we supposed to put that?" Mom shrieked.

"I don't know...move the couch outside? It's an arcade game! What's more important?" he replied, and Mom smiled.

They moved it into the garage, and eventually they would turn my old bedroom into a game room. Kenny was stoked.

The party was over, and Ash was in the garage playing the games, when Kenny came back inside. "This was the best birthday I've ever had," he told me.

"It was pretty great, wasn't it?"

He fingered the edge of his journal. "Yep! Will you take me and Lori on a date tomorrow?"

"Of course."

Kenny looked at me, little wrinkles around his eyes when he smiled. "I'm glad you're happy, Beau. No one deserves it more than you. You're the best brother in the whole wide world."

My heart swelled. "Thanks, but I think that title belongs to you."

"Because of you."

"What?" I asked him.

"I'm happy and a good brother because of you. I knew what to do because I watched you. I write notes when you tell me stuff so I don't forget it, and when I see you do things, I write it down too because you're a hero and I want to be just like you. Sometimes I'd see things, watching you, like when you were sad or lonely or falling in love with Ash, and I made wishes for you. They came true, didn't they?"

My vision blurred as my eyes watered. I thought I might have been the luckiest man alive. "Yeah, Kenny. They came true. And you know what? You've taught me a lot too. You think I'm a hero, and I think the same thing about you."

"I guess that's what brothers do." Kenny shrugged,

and I laughed, hugging him.

Ash, Mom, and Lori came in, and we visited for a while longer before Ash and I got back into the truck to go home.

We spoke about the programs Ash was working on. Nothing was finalized yet with the LGBTQ youth sports program, but Ash had done a few talks at high school GSAs and college sports programs over the past few months. We would still be coaching together next football season. Other than that, Ash was trying to figure out what he wanted to do. He'd never given much thought to what his dreams were outside of football.

We got home, went for a night swim, and then watched a movie. We were naked in bed together later when he wrapped his arms around me and said, "Today was a good day, Campbell."

"Yeah, it was." Linc thought it was funny that Ash still called me by my last name, but I liked it. That was us.

"I like being gay," he whispered a moment later.

"Huh?" That had come out of the blue.

"Remember when I was first trying to be honest with myself but I was still in denial and confused, and I told you I didn't want to be gay?"

"Yeah." I nodded. "I remember."

"That's not me anymore. I like who I am. I'm glad I'm a gay man. I wouldn't change a thing, even if I could."

My pulse went crazy, and I felt a smile in my chest. He had a way of doing that to me. I rolled over on top of him, held myself above him. "Good. I'm glad. You should never be ashamed of who you are. I like that person an awful lot."

"Like or love?" he asked. "Because like is just okay. I'm not sure I'm comfortable with just being okay. You should love who I am."

He'd said the same thing to me in the beginning when I'd said I liked his cock. Fucking Ash. "I love who you are."

"I love you too. *Mine, mine, mine, mine,*" he teased.

I'd always been Ashton Carmichael's, and we would spend the rest of our lives making waves together.

Coming February 8th, 2019

Add to Goodreads

Join Riley's Newsletter

Join Riley's Reader Group

About the Author

Riley Hart is the girl who wears her heart on her sleeve. She's a hopeless romantic. A lover of sexy stories, passionate men, and writing about all the trouble they can get into together. If she's not writing, you'll probably find her reading.

Riley lives in California with her awesome family, who she is thankful for every day.

Other Books by Riley Hart

Beautiful Chaos, Weight of the World & Up for the Challenge with Devon McCormack

Ever After: A Gay Fairy Tale and Of Sunlight and Stardust with Christina Lee

Saint and Lucky
Something About You
His Truth

Jared and Kieran
Jared's Evolution
Jared's Fulfillment

Metropolis Series: With Devon McCormack
Faking It
Working It
Owning It

Last Chance Series:
Depth of Field
Color Me In

Wild Side Series:
Dare You To
Gone For You
Tied to You

Crossroads Series:
Crossroads
Shifting Gears
Test Drive
Jumpstart

Rock Solid Construction Series:
Rock Solid

Broken Pieces Series:
Broken Pieces
Full Circle
Losing Control

Blackcreek Series:
Collide
Stay
Pretend
Return to Blackcreek

Printed in Great Britain
by Amazon